"But I feel we need to keep things strictly business. Or friends, maybe both. But nothing more."

"Sounds good." One corner of his mouth curled up in the beginnings of a smile. "I'm glad you're in agreement."

This made her smile. "I wasn't sure what else to say. You're a nice guy, Trace. And you've been awfully kind to me. It's just that—"

"Don't." The fierceness of his tone caught her by surprise. "I would never expect that of you. I'm not that kind of guy." He cleared his throat. "Like you said, it's just been too long. We're going to be business partners. It's always a mistake to mix business with pleasure."

Pleasure. Mouth suddenly dry, she nodded. "I agree," she managed. "Let's forget it ever happened, okay?"

Dear Reader,

In this story, we once again return to my favorite imaginary town of Getaway, Texas. Emma McBride is one of my all-time favorite heroines. She's strong and resilient and despite everything she's gone through, she still has the capacity for love. Wrongly convicted in the murder of her husband, Emma is determined to clear her name when she finally gets out of prison. She goes looking for her best friend, Heather, with whom she's lost touch, and ends up on the doorstep of Heather's brother, Trace Redkin's, ranch.

Trace has a lot on his plate trying to keep his uncle Will's ranch running and take care of the older man who has Alzheimer's. When Emma shows up on his doorstep, his caring nature won't let Trace turn her away. It also doesn't help that he used to have a crush on her at one time.

Helping Emma clear her name brings danger to both Emma and Trace. As they search for the truth, someone not only wants to make sure they don't find it, but believes Emma has something her deceased husband stole from him. Protecting Emma is hard, but for Trace, protecting his heart is even more difficult.

I hope you enjoy this story of redemption and love amid high-stakes danger!

Karen Whiddon

PROTECTED
BY THE TEXAS
RANCHER

Karen Whiddon

HARLEQUIN

ROMANTIC
SUSPENSE

HARLEQUIN®
ROMANTIC SUSPENSE™

Recycling programs
for this product may
not exist in your area.

ISBN-13: 978-1-335-73808-0

Protected by the Texas Rancher

Copyright © 2022 by Karen Whiddon

All rights reserved. No part of this book may be used or reproduced in
any manner whatsoever without written permission except in the case of
brief quotations embodied in critical articles and reviews.

This is a work of fiction. Names, characters, places and incidents
are either the product of the author's imagination or are used fictitiously.
Any resemblance to actual persons, living or dead, businesses,
companies, events or locales is entirely coincidental.

For questions and comments about the quality of this book,
please contact us at CustomerService@Harlequin.com.

Harlequin Enterprises ULC
22 Adelaide St. West, 41st Floor
Toronto, Ontario M5H 4E3, Canada
www.Harlequin.com

Printed in U.S.A.

Karen Whiddon started weaving fanciful tales for her younger brothers at the age of eleven. Amid the gorgeous Catskill Mountains, then the majestic Rocky Mountains, she fueled her imagination with the natural beauty surrounding her. Karen now lives in north Texas, writes full-time and volunteers for a boxer dog rescue. She shares her life with her hero of a husband and four to five dogs, depending on if she is fostering. You can email Karen at kwhiddon1@aol.com. Fans can also check out her website, karenwhiddon.com.

Books by Karen Whiddon

Harlequin Romantic Suspense

The Rancher's Return
The Texan's Return
Wyoming Undercover
The Texas Soldier's Son
Texas Ranch Justice
Snowbound Targets
The Widow's Bodyguard
Texas Sheriff's Deadly Mission
Texas Rancher's Hidden Danger
Finding the Rancher's Son
The Spy Switch
Protected by the Texas Rancher

Visit the Author Profile page at Harlequin.com for more titles.

Chapter 1

If the cold rain and the jagged flashes of lightning at midnight weren't bad enough, Emma McBride couldn't find the spare key her best friend, Heather, always used to keep hidden under a rock by the ranch house's back door. It didn't help that the back-porch light had burned out and she ended up on her knees in the mud, searching with her numb fingers in the dark. Drenched and shivering, she cursed the undeniable fact that her luck apparently hadn't gotten any better since she'd been released from prison.

Finally abandoning her effort to find the damn key, Emma got up and went around to the dining room window. Heather had often left it unlocked. Naturally, it wasn't.

Just in case, she tried the others. Finally, in what

she believed to be the guest bedroom, she found a window she could push up. Cold and soaked, she managed to heave herself over the windowsill, landing in a sodden heap on the carpeted floor.

Just as she'd staggered to her feet and turned to close the window, a light came on, momentarily blinding her. "What the…?" She spun around, fist up, the fighting instinct that had kept her alive in prison activated.

She found herself facing the end of a shotgun, held by a large and angry-looking man. Heather's older brother, Trace.

"Trace," she managed, hands up. "It's me, Emma. Emma McBride."

Squinting at her, he finally lowered the gun. "I thought you were in prison."

"I was." Gulping air, unable to stop her violent shivering, she wrapped her arms around herself.

"What are you doing here?" he asked, his tone as unfriendly as his expression. "I see you climbed in through that window. Are you adding breaking and entering to your skill set?"

Which meant, she realized, that Trace Redkin, the guy she'd had a crush on all through high school, believed she'd been guilty. Heather had told her the town had been divided, some refusing to believe she could be a cold-blooded murderer, the other ready to see her locked away for the rest of her life.

She might have been too, if her appeal hadn't finally gotten her released for lack of evidence after two years, one month and three days behind bars.

Gathering her scattered thoughts, she lifted her chin. "Is Heather home?"

"Heather got married and moved to California six months ago," he replied. Grabbing a quilt off the end of the bed, he handed it to her. "Here. Wrap yourself up in this. You're freezing."

Grateful, she accepted the quilt. Maybe now, she could get warm. Though what she really wanted was a hot shower and a change of clothes.

Then, Trace's words registered. "Heather is gone?" Just like that, her final option was extinguished. She had no money, nowhere to go. While she'd been incarcerated, her father had died with a will leaving everything to his wife of five years. Emma's stepmother had promptly sold their home and moved to Florida to shack up with her new boyfriend.

Emma had come home with hopes that Heather would let her stay at the ranch until she could figure out where she went from here. Now, not only was she broke, but clearly she was also homeless. It took every bit of self-control she possessed not to break down. "I... I didn't know." When her possessions had been returned to her before being released, she'd still had her old cell phone, but it no longer worked since she didn't have a carrier.

"I'm sorry." Eyeing her, Trace heaved a sigh. "You look beat. Why don't you dry off and I'll see if I can find you something to wear? You can sleep in the guest bed for tonight and we'll talk again in the morning."

"Thank you."

Later, dry and warm and snuggled underneath

clean sheets, Emma fought to stay awake. She needed to try to plan, but fatigue eventually won out and she must have drifted off. The next thing she knew, she opened her eyes to see sunlight streaming in through the window.

For a moment, she had no idea where she was. She sat up in bed, disoriented and panicked, her heart racing, before she remembered.

The ranch. Which now clearly belonged to Trace. Judging by the sunshine, the storm had apparently moved on. Covering her face with her hands, she tried to figure out what on earth she was going to do.

She'd come this far. She'd survived two years in prison, gotten released and now had the opportunity to clear her name. She might not have money, but she had skills. Before her marriage to Jeremy, she'd been known around Getaway, Texas, for her horse training skills. People had brought their horses from all over the country to have her work with them. Maybe, just maybe, she could work out some kind of deal with Trace for a percent of her fees in exchange for the use of his ranch and a place to stay.

Did she dare allow herself to hope? If she did, hope would be strange and wonderful after feeling defeated for so long.

It would all depend on Trace, which meant it could go either way.

She and Trace had never been close, even though she'd once had a huge crush on him. But he was her best friend's older brother, and Heather had teased her mercilessly, until Emma had finally started dating another boy in their high school class.

A quiet tap on the bedroom door startled her. "There's a bathroom down the hall," Trace said, without opening the door. "I put clean towels in there and some toiletries, if you'd like a shower. Plus a set of my old sweats for you to wear while we wash your clothes."

"Thank you," she managed, glad he couldn't see how even this small kindness brought tears to her eyes. Of necessity, she'd had to become tough to survive in prison. She needed to try and draw on some of that toughness now.

Later, showered and clean and feeling human again, she dressed in the faded sweats Trace had left for her. They were huge, though luckily the pants had a drawstring waist. She rolled up the bottoms of the pants and pushed up the sleeves. Since her sneakers were still damp and her socks were apparently in the washer, she padded out to the kitchen in bare feet.

The scent of fresh-made coffee had her mouth watering. Trace stood at the stove with his back to her. "Make yourself a cup of coffee if you want," he said without turning. "I hope you're hungry. I'm about to make scrambled eggs, toast and bacon."

Ache in the throat, once again she found herself blinking back tears. "Thanks," she said. Next to the coffeepot, he'd even set out a clean mug. While in prison, she'd learned to take her coffee black, so that was how she drank it now.

Not sure what to do next, she took a seat at the kitchen table. A moment later, with the smell of bacon frying, she pondered how different this scenario was from how her life had been just a week ago.

"Here you are." Trace interrupted her thoughts, carrying two plates loaded with food over to the table. After placing the breakfast in front of her, he took a seat directly across from her. "Dig in," he said.

In prison, she'd learned to eat as quickly as possible so someone else didn't take her food. Here, she took a deep breath and forced herself to pick up her fork and eat slowly, like a regular person. Even so, when she looked up, she realized she'd finished before Trace was even halfway done.

Oh well. Slightly embarrassed, she took a deep sip of her coffee and watched Trace eat.

"You must have been hungry," he commented, finally pushing his clean plate aside.

"I was. Thank you so much for cooking for me."

He nodded, his brown eyes missing nothing. "What are your plans from here?" he asked.

Nervous again, she drank more coffee to cover. "I wanted to see if I could work out an arrangement with you."

To his credit, he didn't immediately shut her down, as she'd half expected. Instead, he continued to regard her, his expression kind. "What kind of an arrangement?

Oh geez. Blushing, she belatedly realized he might have taken that statement the wrong way. "I don't know if you remember," she began, "but I was once really good with horses."

The understatement of the year.

At his nod, she continued, choosing her words carefully. "I'd like to start training horses again, using your facilities. In exchange for that—plus room and board—I'd give you a percentage of my fees."

When she'd finished, she watched him, waiting for his reaction. He didn't respond right away, clearly considering. He'd matured from a good-looking kid into a handsome man, she realized. A rugged cowboy with more than a fair amount of sex appeal. She imagined he had women chasing after him constantly, which was why she felt the need to clarify. "It would be strictly a business arrangement," she said.

Slowly, he nodded. "I just have one question. Did you do it? Did you kill your husband?"

"No." She didn't even hesitate. "That's why the judge ruled in favor of my appeal and I got out of prison." Deep breath, willing her voice to remain steady. "And one of the first things I plan to do is clear my name."

Whether he believed her or not didn't really matter. Or at least that was what she told herself. Yet a part of her couldn't help but hope that here at least, she could find one person in her corner.

Slowly, Trace nodded. "Heather always swore you were innocent. She hated what happened to you."

The knowledge that her best friend had never given up on her helped. A lot. "I wonder why she stopped staying in touch," Emma mused. "Her letters gradually started tapering off. I continued to write to her, but never heard back."

Trace frowned. "That's weird. I really thought she wrote you. Maybe not as often, once she met Conner, but still."

"Conner," she repeated. "The name doesn't sound familiar. I take it he wasn't from around here?"

"Nope. She met him on one of her business trips to California. He's CEO of one of her client companies. They did a long-distance relationship for a while and then he asked her to move out there."

Heather had always been brave and bold. Those traits were some of the things Emma admired about her. "And then they got engaged?"

Slowly, he nodded. "They lived together for several months and then he popped the question. Since neither of them wanted anything fancy, they got married at city hall." He shook his head. "I wasn't even invited. They texted an announcement and a photograph and that's it."

That didn't sound like the Heather she knew. People change, but still… "How long ago was that?"

"Six months or so." Pushing to his feet, he began to clear the table. "I'll think about your business proposition. In the meantime, you're welcome to stay as long as you'd like."

Though she almost offered to do the dishes as repayment for him cooking the meal, she stayed seated. Maybe she should give him a bit more information. "Would you like to know how much I'm paid to train a horse?" she asked, eyeing his back. "Though it depends on the situation, and the problem, naturally."

Without waiting for an answer, she named her usual price range. "Though that might be outdated now, since it's been a couple years."

When he turned, he met her gaze. "Do you still think you could ask those prices? Even though you clearly haven't worked with horses while you were incarcerated?"

Slowly, she nodded. "All it takes is one horse, one success story. I'm good," she told him, merely stating a fact. "Once word gets out, people will be lining up to secure a spot with me."

"I'm going to be blunt," he warned. "Half this town is convinced you're a murderer. I'm not sure even the best reputation can survive that."

The statement was a blow to her stomach. Sucking in her breath, she straightened, determined to continue. "Again, that's why I plan to clear my name. Since the sheriff's office didn't, I'm determined to find the real killer. As for my reputation? It might be shot here in Getaway—though I have to believe I still have a few friends here who know me well enough to have faith—but outside of this town, it won't matter. My name has been linked to enough success stories that anyone who does their research would welcome my help."

Trace continued to watch her, his expression kind. "Maybe so." He shrugged. "I guess it wouldn't hurt to give it a shot. Though you might reduce your rates at first to draw people in."

Almost afraid to be optimistic, she nodded. "Does that mean we have a deal?"

"Sure, why not. Admittedly, the ranch has been struggling. I could use the extra income. And no one is using that guest room anyway, so you're welcome to have it. I would ask that you agree to help me out around here, at least until you get up and running."

"Definitely," she agreed, once again perilously

close to tears. Giving in to impulse, she jumped up and hugged him, just once, quick and tight, before taking off for her room, where she could allow herself to cry unobserved.

After Emma hugged him and rushed off, Trace didn't move. The instant she'd wrapped her arms around him, he'd battled the urge to tip her head back and cover her mouth with his. Knowing that this would be wrong on so many different levels didn't do anything to help with his sudden, fierce arousal. He could tell himself several different excuses, ranging from the knowledge that he'd been celibate too long—truth—to the fact that Emma McBride was still one of the most beautiful women he'd seen—also truth.

In the end, what mattered was that she was extremely vulnerable right now and he wasn't the kind of man to take advantage. He'd have to work to move past his attraction to her. Surely over time, he'd begin to regard her as a business partner, nothing more, if her plan to start training horses again became a success.

Right now, though, he could definitely use some help around the place. He'd been spreading himself thin trying to do it all alone since he couldn't afford to hire any help yet.

Having Emma here just might turn out to be a blessing in disguise.

He reached for his phone, meaning to call his sister and fill her in, but then hesitated. Maybe he'd wait until Emma was around, so the two women could talk. He had chores to do and he'd best get after them.

He figured he'd show Emma around once she got a bit more settled.

It didn't take long before the entire town was talking about Emma McBride and her return to Getaway. Part of it was due to the flyers advertising her return to horse training that he'd posted for her at various locations. Serenity Rune, the town psychic, had been gracious enough to allow Trace to put one in the front window of her eclectic combination florist, bookstore and metaphysical shop. While there, he'd waited for one of her emphatic pronouncements, but she'd only given him a mysterious smile and wished him well, telling him to send Emma in to see her when she felt up to it.

While he did all this, Emma had insisted on waiting in the truck. When he passed along Serenity's message, she gave a distracted smile and nodded.

After, since they were in town, he stopped at the Tumbleweed Café, intending to grab a burger for lunch. Even Emma couldn't turn down one of their famous burgers, though she'd had to rush off to the ladies' room first. He went ahead and allowed the hostess to seat him, choosing a booth near the front window.

He'd barely sat down when two older women who'd gone to church with his mother rushed over.

"Is it true that Emma McBride is staying with you at the ranch?" Myrna Adams demanded, hands on her hips.

Before he could get a chance to answer, Agnes Long leaned over, close enough to make him slide back in his seat. "Your mother would be so ashamed," she said, making a clucking sound. "How quickly you allowed yourself to be taken in by a pretty face."

"Oh, thank you," Emma said, her voice cheerful. "How wonderful to hear that you think I'm pretty." Her bright smile seemed a bit forced, but who could blame her. She looked pointedly at Myrna. "If you wouldn't mind moving, I'd really like to sit down."

Eyes wide, Myrna shuffled back. Agnes did the same. With both Trace and Emma staring at them, the two women turned around without another word and sailed away.

"Whew." Emma visibly deflated. "When you said half the town thought I was a murderer, I was hoping you might have been exaggerating."

Without thinking, he reached over and covered the top of her hand with his. "I'll help you," he heard himself promise. "In any way possible."

She looked at him, her blue gaze steady. "Even proving my innocence?" she asked. "Or did you mean something else?"

Right then, the waitress appeared, asking if she could get them something to drink. She did a double take when she recognized Emma. "Emma McBride?" she asked, smiling. "You got out?"

"I did." Emma stood and hugged the other woman. "It's so good to see you, Addy. Maybe we can get together and catch up soon."

"Definitely." Still smiling, Addy glanced at Trace. "Can I get you something to drink while you look over the menu?"

"I already know what I want," Emma said, sliding the menu back across the table. "A bacon burger with fries and a Dr Pepper."

"I'll have the same." Trace also handed Addy his menu.

"I'll be right back with your drinks." Addy bustled off.

Emma sat back in her seat, her gaze traveling slowly around the crowded café. "Only a few people are staring at me," she said. "Most of them don't seem to care that I'm here. Especially now that Myrna and Agnes have left."

"I'm sorry about them." Trace felt the need to apologize. "While I knew people would talk—you know as well as I do how much this town loves to gossip—I never expected anyone to be out-and-out rude."

Emma waved his comment away. "That wasn't your fault. If anything, I should be the one apologizing for putting you in that position."

Addy arrived with their drinks, just in time to catch Emma's comment. She set them down on the table before reaching over to squeeze Emma's shoulder. "I heard what happened. Don't you pay any attention to those two old busybodies. Sometimes it seems like they're not happy unless they're making someone miserable."

"I appreciate that," Emma replied.

"I mean it. I'll be back in few minutes with those burgers."

Once Addy had left again, Trace studied Emma. Even subdued and clearly nervous, her beauty made him catch his breath. With her high cheekbones, bright blue eyes and long, blond hair falling softly around her slender shoulders, she looked much the same as when she'd hung around the house with his sister in high school. Though he'd been a senior and she only a freshman, he'd walked around for months with a secret crush on her. He'd never done anything about it, knowing he'd be going off to college while she finished school.

He'd stayed at Texas Tech for three years, working hard on obtaining his engineering degree. Unfortunately, Uncle Frank, the man who'd raised him and Heather, had developed dementia and Heather had needed Trace's help to take care of him.

When he'd left college early, hoping to go back and finish his degree once he'd gotten Uncle Frank's situation stabilized, he'd wondered about Emma. Even though he'd dated a lot while in Lubbock, he'd never entirely forgotten about her.

Unfortunately, by the time he'd returned to Getaway, she'd gotten engaged to Jeremy Miller, a newcomer to town. They'd married a scant week after her high school graduation. Oddly enough, Trace had only met Emma's husband once, when he'd made a trip to town to pick up supplies at the feed store. Jeremy had seemed a nice enough guy, a bit full of himself maybe, but young and handsome and charming. Exactly, Trace had thought, the kind of guy who would suit a girl like Emma.

Preoccupied with taking care of his uncle and trying to keep the ranch afloat, Trace had lost track of Emma and Jeremy until the news broke that Jeremy was found shot to death inside a burned-out vehicle on the outskirts of town, right after asking Emma for a divorce.

"Here you are." Addy returned, bearing two hamburgers with all the fixings, and fries. "Is there anything else I can get you?"

When they both shook their heads, she told them to enjoy their meal and sauntered off.

Emma dug into her burger as if she hadn't eaten in days. Chewing, she made little sounds of pleasure low in her throat. "This. Is. So. Good," she commented in between bites.

Though he hadn't yet taken a bite, he nodded. Even watching her eat turned him on, which meant he might be setting himself up for a world of trouble. Forcing his attention to his own meal, he picked up his own hamburger and began to eat.

"That was amazing," Emma commented.

He looked up, realized she'd cleaned her plate and grinned. He finished the last of his burger, ate a few more of his fries and then asked her if she wanted any.

"You don't want them?" The sparkle in her eyes dimmed as someone else approached their table.

"You're the last person I expected to see in here," the burly young man said. Trace recognized him since his sister had dated him in high school.

Emma recognized him too. She'd gone all poker faced, her posture stiff. "Eric Stillwell," she said, her voice cool. "How have you been?"

"Better than you," he responded, his snide tone matching the curl of his lip. "Why the hell would you think you could come back here anyway?"

"That's enough." Trace stood. Despite Eric having been the quarterback for the high school football team, Trace had six inches and maybe forty pounds on him. "If you can't be pleasant, then you need to leave."

Instead, Eric glared at Emma. "I liked Jeremy," he told her. "He might have been new to town, but he was a lot of fun. I won't ever forgive you for what you did to him. I don't know how you got out so quickly, but you definitely should have gone somewhere else."

"I got out because I won my appeal," she responded, twin spots of color blooming high on her cheekbones. "The judge ruled that there wasn't enough evidence to convict me, especially since Jeremy's mistress, Amber, recanted her made-up story."

Eric's mouth opened and then closed. "Whatever," he finally said. He looked from her to Trace, who still stood. "I'm surprised you're letting her use you, man. I hope the next thing we hear about isn't that you are dead."

After dropping that parting shot, Eric turned and sauntered away.

Unclenching his fists, Trace sat back down, glancing at Emma. She'd gone pale, but seemed composed. "Are you ready to go?" he asked.

Slowly, she nodded.

Trace signaled the waitress for the check. Once she'd brought it, he paid and left a generous tip. Addy hugged Emma, and the two women promised to get together soon.

As he stood, he offered Emma his arm. Surprise flickered across her face, but she took it. Then they left the café together.

Once inside his pickup, Emma turned to him and put her hand on his arm. "Thank you," she said. "I appreciate the show of support."

Trace had always been one to speak his mind. "No problem. You didn't deserve that nonsense. I hope you understand that."

She grimaced. "Now you see why I want so badly to clear my name. I know I'm innocent, and the appeals judge overturned my conviction, but in the minds of a lot of these people, I killed Jeremy. I need to find out who really shot him."

"Don't you think doing that might be dangerous?" he asked.

Judging from her expression, the thought had never occurred to her. "What do you mean?" Then, before he could formulate his response, she answered her own question. "You mean the real killer might try to stop me?"

"Exactly."

Her chin came up. "Then I'll just have to be careful. I managed to survive in prison, which wasn't easy. I'll survive this too."

Though he had to admire her pluck, he made a silent vow to do what he could to protect her. No matter what it took.

Chapter 2

Back at the ranch, Emma excused herself and went to her room. She'd been careful not to reveal the extent of her discomfort around Trace, but the ugly reactions to her presence in the café had shocked her.

Emma had never considered herself a brave person, until she went to prison for a crime she hadn't committed. All along, stunned by Jeremy's sudden request for a divorce and then his subsequent death, she'd been numb. Naive enough to have complete faith in the judicial system, certain she'd be acquitted, at first she hadn't been able to process her conviction. After all, there was nothing but hearsay evidence against her. One woman—a complete stranger named Amber Trevault, who'd claimed to be Jeremy's mistress—had testified that Emma had made death threats against Jeremy and that he worried his wife was unhinged. The prosecution had tied that to his divorce request and a jury had evidently felt all that was enough to convict her.

Walking into the women's prison for the first time, Emma had built a fortress around herself. She'd read enough and watched enough television to know that how she presented herself would determine her standing among the other inmates.

"You survived," she reminded herself. If she could make it through twenty-four months incarcerated, only to be released on appeal, she definitely had the strength to not only rebuild her life but to figure out how to clear her name.

She'd made lots of plans while waiting to be released. The thought of going home had brought her so much joy. One thing she hadn't expected had been so much rancor from people she'd known her whole life. The short stop at the Tumbleweed Café had been an eye-opener. It still shocked her that people she'd known all her life could judge her so harshly for a crime she hadn't even committed. Her early release from prison should have at least given them reason to think.

They knew her, damn it. She wiped a stray tear away. She'd gone to school with them, attended church with them and trained their horses. How they could believe her to be a murderer, she'd never understand.

Jeremy had been popular, a charmer, but he'd only relocated to Getaway a month before they'd started dating. Just a year older than her, and a definite city boy, he'd been used to the kind of night life Houston could offer, something sorely lacking in her small West Texas town.

He'd decided to make his own party wherever he went. He'd charmed Emma, even made her love him, and then less than a year into the marriage had decided she bored him. In typical Jeremy fashion, he'd asked for a divorce at the same time as telling her he'd met someone else.

And then he'd been found shot to death in a burned-out car. Immediately, law enforcement had focused on the spurned wife. In disbelief, she hadn't stood a chance.

But that was the past, she reminded herself. From now on, she needed to focus on her future. Rebuilding her life and clearing her name.

Thank goodness for Trace. Learning Heather had moved away had been a complete surprise. Luckily, Trace had been willing to take her in. She suspected her help would be more welcome than he'd admitted.

While she hadn't seen more than the house, the ranch that she remembered had fallen into a bit of a decline.

Pulling herself together, she decided the time had come to check out the rest of the place.

Trace was in the kitchen when she emerged, going through the mail. He looked up when she came in and smiled. "I'm about to go check on some fencing. Would you like to go with me?"

"Definitely. Do you have an extra horse I can ride?"

"I do. Do you think you remember how?"

It took a second for her to realize he was teasing her. She shook her head, allowing herself to laugh. "I think we might just become good friends," she said, a light warning not only to him, but to herself. All she needed in her life right now was a friend. Nothing more.

"I agree," he responded. Grabbing his hat, he headed toward the back door. "Let's go. When we get back, I think I'll call Heather. I'm sure she'd enjoy catching up with you."

"I'd like that," she replied.

As they walked through the yard, she spotted the round pen and the larger riding arena. They looked decent, though grass had been allowed to grow up through dirt here and there in both places.

Trace noticed the direction of her gaze. "I'll work on those, I promise," he said. "They haven't been used at all since Heather left. I mostly raise cattle here."

"I can help. I'm definitely going to need them once I start getting clients."

The barn sat on the other side of the larger arena. She braced herself for what she might find inside. On the outside, the barn appeared sturdy, some new boards nailed alongside old. Though it could have used a fresh coat of paint on the exterior, it seemed well maintained. So far, so good.

She waited while Trace pulled the heavy sliding door open and followed him. The cement aisle between the six-stall barn was clean. Inside, there were three horses in stalls. Emma stopped, inhaling deeply. The familiar scents of horse and hay and leather were some of her favorite things. She stood stock-still and let herself breathe it all in. Once, she'd taken such things for granted. She wouldn't ever again. Far too much time had passed since she'd smelled them.

"Are you okay?" Trace asked, turning to eye her curiously.

Slowly, she nodded. "I never thought I'd be able to breathe the scent from inside a barn again."

This made him smile. "You can tell you're a country girl. Not everyone likes the smell of manure."

"Manure," she repeated, taken aback for a second, though he was right. "That's just part of being around horses. One of the best smells in the world."

Still smiling, Trace shook his head. She decided she really liked his smile. It made her warm inside. Maybe they could actually be friends as well as business partners. She'd like that. She could always use more friends.

She eyed the three horses. All appeared healthy, well taken care of and curious. They'd come to the front of their stalls and poked their heads out over the half door.

Trace pointed to a stocky gray mare. "You'll be riding her. Her name's Libby. I'll take Jack. He's the gelding in the stall next to her."

"What about that one?" Emma pointed toward the third horse, a flashy black-and-white paint who watched them intently.

"That's Daisy," he replied. "She's skittish. Not rideable. In fact, I'm hoping maybe you can work with her. She was Heather's horse before she moved away."

Emma went over to the horse and scratched behind her ears. "Is she getting any exercise?" she asked.

"I try," he answered. "She gets let out in the pasture with the others. But she hasn't been ridden in a good while."

"She probably misses Heather." She looked up in

time to catch his expression of disbelief. "Horses do miss their people, you know. Either way, I'll start working with her tomorrow if that's okay with you."

"Sounds good." He led the way to the tack room. Most of the saddle holders were empty. She counted three Western saddles and one English style.

"Let me guess." She pointed. "Heather's?"

"Yep. She left everything behind when she moved to the West Coast. I don't think she'd mind if you used her tack."

"Just to be sure, we can ask when we call her later." Waiting for him to choose his saddle, he hefted one up along with a pad, and then she selected the one closest to her.

Saddling up Libby felt familiar and strange. She tightened the cinch, double checking it before she turned to look at Trace. "What bridle and bit?"

"I'll get it." A moment later, he returned and handed one to her. "Just a basic snaffle bit."

"Mild on the mouth," she said. "I like it."

She led her mare out into the aisle before stepping up and swinging her leg over. Once settled in the saddle, she again took time to appreciate the sensation.

"Is everything all right?" Trace asked, leading his gelding over to her. "You just had a weird look on your face."

"It's…this." Shifting her weight in the saddle, she gathered up the reins and managed a watery smile. "I know you can't really relate, but I missed this so much. All of it. The barn, the horses, this ranch. I wasn't really sure when—or if ever—I'd see any of it again."

His gaze sharpened. "You missed this ranch?"

"Of course. My home away from home. I think I spent more time here than I did with my own family."

"I heard about your father," he said, getting up on his horse with effortless grace. "I'm sorry for your loss."

"Thank you. The hardest part was not being able to see him before he died. Or being allowed to attend the funeral." Then, because the discussion was making her morose, she nudged the horse forward. "Where to?"

He pointed west. "I've got a hundred head pastured over there. I need to check on them, plus the fifty head that are on another pasture. I figure this will be a good way to show you around the place."

As if she hadn't ridden down every dirt road and through every pasture in her younger years. Still, she relished not only the experience, enjoying the feel of being on horseback again, the sunshine on her skin and the fresh air, but the opportunity to see how the rest of the ranch might be faring. From what she remembered, Heather and Trace's uncle Frank, had kept a decent-sized group of ranch hands.

"Uncle Frank," she exclaimed out loud, bracing herself in case of bad news. "Where is he? Is he all right?"

Trace turned in the saddle to look at her, his cowboy hat shadowing his face and hiding his expression.

"He has dementia. I tried to take care of him at home, but he got worse and worse. After he ran away twice and almost burned the house down another time, I had to put him in a facility where professionals could take care of him."

"I'm sorry," she said, meaning it. "I always liked him."

Trace lifted his chin. "I searched all over for the best memory care facility. He's in a very good place in Midland. I make sure and go and see him at least once a month."

"I imagine you did." Those kind of care places were expensive, she'd heard. Very expensive. Which would explain the lack of ranch hands and why Trace was trying to garner any extra income he could. Now she understood why he'd agreed to her offer of a horse training partnership. He had nothing to lose.

Then she'd better make damn sure to succeed.

They continued to ride toward the back pasture. The sound of the horses' hooves on the hard-packed ground felt comforting, even reassuring. Life did go on and the fact that she'd been able to return to doing things she loved like riding brought no small measure of happiness.

With the flatness of the arid landscape, she could see the herd in the distant field up ahead. When they reached the gate, Trace dismounted and opened it, waiting until she'd ridden through before closing it and then getting back on his horse. In her time in prison, she'd taken up sketching as a hobby and felt she'd gotten pretty damn good. Right now, eyeing the handsome, broad-shouldered cowboy riding in front of her, she ached for a pencil and pad. Since she had none, instead she tried to burn the image into her memory. The blazing Texas sun, the bright blue, cloudless sky, the brown grass stretching to the horizon and the large herd of cattle ahead. All this, the animals, the West Texas landscape, had been hard-wired into her DNA and become as much a part of her as the beating of her heart.

"Earth to Emma." Trace's deep voice intruded into her thoughts.

She blinked and realized he'd stopped and turned to watch her. She'd been so lost in those thoughts that she'd nearly run her horse into the backside of his. Not a good thing, under any circumstances. Lack of attention could get a rider thrown off and hurt. She knew better.

"Sorry." She summoned up a smile. "This is all so awesome to me, especially after being locked inside a prison for a couple of years. I let myself get lost inside my own head. It won't happen again."

His warm smile sent a blaze of heat all the way to her toes. Startled, she shook her head, as if by doing so she could cause the heat to dissipate.

"Come on," he said, urging his horse forward. Immediately, she followed, enjoying the smooth cadence of her mount's lope.

When they reached the herd and slowed, a few of the cattle raised their heads and eyed them curiously, though most avoided acknowledging their presence. Trace circled around them, checking them out, moving from one cluster of animals to another.

A large stock pond separated one group from another, and Trace and Emma rode around it. Here and there, a twisted tree provided a little shade. Some of the cattle clustered underneath, taking advantage.

Trace continued to move forward. "The second pasture is just over that rise," he said, pointing to a large bump of dirt that made a long hill.

She nodded. "I'll follow you," she said.

A moment later, they heard an unmistakable rattle coming from an area to their left. They managed to control their spooked horses, aware it was imperative to move quickly away from wherever the snake might be.

Just then, Emma's horse's snorted, shying sideways, and tried to rear. Easily, she managed to control the now terrified animal, moving them both in the opposite direction of the snake.

"Come on," Trace urged, motioning her forward. She didn't hesitate, using her heels to send her horse moving forward.

Together, they rode maybe fifty feet away. Then Trace stopped and dismounted.

"What are you doing?" she asked.

"Hang on to my horse." He handed her the reins. "I've got to go take care of that rattler. I can't have it biting any of my livestock."

Slowly, she nodded. She'd been born and raised in Getaway. She knew how ranches dealt with rattlesnakes. Still, she hadn't seen a shotgun and mentioned that to him.

"True. I'd prefer that, but I always carry a pistol." He reached into a saddlebag and showed her. "It'll do. It would take too long to ride back to the house and get my rifle out of the truck."

"Are both of these horses used to gunshots?"

"I think so, but why don't you take them over to the other side of the pond just in case."

After doing as he requested, she decided to continue on, intending to get as far away as possible before Trace discharged his pistol.

The gunshot rang out loud, echoing in the previously tranquil air. Emma's horse, Libby, reared up, pawing the air. She struggled to control her and to hang on to Trace's horse, Jack, but when her own mount started bucking, desperate to unseat her, she could only focus on one thing. Getting Libby back under control.

Glancing up from the dead snake, Trace saw Emma's struggle. Libby suddenly turned into a bucking bronc, using every trick in the book to unseat her rider. Meanwhile, Jack bolted, hightailing it across the pasture, reins trailing behind him.

"Damn it." Trace started walking toward Emma, careful to keep on the lookout for any more snakes, well aware that when there was one, there usually was another. Somehow, Emma managed to not only stay on Libby's back, but at the same time, she brought the horse around in a tight circle, gradually regaining control.

By the time he reached them, Libby was calm. And Jack had stopped running long enough to graze.

"Are you all right?" he asked. Judging by her triumphant smile and flushed face, the answer would be affirmative.

"I still have it, Trace!" she exclaimed. "I haven't forgotten how to communicate with horses!"

"Yes, you do." He walked over to Jack, retrieving him and getting back into the saddle. "Let's go finish checking out the herd and then we can head back to the house."

She nodded. "Lead the way. I'm just glad we avoided that snake."

After they'd made a complete circle around the

second group of cattle, checking the fence as they went, they rode back the way they'd come. After going through the gate back into the first pasture, he kept them on a direct path toward the barn.

Once there, Emma made no move to dismount, instead glancing longingly toward the dirt road that ran the length of his acreage. "Do you have time to take a short pleasure ride?" she asked. "It's just that it's been so long since I've been on a horse and I'm not ready to give it up yet."

How could he do anything else but humor her? He couldn't imagine what it would be like to be locked away from fresh air and sunshine and animals for two entire years.

"Sure." He kept his tone easy. "There's a guy with a bunch of alpacas down the road a piece, across from my land. They're interesting to watch."

This news made her practically bounce in her saddle. "Awesome. I can't wait to see them."

They rode at a leisurely walk. Watching Emma, with the almost childlike joy she found in ordinary activities, made him realize it had been a long time since he'd done anything for fun. These days, all he seemed to do was work.

Rounding the turn, he pointed out the alpacas grazing in a field. The shaggy animals, resembling llamas only smaller, ignored them.

"They're much more timid than llamas," Trace pointed out. "They prefer to stay with their herd, so they probably won't be wandering over to check us out."

"That's okay," she said, her attention focused on

the beasts. "I'm just enjoying watching them do their thing."

And Trace was enjoying watching her. He didn't know what it was about Emma McBride, but he found her fascinating, among other things. She brought a brightness to his days that he hadn't even realized he was missing.

The thought so startled him that he nearly missed whatever she said next.

"I need to ask a favor." Expression troubled, Emma appeared uncomfortable. Shifting her weight in the saddle, she wouldn't meet his gaze. "I know you don't owe me anything, and I can see money is tight around here, but I need to ask for a small loan."

Though he didn't know her all that well, he could see how much it pained her to ask.

Still, right now money was so tight, after he paid the monthly charge for Uncle Frank's facility, every month he had to budget carefully to even survive. And some days, even that was a stretch.

Swallowing, he tried to find the right words to let her down easy.

"Never mind," she said hurriedly before he could speak. "It's just that I left prison with nothing. I have no clothes, no toiletries…" Shaking her head, she lifted her chin. "But none of that is your problem. You were kind enough to let me stay here. Maybe I should see if I can find work in town to bring in an income until I get some horse training clients."

Work in town. Despite what had happened at the Tumbleweed Café, Trace knew she didn't understand the amount of gossip and rancor that still swirled around town about her. While she'd grown up there and had been well loved, Jeremy had been a charmer, a real smooth talker. With his internet brokerage and his wild promises of riches to come, he'd quickly gained numerous clients. And friends. Of both sexes. Heather had even talked about Jeremy nonstop.

On a few of his trips home during breaks from college, Trace had seen the man a few times. He'd seen him around in the Rattlesnake Pub, always surrounded by a crowd of young men his age. Women had apparently also loved Jeremy, judging by how many sought him out and hung all over him. The fact that he'd been dating Emma didn't seem to faze anyone, least of all him.

Emma had rarely accompanied her boyfriend on his party-with-the-guys nights. Trace had wondered a few times how someone like her had fallen for a man like Jeremy. Maybe she'd changed while he'd been away at Tech. He'd thought about asking his sister, since she and Emma were still close, but hadn't wanted to betray his interest.

Either way, something about Jeremy hadn't sat right with Trace. The guy seemed too fake, too full of himself, and his naked ambition had been off-putting. He appeared, at least to Trace, to see everyone and every chance meeting as a business opportunity.

Luckily, Trace, as a broke college student, hadn't been the kind of person to even register on Jeremy's radar. Trace had gone back to school, and Jeremy and Emma had gotten married.

"Sorry to have bothered you." Emma urged her horse ahead, her posture dejected.

Realizing he'd been lost in his thoughts too long, Trace went after her, until his horse had reached her side. "Wait," he said. "I can take you shopping." He didn't want to tell her he'd have to put whatever she purchased on one of his credit cards, because right now he didn't have the spare cash to give her.

"Whoa," she told her horse, halting. She went still, her gaze searching his face. "It's okay. I'll start looking for a job in town tomorrow."

Since he didn't have the heart to tell her that might be more difficult than she thought, he simply nodded. "You'll still have a few things to tide you over until then. I've got to run into town tomorrow anyway. We can stop at the discount store on the east side of town."

She opened her mouth to speak and closed it again. "Thank you," she finally managed, her voice shaky. "I promise I'll repay you as soon as I'm able." With that, she urged her horse into a jog and headed back toward his ranch.

Once there, they brushed their horses down before returning them to their stalls.

She offered to help him with any chores, but he told her to go ahead and hang out at the house. What he didn't say was that he needed some time away from her to clear his head. He wasn't sure how or why she had such a strong effect on him, but he needed to get that under control. He'd found hard work to always be a good remedy for any problem.

When he came back inside after feeding the livestock, driving hay out to the pastures and then stopping in the barn to tend to the horses, he was surprised to find Emma in the kitchen, busily stirring something in a saucepan on the stove.

"I thought I'd make breakfast for dinner," she said, reaching for a mug of coffee. "I couldn't find any bread or sandwich fixin's, so I hope that's all right."

"Sure," he replied, genuinely grateful. "Picking up groceries is one of the errands I need to take care of while we're in town."

"Oh good." Her smile lit up her face. "I've started a list. Nothing major, but some staples for meals for next week."

His stomach churned. "I should warn you, I'm on a really tight budget."

"No worries. I kind of figured that, so everything I plan to make is not only inexpensive, but will stretch to more than one meal."

Relieved, he nodded. "What are you making?"

"Oatmeal. The good, old-fashioned kind. I didn't find any raisins to put in it, but that's okay. I cut up an apple and cooked the pieces in brown sugar and lemon juice."

He managed to hide his pleasure. "That sounds delicious."

While she continued to stir the oatmeal, he got his own cup of coffee and sat. "Is there anything I can do to help?" he offered.

"No, nothing." Clearly in a better mood, she spooned the oatmeal into two bowls, added the apples and carried them over to the table. Then she got the milk out of the fridge and placed it between them before sitting down. "Maybe I can get a job cooking at one of the restaurants in town. That way they could hide me in the kitchen where people couldn't see me."

This made him smile. Maybe she understood more

about the situation in town than he realized. After all, the way people had acted toward her at the café must have opened her eyes.

She poured a little milk on her oatmeal and slid the jug over to him. He did the same, taking another gulp of his coffee before trying a bite. It was perhaps the best oatmeal he'd tasted in his life.

"Wow," he said, inclining his head toward her. "This is really good."

His compliment turned her smile into a grin. "I'm glad you like it. After all you're doing for me, cooking for you is the least I can do."

For some reason, he couldn't seem to look away from her. As they locked gazes, her smile faded. Damn it. Jumping to his feet, he carried his bowl over to the sink and began rinsing it. His heart beat fast and a low thrum of desire ran through him. He wouldn't turn around until he had it under control. Emma had been through enough. He refused to even consider taking advantage of her vulnerability.

"Is something wrong?" she asked as the silence stretched out a bit too long. She sounded concerned, clearly not affected the same way he'd been.

"No." Leaving the bowl in the sink, he turned. "I can clean up this."

Smiling, she nodded. "Thanks."

"It's the least I can do, since you cooked."

Once he'd finished washing the dishes, he turned to find her still in the kitchen, hovering but clearly trying not to.

"What else is on the agenda for today?" she asked.

"Do you need my help with anything before we turn in for the night?"

He tried to rein in his scattered thoughts. All he could think about was sharing his bed with her. Which was not going to happen. "We're done. I thought we could watch the news."

"Okay." She sat on the couch, her eyes drifting closed. After covering her mouth while she yawned several times, she finally pushed to her feet. "I think I'm going to turn in for the night."

"Sleep well," he told her, keeping his voice casual.

The next morning, she padded into the kitchen right after he'd sat down with his first cup of coffee. With her bare feet and her disheveled hair, she looked so adorable he nearly choked on his drink.

"Good morning," she said softly. "Did you have a restful night?"

"Yes." Which was a lie. But she didn't need to know he'd tossed and turned in his bed, aching for her. "How about you?"

"I did." She got herself a cup of coffee and joined him at the table. "What's on the agenda for today?"

"I'm not sure," he finally admitted. "Other than our planned trip into town. Are you still planning on working with Daisy?"

"The paint mare? Yes." Clearly, the prospect made her happy. She beamed at him. "I was going to do that after we get back, if there's enough time. If not, I'll start in the morning."

Checking his watch, he nodded. "You should be okay. Are you ready to go? I just need to clean up a bit before I drive you."

"You know what, you don't have to do that. If it's okay, I was thinking I could just borrow one of your vehicles. I couldn't help but notice you have a couple older ones parked on the side of the drive."

"One of those doesn't run," he replied. "The old pickup. I've been working on the other one—the Jeep—in my spare time. It runs, but I wouldn't call it trustworthy."

Considering, she tilted her head. "Are the registration and insurance up-to-date on it?"

The question made him wince. He could barely afford the insurance on his pickup, never mind on an old Jeep he never drove. "No."

"Well, then that won't work. I can't risk doing anything even remotely illegal." She thought for a moment. "Maybe I can walk to town."

"It's a good ten miles," he pointed out. "Not doable. We discussed this yesterday. I have to go anyway. I'll drive you."

Still, she appeared reluctant. She opened her mouth as if to say something and then closed it without speaking.

"What is it?" he asked.

Her sigh sounded shaky. "It's embarrassing, Trace. I'm having again to rely on your charity. On top of that, I have no idea how people are going to act toward me when I try to find a job. I'm not sure I want you to witness it."

His heart squeezed. "Let me be your friend, Emma. You need to have someone who has your back."

Chapter 3

Let me be your friend. How long had it been since someone had made that kind of offer and meant it without any strings attached? Too long. Making friends in prison had been based on what one could do for the other. Not real friendship, except for the romantic relationships that sprang up here and there. Emma had kept herself apart from all of that, aware she had to be careful who to trust and stayed safe by trusting no one.

But Trace was different. He'd taken her in, offered her a business opportunity and his help, and hadn't asked for anything in return. She couldn't put in words how much she valued that.

Slowly, she nodded, using her hand to move a wayward strand of blond hair away from her face. "Thank you. I appreciate that, Trace. I promise I won't forget it."

She straightened up the kitchen while Trace went to clean himself up, and then they got in his pickup and made the drive to town. Their first stop, Trace told her, would be the discount store on the other side of town. After she'd picked up a few essentials, he'd take her to fill out applications wherever she wanted, before finishing up at the grocery store.

Essentials. She'd made a short list, planning on getting the discount brand of everything from shampoo and conditioner to deodorant and soap. She'd need a few clothing items too. At least a week's worth of underwear, a few bras, socks, T-shirts, a pair of pajamas and jeans and shorts. She had no idea what her budget was—and was afraid to ask—but she figured if she stuck with the least expensive items she could find, she ought to be okay.

Still, her stomach churned at the thought of accepting charity from a man she barely knew.

He squeezed her shoulder, startling her. "It's all going to be all right," he said, almost as if he knew her thoughts. "Wait and see."

"Optimism," she mused. "It's been a while since I've allowed myself to feel that."

"That's not true." His smile lifted her spirits. "You came here with a plan. Not only to reestablish your horse training business, but to clear your name. Even now, you're planning to get a job to support yourself until your horse business is up and running. If that's not optimistic, then I don't know what is."

Despite herself, she couldn't help but smile. "You're really kind, Trace Redkin. Thank you."

With a nod, he removed his hand and focused his attention back on the road.

They pulled into the crowded parking lot and scored a space close to the front door. Emma took a deep breath to steady her nerves before opening her door. "Hopefully, we won't run into anyone who recognizes me," she said, her voice tight.

In response, Trace once again squeezed her shoulder. Then, side by side, they headed into the store.

Checking her list, she made quick work of getting what she needed, buying the generic brand of everything when possible. Once she'd finished with the toiletries, they went to the women's clothing area. Once again, she quickly got what she needed without trying anything on. She hoped she didn't regret that later, but hated the idea of making Trace wait.

In the shoe area, she grabbed a pair of discount sneakers and flip-flops. Finally, she had everything. She'd have to make this last until she had her own income coming in.

Through it all, Trace stayed stoically in the background, either scrolling through his phone or people watching. He didn't hover or make her feel uncomfortable in any way, for which she was beyond grateful.

They were walking toward the checkout when she heard someone call her name.

"Emma? Is that really you?"

Dread coiling in her stomach, Emma raised her

head. An older woman barreled toward them with the intent focus of a charging bull.

Jeremy's aunt Becky. Of all the people to run into, Emma ranked her up there as one of the worst.

"It *is* you." The woman stopped three feet away, her large bosom heaving. "How *dare* you show your face in this town! You belong behind bars for the rest of your life."

Despite the screeching and the way several other people turned to stare, Emma attempted to move past Becky toward the checkout. Becky, however, was having none of that.

"Don't you walk away from me," Becky bellowed. "Murderer!"

Trace stepped forward, placing himself between the two women. "Ma'am, I suggest you move along. Store security is heading this way and I think you're about to be thrown out."

Red-faced, Becky eyed Trace with the same amount of disgust one might show a particularly ugly spider. "Who are you? Let me guess. Another hapless man taken in by a pretty viper—"

Luckily for her, the store security guard reached them at that exact moment. "Is there a problem here?" the uniformed man asked.

Hands clenched into fists, Trace nodded. "This woman verbally assaulted us."

A small crowd of onlookers had gathered and they murmured agreement. Meanwhile, Emma kept her chin up, refusing to allow anyone to see she was blinking back tears. "I'd just like to check out," she murmured. "Please keep that woman away from me."

The guard reached for Becky's arm. "Ma'am, I'm going to have to ask you to leave."

"Don't you dare touch me," she shrieked. Finger shaky, she pointed at Emma. "That woman is a murderer. She killed my nephew. She's the one you need to ask to leave."

Trace took Emma's arm. "Come on," he said. "Let's go pay for this stuff. I've still got groceries to buy."

Turning their backs on Becky and the security guard, they made their way to the self-checkout and began ringing up their purchases.

The security guard must have called for backup, because two more came running. It took all three of them to hustle the still-ranting Aunt Becky away.

While she scanned her items, Emma swore she could feel the onlookers' stares boring into her back. She kept her spine straight, and pretended not to notice.

When she'd finally finished, with everything in bags and in her cart, she stepped back. Trace glanced at the total for her items. Expressionless, he inserted his credit card into the register.

Denied flashed across the screen. "Please try again."

Trace glanced at Emma, a flash of panic on his face. "I must have used the wrong card," he murmured, yanking that one out and digging in his wallet for another. Attempting to get the card in the slot, he fumbled and dropped it.

"Is everything okay?" a quiet voice asked. Both

Emma and Trace looked up at the white-bearded man standing there.

"Cliff," Trace said, clearly shaken. "One of my credit cards isn't working. I have no idea why." He finally succeeded in dislodging a second card from his wallet and, hand shaking, went to use it.

"Let me," Cliff said, stepping in front of Trace and inserting his own card. As the receipt printed off, he turned to Trace and smiled. "You can pay me back later." Then he walked away.

Clearly stunned, Trace stared after him. Emma gathered up the receipt, took Trace's arm and, pushing the cart, steered him toward the exit.

They walked to his truck in silence, and Trace pitched in when she began loading the shopping bags in the pickup bed. She got in the passenger side and buckled in, waiting while he did the same. Still quiet, he started the engine, backed out and began the drive home.

"I'm sorry," she said softly. "You should have told me. I would have figured out a way to manage."

"I don't know why that card got declined." The bitterness in his voice made her swallow hard. "Maybe they haven't posted my payment yet."

Too well she understood his pride. "Trace, I…"

"Basic necessities, Emma. That's all you asked for. I watched you shop. You got the least expensive version of everything." He shook his head, his expression still distraught.

She decided not to say anything else, at least until they were safely back home. It was only when they pulled into his driveway that she realized not only had he not stopped at the grocery store, but she'd completely forgotten to fill out some job applications in town.

"What about the food?" she asked softly. "We didn't pick any up."

Putting the truck into Park, he turned to face her. "I don't have any cash," he said. "If my credit card wouldn't work there, it wouldn't work at the grocery store either. I need to find out what the problem is. Once I get that straightened out, then I can get food."

Nodding, she fought back rising worry and failed. "I didn't know things were this dire with you."

"Why should you? You've been here all of two days and barely know me." He shrugged. "It is what it is. Paying for Uncle Frank's care is taking every cent I have. I live in fear what will happen when I can't afford to make that payment."

"Can't you sell off some cows or something?" she asked.

His smile seemed sad. "If I sell off too many more, I won't have a cattle ranch. Spring is calving season. I'd hoped to invest in a new bull since the one I have is getting old, but that's not looking likely at the moment."

He got out and she followed him. "What other sources of income do you have?" she asked.

"I've got a couple of fields planted with cotton. Once I harvest that and sell it, that will bring in some money." He glanced sideways at her. "That's why I kind of jumped on your idea of running your training business from here and cutting me in on a share of the profits."

"What about Daisy?" she asked, thinking of the beautiful paint mare she'd met earlier in the barn. "What exactly is wrong with her? I know you said she's not rideable. What does that mean? Has she ever had a saddle on her back?"

"Oh, she's broke," he replied. "You can saddle her up, put a bridle and bit on her, even climb up to ride. But she won't walk or jog. All she wants to do is run."

"Do you know if she was a racehorse somewhere?" Though a paint racehorse wasn't the norm, there were specialized events for certain breeds.

"I don't know much about her at all. A delivery service brought her to the ranch and Uncle Frank accepted the delivery." He shook his head. "He was so proud. Said he bought a new horse for his own birthday gift. He's the one who named her Daisy. Her APHA registered name is something totally different."

"I was thinking Daisy was an odd name for a horse." She chuckled. "Though I've heard worse."

"Uncle Frank loved that mare. Luckily, he never tried to ride her. At his age, I have no doubt he would have gotten badly hurt."

"What do you plan to do with her?"

"Assuming you can train her?" He went to the refrigerator and grabbed a couple bottles of beer. "Want one?"

"Sure. Yes, after I train her—" she chose to be positive "—will you sell her?"

"Maybe." He opened both bottles and handed her one. "I haven't really thought that far ahead. She still technically belongs to Uncle Frank. I'd have to get his permission, have him sign off on the sale. I'm afraid he wouldn't understand."

Which explained why Trace had kept that mare, providing feed and shelter even when the horse was of no use to him or his operation. Well, she'd fix that. First thing. Right now, she'd pretend the sadness in Trace's voice didn't affect her at all.

Taking a sip of the beer, she sighed. "I'll do an assessment on Daisy tomorrow. Once I know more about her, I should be able to give you an approximate timeline of how much work she'll need."

"Thanks. I appreciate it."

She nodded, suddenly tongue-tied. In prison, she'd allowed herself to dream about what her life would be like once she got out. She'd never had the slightest doubt she'd come back to Getaway. But even in her wildest dreams, she'd never imagined she'd be staying with a rugged cowboy who was not only handsome, but kind and generous too.

Oh no. She wasn't going there. Not now, not ever. She had too much to do to allow herself to get caught up in any sort of romantic entanglement. Since she now accepted that it would be unlikely anyone in Getaway would hire her, she'd focus on two things. Restarting her horse training business, and equally important, clearing her name.

Excusing herself, she went to her room to collect her thoughts.

Never in his life had Trace Redkin accepted charity, and he wasn't about to start now. First, he had to figure out a way to scrape together enough money to pay Cliff back, and then purchase some groceries. Uncle Frank's monthly social security check had been deposited in their joint bank account, but Trace didn't dare touch it. He always used that to help make the payment for his uncle's memory care facility.

Lately, Heather had been good about sending money once or twice a month. After a candid conversation with her detailing the cost of Uncle Frank's place plus keeping the ranch going, she'd made her own decision to help out. After all, Uncle Frank had raised them both and was more of a parent to them than their own father, who hadn't bothered to make contact since dropping them off on his brother's doorstep when they'd been small.

Maybe she'd understand if he called her and told her he needed a bit extra this month. It was past time she learned about Emma's arrival anyway.

Pulling out his phone, he dialed her number. The call went straight to voice mail. He left a message asking her to call him back and then began rummaging through the cupboards to see what he could pull together for them to eat for dinner.

"I can do that," Emma said, startling him. She must have returned without him realizing. "I'm really good at improvising meals. I also want to apologize for giving you another mouth to feed when you least need one. I promise I'll do my best to start bringing money in. I plan to reach out to some of my former out-of-area clients tomorrow."

He started to speak, intending to tell her he was actually glad to have her company, when his phone rang. Heather. Great. The last thing he needed was having Emma hear him asking his younger sister for money.

As expected, Heather squealed when she learned Emma was there. "Seriously? Let me talk to her right this instant."

Amused, he passed the phone over. "Emma, it's Heather."

Emma snatched the phone from his hand. "Heather! I can't believe it. We have so much to catch up on." Talking ninety to nothing, she walked outside, phone pressed up against her ear.

Shaking his head, he watched her go. And then he continued looking for something to put together that might make a meal.

He located a can of tuna, a can of peas and some boxed macaroni and cheese. Uncle Frank had made a tuna-casserole-type dish for him and Heather when they'd been small with these ingredients. If Trace remembered right, it had been pretty darn tasty and as a bonus, made enough for more than one meal.

He started a pot of water boiling, listening for Emma and hoping she didn't hang up before he got a chance to talk to his sister.

Emma came back into the kitchen just as he was about to start mixing everything together. She was no longer on the phone.

"That looks interesting," she said, handing him his cell. "Heather said she will call you back later."

"Thanks." He gestured toward the table. "Dinner's just about ready."

"A man who cooks," she teased, pulling out a chair and taking a seat. "Such a wonderful thing."

Their gazes caught and he sucked in his breath as a shot of attraction jolted through him. Damn if he didn't almost drop the bowl he'd gotten out to combine everything in. Luckily, he got ahold of himself just in time.

The next several minutes, he kept busy draining the macaroni and mixing everything up. While he did that, she set the table. He wasn't sure why, but he felt suddenly overly conscious of her every movement.

Finally, he had the humble concoction prepared.

"That smells good," she offered.

He glanced at her, not sure if she was joking or serious. Her bright blue eyes once again met his, making him swallow.

"Here you go," he managed, clearing his throat. He placed the bowl on the table and took a seat across from her. He didn't like the way he twisted up inside, as if he'd reverted to adolescence again and had a crush on a girl.

That was not a place he was eager to revisit, ever.

After they'd eaten their fill, enough remained for a second dinner.

"Way to dine on a dime," Emma said, holding up her hand for a high-five.

Smiling despite himself, he slapped his palm to hers. "I've gotten pretty good at that sort of thing," he admitted.

"Since you cooked, let me do the dishes." Without waiting for his agreement, she began clearing the table.

"I'm going to go check on the horses," he said. "It's time to give them their evening feed."

Odd how leaving the house felt more like escaping than anything else. He shook his head, trying to gain the confidence to get a grip on this unwanted attraction.

Once the horses had been taken care of, he walked to collect the mail from the mailbox at the end of his drive.

Hoping there weren't too many bills, he flipped through it as he walked back toward the house. One envelope in particular caught his eye addressed to Emma written in all capital letters. There was no return address and the sender either hadn't known Emma's last name or hadn't bothered to write it.

This worried him on numerous levels, though he admitted it was possible he had become paranoid. Of course, considering the level of vitriol displayed toward her in town, maybe not.

Carrying the mail into the kitchen, he found Emma working on his laptop. "Who besides Heather knows you're here?"

She glanced up, appearing unconcerned. "No one. Oh, maybe the people we ran into in Getaway the few times we've been there. Why?"

"This came for you." He handed her the letter, trying to pretend he didn't notice her trepidation, and then moved past her to check out his own mail. He hadn't called his sister back after her conversation with Emma, though he'd shot off a quick text. Given the urgency, she'd told him she'd already sent a check. There likely hadn't been enough time for it to arrive yet, but he couldn't help but look.

Rifling through the advertisements and bills, he

tried not to be überconscious of Emma opening her mail. But he turned quickly when Emma gasped.

"What's wrong?" he asked, putting down the mail and crossing the room to her side.

"This letter." She held out a twice-folded piece of lined notebook paper. "It makes no sense. I was worried it might be some kind of hate mail from one of those awful people in town, but it's not. Instead, it's…"

Clearly at a loss for words, she waved the paper at him. "Read it for yourself."

He took it from her, scanning the handwritten note, printed again in block letters:

I want my money and I know you have it. Be ready to hand it over. I'm coming for it and you soon.

No signature, nothing else but the cryptic couple of sentences. Strange. He read it again.

"What money?" he asked. "Do you have any idea what this person is talking about?"

"No." She shook her head, expression dismayed. "None whatsoever. I'm thinking maybe they sent it to the wrong person."

"Since your name and my address is on the envelope, that'd be doubtful."

"I know." Carefully, she folded the paper on the exact same lines and reinserted it into the envelope. "I'm going to hang on to this just in case."

He didn't blame her. With the way her life had gone lately, who knew what might happen. And the letter writer had been creepily specific, saying they were coming for her soon.

Right then, he made a snap decision. "Do you know how to handle a pistol?"

Her head snapped up. "I was raised here in West Texas," she replied. "Of course I do. My daddy taught me how to shoot. I just don't own a gun."

"It just so happens I have a couple of extras. I'll let you try a few out and pick which one you like the best."

Slowly, she nodded. Instead of reassuring her, his offer appeared to have worried her. "Do you really think this threat is serious?"

"Who knows? But it's better to be safe than sorry, right?"

She thought about it for a moment. "Yes. You're right. Especially since I intend to clear my name. The true killer isn't going to take too well to that."

"How are you going to do that?" he asked, genuinely curious.

"Well, I'm going to start by talking to Rayna. She was the sheriff when all this happened and I'm hoping she'll let me take a look at what evidence they might have collected."

"Makes sense. And then what?"

"I want to talk to Amber Trevault. She was Jeremy's mistress. I'm hoping she'll tell me why she made up testimony against me. One doesn't knowingly commit perjury without a good reason."

He couldn't help but admire her logic. "You've obviously given this a lot of thought."

Her wry smile had him smiling back. "I had two

years to think about it. Actually, I thought of little else."

"I can't say I blame you. On top of losing your husband, it must have been tough being locked up for a crime you didn't commit."

"You don't know the half of it." Eyeing him, she took a deep breath. "Jeremy ran an online brokerage. Since he and I lived with my dad and stepmother, and she sold everything once my father died, I have no idea where to find those records. I'm hoping Rayna will have some of that. Client information, all of that."

"Do you think one of his clients killed him?" he asked, intrigued despite himself.

"Who knows? It's possible. Someone did. The only thing I know for sure is that it wasn't me."

He believed her. But then again, he'd always felt they'd sent the wrong person to prison.

He went back to sorting through the mail. Heather apparently had picked up on Trace's desperation, because she sent the check by next-day delivery. More grateful to see five hundred dollars than he'd ever been, he looked up and smiled at Emma.

"I'm going into town to make a stop at the bank and then the grocery store." He waved the envelope at her, trying hard not to feel ashamed that he had to rely on his sister for help.

"Heather came through."

"Does she pitch in to help with Uncle Frank's monthly bill too?" Emma asked.

"Not really. She's got her own life going on there in California. It's enough that she helps out when she can."

"You sound angry."

"Do I?" He shook his head. "I'm not. More bitter than anything else. I'm the older brother. She shouldn't have to be helping me make it."

To his gratification, she immediately came to his defense. "She's family, Trace. Family helps each other out, especially in tough times. I know Heather. She'd do more if she could."

Since his sister had said something similar, he knew Emma was right. "Thank you for that," he said quietly, meaning it.

"You're welcome," she replied, smiling. And then to his utter shock, she came and wrapped her arms around him.

The feel of her slender body pressed against him sent his heart into overdrive. He froze, afraid to move, fighting against the sudden surge of desire that had him suddenly, fiercely, hard.

She must have felt him—how could she not?—and drew back slightly, a question in her blue eyes. Her lips parted, and he did the only thing he could think of. He covered her mouth with his and kissed her. Not a chaste, friendly kiss either, but an open-mouthed, damn-if-I-don't-need-you kind of kiss.

In response, she might have done any number of things, including pulling back and slapping him, and he wouldn't have blamed her. Instead, after the barest of hesitations, she kissed him back with just enough passion to make his head swim. Then, she pushed him away, laughing.

"None of that, Trace," she told him, her eyes sparkling. "I think we've both been alone too long."

Her words had the same effect as a cold shower would have. Shaking his head, he vacillated between feeling like a fool and wanting to laugh. Either way, she was right. Getting involved would be a huge mistake.

"I'm sorry," he began, his voice stiff, his body still tight.

"Don't be." She waved his apology away. "I get it. Believe me. It's been over two years for me. There's a lot to say for close proximity. We just…can't."

Damn if he didn't wish he could get to the same place as her. He swore he would. Soon. Just not right now, with desire still clawing at him, imagining how hungry she must be if she'd gone two years without. It hadn't been nearly that long for him, though he'd say six months sometimes felt that way.

He realized she was staring at him, clearly perplexed.

"Are you okay?" she asked, a trace of humor mingling with the concern in her voice.

"Yes. Of course." He looked down at the check he still held in his hand. "Did you want to go to town with me or not?"

"I do. Give me five minutes and I'll be ready." With that, she flounced from the room, leaving him still aching, looking at the spot where she'd been.

Chapter 4

That kiss. Wow. Staring at herself in her bedroom mirror, Emma touched her still-swollen lips and tried not to think about how easy it would have been to give in and let desire take over.

But these days, she wasn't about easy. She'd learned the hard way she couldn't afford to sit back and let the current carry her where it may. She'd been blissfully ignorant in her perceived security before and look where that had gotten her.

She put on mascara and lip gloss, dragging a brush through her hair before turning to go. In prison, she'd taken great care to keep her hair up in as tight a bun as possible. She'd seen other women get grabbed by their hair and didn't want to present that opportunity. Now, she luxuriated in the feel of it swirling around her shoulders. Funny how the smallest of things could bring such pleasure.

Gathering herself, since she needed to snap out of it, she took a deep breath and walked back into the other room.

"Do you mind if I stop off at the sheriff's department while we're in town?" she asked. "I'm hoping I can get a chance to talk to Rayna. I really need to get started."

"No problem." Walking to the door, he jingled his keys in his hand. "I'll drop you off on my way to the bank."

"Thanks." Following him outside to his truck, she climbed up, buckling her seat belt.

Once they were on the road, he glanced at her. "How long do you think you'll need with Rayna? I can do the food shopping while you're there if you think it's going to be a while."

"I'm not sure." She hesitated, not wanting to overstep. "Is it okay if I go to the grocery store with you? I have a small list. I've been doing some meal planning. Inexpensive meals, I promise," she added. "I've got all the meals planned out for the next week."

"Sure, if that's what you want." Signaling, he turned right, taking the two-lane road into town. He barely looked at her, keeping his attention on the road. "Listen, Emma. I'm sorry for what happened back there."

"The kiss?"

"Yeah." He sounded miserable. "I didn't mean to take advantage of you. I can promise it won't happen again."

Squelching the tiniest bit of disappointment, she nodded.

"Okay." She watched him carefully. "I'm not upset and you didn't take advantage. But I feel we need to keep things strictly business. Or friends, maybe both. But nothing more."

"Sounds good." One corner of his mouth curled up in the beginnings of a smile. "I'm glad you're in agreement."

This made her smile. "I wasn't sure what else to say. You're a nice guy, Trace. And you've been awfully kind to me. It's just that—"

"Don't." The fierceness of his tone caught her by surprise. "I would never expect that of you. I'm not that kind of guy." He cleared his throat. "Like you said, it's just been too long. We're going to be business partners. It's always a mistake to mix business with pleasure."

Pleasure. Mouth suddenly dry, she nodded. "I agree," she managed. "Let's forget it ever happened, okay?"

"Done." He reached for the radio knob and turned it up. KLLL 96.3, a country music station out of Lubbock, came on, playing a popular Keith Urban song.

The music of home. Finally relaxing again, she sat back in her seat, letting the song take her away.

When they pulled up to the sheriff's office, Trace parked at the curb to let her out. "We need to get your cell phone added to my plan," he said. "All you need is a carrier."

"Maybe," she allowed, getting out. "But since I

don't have one, please just wait for me after you're finished with the bank."

He nodded. "Will do. Good luck."

Watching as he drove off, she turned to face the building. Squaring her shoulders and ignoring the way her stomach twisted, she walked to the door and went inside.

Mary still sat at the front desk. She looked up when Emma entered and blinked, clearly not recognizing her for a second. Then, as she realized who Emma was, she got to her feet.

"Emma McBride? Is that you?" Coming around the counter without waiting for Emma's answer, she wrapped Emma up in a fierce hug. "It's so good to see you. I heard you were out."

"I am. My case finally went to appeal. The one witness against me recanted her testimony and without that, they had no evidence."

Releasing her, Mary nodded. "I always knew you were innocent. I've known you since you were a toddler. You don't have a mean bone in your body."

"Thank you." Emma took a deep breath. "Is Rayna in? I was hoping to have a word with her."

"She is. Let me tell her you're here."

But before she could, Rayna walked up. She wore her unruly red hair in a neat braid. The sheriff's face lit up when she saw Emma. "I wondered when I'd be seeing you," she exclaimed, rushing over for a quick hug. "I've seen some of your advertisements in town, so I knew you were out. Come on back to my office and we'll talk."

Emma followed, trying to push away the bad

memories. She'd only been to the sheriff's office once—on the day she'd been arrested and booked for murdering Jeremy—and she couldn't help but remember how awful she'd felt. Frightened and confused, but still confident that her arrest had been a terrible mistake that would soon be corrected. How wrong she'd been.

When they reached Rayna's office, Rayna gestured at a chair across from her desk and closed the door. "Have a seat."

Still attempting to push away the queasy feeling, Emma did.

Meanwhile, Rayna turned to the credenza behind her and retrieved a fat manila folder.

"I took the liberty of putting together a copy of every bit of our preliminary investigations. I had a feeling you'd want to see them." She slid the folder across her desk toward Emma.

"Thank you," Emma said, taking it. "This is exactly what I wanted to talk to you about. I want to clear my name."

"I figured you would." Rayna dropped into her chair, which creaked as she leaned back. "I'd do the same thing if I were in your shoes."

"How long may I keep this?" Emma asked, lifting up the folder.

"It's yours. Everything in it is a photocopy. We still have all the originals. If there's anything else I can help you with, I will."

Still, Emma didn't move. "There's just one thing I'd like to know. When I was arrested and charged, did you really think I'd done it?"

Rayna's expression stilled. "My job is to look at the evidence," she finally responded. "I can't let personal feelings get in the way of that. And at the time, all the evidence we had made you a likely suspect. It was up to the court of law to actually determine you guilty or not."

Which they had. Still... "I'd ask what evidence, other than that woman's testimony, but I'm guessing everything will be in this folder."

"Yes." Rayna hesitated. "I kept up with your case, you know. My gut instinct told me you weren't guilty, despite the evidence. Unfortunately, I can't always go with my instincts. I want you to know, I tried and tried to find something else, anything that might indicate you hadn't done it. I wasn't successful."

"I understand," Emma said, even though she really didn't. She pushed to her feet, once again battling bitterness and struggling to keep her emotions from showing.

"Hey." Rayna stood too. "I recognize that expression. I've been in a similar situation, years ago. It's perfectly normal to feel resentful, as long as you don't let it consume you."

Somehow, the sheriff's words helped, even if just a little.

"I won't," Emma promised. She shook Rayna's hand. "Thank you for all your help."

"No problem. By the way, we have several of Jeremy's possessions in our evidence locker. I'll work on getting those to you as soon as possible."

Possessions? Emma managed to find her voice. "That would be great."

"All right then. Let me know if you need anything or if I can help in any way."

"I will." Moving toward the front door, Emma clutched the folder to her chest, allowing herself to feel optimistic for the first time.

As she walked outside, she spotted Trace's pickup truck parked at the curb. She climbed up inside, smiling.

"How'd it go?" Trace asked. "You seem pretty pleased."

"Rayna gave me this." She held up the folder, explaining what it contained. "I have to admit, I was nervous. After all, her office arrested me. But honestly, I have to admire her professionalism. She managed to make me feel better and offered to help me any way she could."

"That's great." He put the truck in gear and pulled away.

"It is," she agreed. "Unfortunately, she let me know that she tried really hard to find any evidence pointing toward someone else. She said she found nothing. This worries me. She's a trained law-enforcement officer. If she couldn't unearth any clues, how can I possibly hope to?"

They pulled into the grocery store parking lot. At this time of the day, it was only half full. "I don't know, Emma," he finally replied. "But I have faith in you. If anyone can, you will. You have more reason to dig hard than anyone else."

Yet again, he lucked out and secured a parking spot close to the door. "Come on," he said, jumping out. "We've got some food shopping to do."

Reluctantly leaving the folder on the seat, she got out too. "Would you mind locking the truck?" she asked. Though she knew no one usually locked anything in this small town, she couldn't take a chance on the folder disappearing. She knew Rayna had put a lot of effort in compiling it and would hate to have to ask her to do it again. Plus, neither of them would want a random person seeing all the private information inside.

"No problem." He clicked the key fob until the horn sounded. "There."

"Thank you." Side by side, they entered the store. Trace grabbed a shopping cart and Emma dug her shopping list from her jeans pocket. "Do you have a list too?" she asked him.

"No." His expression seemed a bit grim. "I just get the essentials. Bread, milk, eggs, lunch meat, cheese. Stuff like that."

"They're all on my list. Even though it's been a long time since I've done this, I remember how." Glancing at him, she interpreted his dark look to money concerns. "Don't worry. I promise you, I am budget friendly. We should get dinners for two weeks without spending very much."

Though he nodded, he didn't appear convinced. "Let's get this over with," he said. "I still need to stop at the feed store and get grain for the horses."

Which she interpreted as *Don't blow through all my cash.*

One thing Trace didn't know about her was that when she and Jeremy had first married and moved in with her family, they'd all been extremely strapped for money. She'd taken over the meal planning for their family, a move her stepmother welcomed as it meant she wouldn't have to cook. Emma had learned well how to stretch a dollar, and those skills would come in handy right about now.

They went down every aisle, Trace pushing the cart while she grabbed the items on her list. "I'm making spaghetti with meat sauce one night," she said. "That will last for a couple meals. Meat loaf with mashed potatoes and peas—another inexpensive couple of meals, plus meat-loaf sandwiches are the bomb."

Her comments coaxed a reluctant smile. "You are pretty good at this," he said. "Plus those are all things I like."

"Good." She also grabbed a whole chicken, knowing she could roast it and use the meat for casseroles too. Shredded cheese, two cans of diced tomatoes with chili peppers and some corn tortillas were also added to the cart.

Lost in her thoughts, she whistled quietly as she walked along, so intent on searching for the next item that she nearly walked into someone. She barely stopped in time.

"Oh, I'm sorry," she said, laughing, slightly breathless. "I wasn't paying attention."

The man turned, his annoyed expression giving way to shock. "You!" he exclaimed. "Who the hell let you out of prison?"

At first, she couldn't place him. And then she realized he'd been one of Jeremy's drinking buddies, Brandon. "Excuse me," she said, trying to move past.

But he grabbed her arm. "Answer me," he demanded.

Trace moved quickly, pulling her away and putting himself in between her and Brandon. "Is there a problem here?" he asked, the steel undercurrent in his voice a warning.

Brandon's gaze narrowed. "Well, isn't this nice. Trace Redkin and Emma McBride. Let me guess. A blue-eyed blonde can be very enticing. I never figured you for a sucker, buddy."

For a heart-stopping second, Emma thought Trace might hit him. Instead, he shoved the cart past and indicated to Emma to move with it. Trace didn't turn around, not even when Brandon started to laugh, muttering the word *coward.*

"I didn't want to get into a fight in the grocery store," Trace explained. "There'd be bond and legal fees and all that. Also, it wouldn't help your case any. Who was that guy?"

"One of Jeremy's friends. Brandon something or other. He had a group of guys he used to hang with. I imagine they're all convinced I killed their friend." Blinking back tears, she tried to concentrate on the last items on her list. "I didn't know coming home would be this bad. I need to hurry up and figure out who really killed Jeremy so these people can stop hating me."

He nodded. "Agreed. I'll help any way I can."

By the time they'd reached the last aisle, she had everything on her list. Oatmeal and eggs and pancake mix for various breakfasts, sandwiches for lunch, and different dinners. She grabbed a bag of apples for snacks, and then turned to look at Trace. "I'm done. Is there anything else you need?"

Eyeing the cart, he shook his head. "The only items I knew for sure were milk, eggs and bread. It looks like you've got that covered."

They managed to check out without any more incidents, though Emma couldn't help but keep glancing over her shoulder, worried that Brandon might return.

She held her tongue all the way out to Trace's truck, silent while they loaded up the bags in the back. He pushed the cart back while she got in and buckled up.

Only once they'd left the parking lot did she allow the emotion that had been building up since Brandon grabbed her to bubble to the surface. "This is awful," she said, keeping her gaze averted. "I guess I didn't really think much about what others might think. Getaway is my hometown. I was born and raised here. Anyone who knows me knows there's no way I killed Jeremy."

Heaven help her, he squeezed her shoulder. "That's all that matters, Emma. All you can do is move forward with your life. You were acquitted."

"That doesn't seem to matter to anyone in town." Perilously close to tears, she fought the urge to lean into his touch. Deep breath in, exhale. And repeat. Finally, she felt composed enough to look at him. "You're right about moving forward. Once I figure out who really killed Jeremy, all those awful people can eat crow."

Trace tried not to doubt that Emma would succeed, even if Rayna and her team of trained law enforcement personnel hadn't. Someone had murdered Jeremy and if she began with attempting to find a reason, she might have better luck. While he felt confident Rayna had tried every avenue, since Emma had been Jeremy's wife and even now would own his half of his business if she hadn't gone to prison for his murder. That meant she'd be able to inquire into things that no one else could. As long as she didn't place herself in danger, he'd stay back and let her do her thing. He imagined once the real killer got word of her search, he or she might take steps to stop her. If that happened, Trace knew he'd be sure to have Emma's back.

Once they arrived back at the ranch, they made short work of carrying the grocery bags into the house. He told Emma she could put them away wherever she liked, which made sense since she planned to be doing all the cooking.

He had mixed feelings about that. On the one hand, he kind of liked having someone there who clearly enjoyed making the meals. On the other, having a woman cooking for him felt too intimate, too...cozy. The exact opposite of what they'd agreed to be.

Leaving her puttering around in the kitchen, he headed out to the barn. Saddling up his horse, he rode out to check on his herd and to clear his head. When he'd issued his admittedly impulsive invitation to Emma, he'd never imagined the potential repercussions. Being around a beautiful, sexy woman 24/7 had begun to wreak havoc on his equilibrium.

His cell phone rang just after he'd ridden out. The caller ID showed an unknown number, which generally meant a spam call. Just for the heck of it, he answered. "Hello?"

"I'd like to speak with Emma McBride," the male caller said. His voice sounded gravelly and slightly distorted. Something about it had Trace on full alert.

"Where'd you get my number?"

"On one of Emma's flyers. Don't tell me you didn't know she was posting them all over town advertising her horse training business."

That was right. Since she didn't have her own phone, Trace had let her use his number. Maybe this person was a potential client. "Are you calling about having her train a horse?"

"None of your business," the man immediately responded. "As I said, I'd like to talk to Emma."

Though he didn't want to screw things up for her, something about this phone call was off. The caller was too evasive, for one thing.

"May I say who's calling?" Trace asked, making one last attempt at normalcy.

"Her lover," the man sneered. "Translation—none of your business. Just put her on the phone."

Trace glanced back toward the house. "She's not available right now. If I can get your name and number, I'd be happy to have her call you back."

Instead of responding, the caller hung up.

Strange. And worrisome. Trace immediately thought of the cryptic letter Emma had received. Could this phone call have something to do with that?

Distracted, he made quick work of his ride. After making sure everything was fine with his herds, he rode back to the barn. He unsaddled and brushed Jack down and put him in his stall. Apparently, Emma had come and gotten Daisy and let her loose in the round pen, which meant she intended to work with the horse soon.

As he walked toward the house, he debated whether or not to tell her about the call. While he didn't want to worry her, he felt she needed to know, especially if this might somehow be related to her husband's death.

She came out the back just as he came through the gate into the yard. She'd put her long hair back in a neat ponytail. "Hey," she called out, smiling. "I wondered where you'd disappeared to."

"I went to check on the cattle," he replied, hating the way her smile faltered as he drew close.

"What's wrong?" she asked, tilting her head to look up at him. "Are the horses all right? The cows?"

He exhaled. "They're fine." And then he told her about the call. When he'd finished, she didn't speak right away.

Waiting, he searched her face for some hint of how she felt. He saw no fear. Instead, she lifted her chin and met his gaze, determination flashing in her eyes. "I bet this has something to do with that letter asking for money. And they're both probably tied in to Jeremy's murder. I just have to figure out how."

"I agree." He nodded. "Remember, I'll help you any way I can." Even if it meant trying to keep her safe, he added silently.

"Thanks. I'm on my way to exercise Daisy. After that, I'm going to saddle her up and see how she does," she said, her smile back. "Then, I'm going to make a few phone calls to previous clients to see if I can find anyone with a horse in need of training."

"I'm sure you will. After all, your horse training skills are legendary."

"Were," she corrected. "They were legendary. Now, it seems as if everyone has completely forgotten I ever existed."

He noticed she didn't speak in a self-pitying way; no, it seemed more a statement of fact. "Give it time," he said. "All you need is one success story and people will be clamoring to work with you again."

"I hope you're right." With a quick wave, she turned to go.

He watched her walk all the way to the barn, no doubt to get her tack. Then he forced himself to turn away. He knew he should go back inside the house. A big cattle auction was coming up the next weekend in Lubbock and he had high hopes of getting a young bull for breeding purposes. The one he had now was getting old and tired and he wasn't sure how much longer the animal would last. To pay for the bull, he'd need to sell of a few of his good heifers, but the trade-off would be worth it.

After reviewing the animals listed for auction, he had his eye on a particular bull. Young and not a proven stud, but with good bloodlines. If things went well, he hoped to bring the animal home. Expanding his herd was imperative if he wanted to grow his business.

Since he didn't have anything pressing at the moment, he decided to remain outside and watch Emma work Daisy. Uncle Frank had named the paint horse and while Trace hadn't been fond of the name, he hadn't had the heart to change it. His uncle had viewed Daisy more as a pet than an animal meant to be ridden. Which might also be because no one had ever successfully ridden the mare.

The thought made him snort. Even Trace hadn't been able to do much with Daisy. He'd tried. She'd allow a rider to mount up, but beyond that, she apparently considered herself a bucking bronco. He'd told Emma the horse was skittish. That might have been the understatement of the year.

Emma had saddled Daisy up and was now lounging her. He walked to the edge of the round pen and, leaning on the top rail, watched.

The horse worked well enough. She seemed attentive, going from a jog into a lope upon command. She didn't appear to mind the saddle on her back either, but then she never had. It was only when someone got on the saddle that the mare went berserk.

Finally, Emma appeared to judge Daisy warmed up enough.

"Whoa," she said, allowing the horse to slow to a walk and finally a halt. "You said she's not rideable," Emma said, glancing at Trace. "Can you elaborate? What exactly does she do?"

"She bucks," he replied, grimacing. "And not just little hops. More like a rodeo bronc. I don't have any idea why."

"Hmm." She eyed Daisy thoughtfully. "It's been a few years since I've been tested by a bucker. I hope I remember how."

It took him a moment to realize she was kidding. "Well then, this ought to be entertaining," he said.

"Maybe so." Leaning close to Daisy, she scratched behind the horse's ears. Daisy leaned in for this, clearly enjoying it. "It's okay, girl," Emma crooned. "You're going to be a good horse, aren't you?"

If Emma had been anyone else, Trace might have laughed. But she'd had a reputation before. Even hardened ranchers and horse breeders had sworn she could communicate with horses. Who was he to doubt her?

Daisy's ears twitched, a sure sign that she was listening. Entertained, Trace continued to watch silently.

Emma kept up a steady stream of conversation, all in the same soothing voice. First, she leaned into the mare's side, keeping her weight there for a moment, before leaning back. She repeated this several times. At first, Daisy stomped her front feet, indicating her displeasure, but to Trace's amazement, made no attempt to sidestep in order to get away.

All very impressive, but so far Emma still had both feet planted firmly on the ground. Trace had made several attempts to ride Daisy, none of them successful. He really wanted to see what Emma could do.

Next, she put one foot in the stirrup and swung her leg over, sitting down carefully in the saddle. While Daisy showed the whites of her eyes and her ears twitched, she didn't move. Yet. Trace knew the second Emma tried to make the mare move, she'd let loose. "Be careful," he advised.

Ignoring him, Emma continued simply sitting in the saddle, absolutely stock-still. Daisy pawed the ground, but since Emma didn't move, neither did she.

After a few minutes of this, Emma slowly and carefully dismounted.

"That's all for today," she said, smiling as she patted Daisy's neck. "You were a good girl."

"She was," Trace seconded. "I'm surprised you didn't try to ride her more."

Emma cast him an amused look. "These things can't be rushed. I need to earn her trust first. Only then can I ask her to carry me on her back."

"Interesting. I look forward to seeing the result."

"Good." With a nod, Emma turned and led the horse back to the barn.

Again, Trace watched her go, this time allowing himself to admit she caused an ache deep inside him. Only once she and Daisy had disappeared inside did he force himself to return to the house.

That night, after eating Emma's home-cooked meat loaf, Trace tried to shake off the overly domestic feeling and excused himself. Though he'd told Emma he needed to stop in at the barn, which was true, he also planned to take a walk, hoping to clear his head.

To his relief, Emma hadn't asked to go with him. During dinner, she kept sneaking glances at the fat folder she'd picked up at the sheriff's office. He figured she'd appreciate being left alone to go through it.

Outside, he breathed deeply. While the sun had crossed below the horizon, true darkness had not yet fallen. Still, the sounds of the night—a chorus of crickets, the throaty bellow of bullfrogs out in the pond—had already begun. Trace couldn't imagine living anywhere but in the country. Even back when he'd attended Texas Tech and lived in the dorms in

Lubbock, he'd felt like a fish out of water. Every chance he'd gotten, he'd hightailed it back to Getaway and to the ranch.

After he made sure the horses had feed and water, he walked down to the end of the drive. Pulling out his phone, he called his sister. Heather answered on the first ring.

"Hey you," she chirped. "I'm glad to hear from you. How's everything going? Is Emma all right?"

"She seems fine," he replied. "Despite the way people in town are treating her."

After he'd explained what had happened both times they'd gone into Getaway, Heather swore. "That's so wrong. They obviously don't know Emma like I do."

They talked about a few other things. Uncle Frank, the state of the ranch, his current cash situation. Several times he considered telling her about kissing Emma, but didn't want her to make more of the incident than necessary. After all, both he and Emma had admitted the kiss had been a mistake.

What he didn't understand was why that bothered him so much. Or why he couldn't stop thinking about how badly he wanted to kiss her again.

In the end, he said none of this to Heather. He did tell her about the note Emma had received and the phone call. He also mentioned Emma's visit to the sheriff and her determination to clear her name.

"I can't say I blame her on that," Heather replied. "Is she around? I'd like to talk to her."

"She's back at the house, looking through the information Rayna gave her."

"Oh. Then where are you?" she asked.

He almost hated to respond. His sister knew him too well. "Taking a walk." Which meant he needed to think.

"That bad, is it?" Heather made a tsking sound. "What's got you riled up? Your finances or your houseguest? Are you already regretting allowing Emma to stay?"

"Why do you assume something's bothering me," he asked.

"Because you always go for a walk when you're trying to figure something out," she snapped back. "You might as well tell me, brother dear. What's going on?"

No way could he tell her the truth—that Emma's presence made him yearn for things he'd never much cared about before. So he settled on a half-truth, something that was part of his worries, even if not all of them.

"I'm concerned about Emma's quest to find Jeremy's real murderer," he allowed. "And also about the way people in town have been treating her. I'm worried about her safety."

Just then something whizzed past him, lodging in a nearby tree with a thud. "I've got to go," Trace said, cutting Heather off midsentence.

Ending the call, he dropped the phone in his pocket. A large arrow, the deadly kind used by bowhunters, had lodged in the tree, barely a few feet from his head.

Chapter 5

After taking care of the dishes, Emma settled at the kitchen table with the folder Rayna had prepared for her. The papers were in chronological order, with the oldest on top. Steeling herself, she began to read about the caller who'd discovered the burned-out vehicle in a field outside of town.

The investigation had been very detailed and, as far as she could tell, by the book. The coroner had come out from Abilene, examined what was left of Jeremy's body—which wasn't much after the fire had consumed him. He'd been identified by his dental implants. Reading this, she remembered how Jeremy had been so proud of his perfect teeth, and now she understood why. Cosmetic dentistry was expensive. Why not show off what he'd paid for?

The copies of the photos turned her stomach. Still, she forced herself to study them intently.

Sitting back, she swallowed and then got up to get a drink of water. Though she'd had two years in prison to come to terms with all this, in the space of a few days, she'd gone from being happily married, to her husband asking for a divorce and leaving her, to learning he'd been killed. And then, while she'd been struggling to process everything, she'd been arrested and charged for a crime she hadn't committed. She'd only learned about his mistress when the woman had testified in court. Amber Trevault. Still in disbelief, Emma had studied her while Amber had been on the stand, trying to see what Jeremy had seen in her that he hadn't seen in Emma.

As far as appearances went, Emma and Amber had been complete opposites. Emma had a slender, athletic build. Jeremy had always said she was perfectly proportioned. Amber was all lush curves, wavy flame-colored hair, and dressed far too stylishly for a small West Texas town.

Emma had listened as, while under oath, Amber spewed lie after lie in her testimony. According to her, Jeremy had lived in constant fear for his life due to all the threats Emma had made. Not only had Emma been abusive, Amber claimed, but she'd made several attempts to kill Jeremy. He'd finally asked for a divorce and left her. Even so, Emma had clearly succeeded in making good on her threats.

Barely able to comprehend what she'd been hearing, Emma had opened her mouth several times to refute the other woman's testimony. Only her court-appointed attorney's hold on her arm had prevented her.

By the time Emma took the stand, she could tell from the distrustful looks the jury shot her way that they'd already made up their mind. She'd been painted a jealous wife, vengeful and cruel. Despite the fact that several of these people knew her, they believed Amber over her.

With only circumstantial evidence, Emma had been convicted based upon Amber's testimony. Emma's attorney had promised to appeal, though Emma hadn't had much faith in that actually happening.

It took two years. Amber had recanted her testimony. And now Emma was finally free and determined to find the truth.

Taking a deep breath, she sat back down and resumed her study of the folder.

So engrossed was she in reading the details of the investigation, she didn't notice Trace coming in.

"Emma."

Something in his voice had her raising her head in alarm. "Look." He lifted his hand to show her a long arrow, a lethal-looking thing with a sharp point. "Someone shot this into a tree while I was out walking. I couldn't see who."

Dumbfounded, she eyed him. "Why? Why would anyone do such a thing?"

"Probably to deliver this note," he said, his tone dry. He handed her a piece of paper with a jagged hole in the middle. "It's for you."

"What does it say?" She made no move to take it, even though he held it out to her.

Understanding that she wanted him to read it to her, he cleared his throat:

"Where is my money? I will call you at noon tomorrow and you'd better have a plan to get it to me."

"Again about money." She frowned. "I wonder if this is one of Jeremy's former clients. He handled a lot of investments and I'm not sure what happened to his business after he died and I was arrested. There could be quite a few people wanting whatever dividends they might have earned from investing."

"All of that usually goes directly to the investor," Trace pointed out. "Jeremy would have only handled things if they wanted to make a trade or a new investment or cash-out."

"Oh. I wasn't sure how all that worked." She eyed him curiously. "Do you invest in the stock market?"

He shrugged. "I did a little day trading back in the day. Mostly for fun. Nothing major."

"Well then, if this person wanting their money isn't talking about something Jeremy handled for them investment-wise, what do they mean?" she asked.

"Your guess is as good as mine." He looked from the arrow to the note. "But they're serious. This is a hunting arrow. It can take down a full-size buck. The idea that someone shot this at me…"

His words made her shiver. "I agree. Since he says he'll call me tomorrow, I'll just ask him. I'm guessing he doesn't understand that I have no idea what he's talking about."

"Have you mentioned any of this to Rayna?" he asked, his expression grim.

"No. I plan to, but since I have no idea what he's talking about, I honestly think it might be some kind of mistake. Either that, or a huge misunderstanding."

"I don't like that he not only knows where you live, but that he's clearly stalking you." Raising the arrow, he shook his head. "Something like this can go sideways really fast."

Her stomach churned. "Hopefully, I can get this all cleared up when I talk to him tomorrow." She gestured toward the folder. "Dealing with some lunatic is the last thing I need right now. I'm still trying to go through all the information Rayna compiled on Jeremy's death."

"Just curious. What made you marry him?" he asked.

The question took her by surprise. "What do you mean?"

He looked at her, his expression neutral. "I don't know. I met him once or twice. He didn't really seem like he was your type."

"How would you know what's my type?"

Rubbing his jaw, he gave her a sheepish smile. "You're right, of course. I'm just going on what I knew of you from hanging out here with Heather and things she'd said."

"Heather never really liked him," Emma remembered. "And in hindsight, I think Jeremy pretended to be someone he wasn't. We weren't actually married that long. I was shocked when he told me he wanted a divorce. Even more stunned when he turned up dead and I learned he had a mistress."

"I can imagine. What you have to try and figure out is why someone wanted to kill him."

"True." She thought back. "As far as I could tell, he had a lot of friends."

"Where there are friends, there are almost always enemies," Trace said. "I'm sure Rayna checked into it, so maybe there's something in that file."

"I'm sure there are. And knowing her, she likely investigated all of them thoroughly." Taking a deep breath, she decided to go ahead and speak her thoughts. "I can't help but feel this guy who's asking for his money is tied into Jeremy's death somehow."

"I'd thought the same," he admitted. "But if that turns out to be the case, he's definitely dangerous."

"I'll keep that in mind," she said, her tone dry. "He's just one more thing to add to my list of people to investigate. The only problem is that I have no idea who he is."

Somehow, she made it through the rest of the evening. When she went to bed, she tried not to think about who might have sent the note and what they'd have to say.

The next morning, she kept busy cleaning the kitchen and doing meal prep for later on in the day.

A nervous wreck as she counted down the minutes until noon and the promised phone call, Emma couldn't help but pace. Trace sat at the kitchen table and watched her, his expression kind. He'd placed his cell phone on the table, so she could answer it when it rang.

Wanting to be prepared, she'd made a list of questions for which she hoped to gain answers. She'd ranked them in order of importance, well aware that the mystery caller might be reluctant to answer.

Nevertheless, when the phone rang at exactly noon, she about jumped out of her skin.

Panic-stricken, she stared at the phone and then at Trace.

"Answer it," he urged.

Heart pounding, she snatched it up off the table, accepted the call and said hello.

"Do you have my money?" the man asked. "I'm tired of waiting. Next time, I just might shoot an arrow into your boyfriend's head."

The threat so unnerved her that she nearly lost her train of thought. But then she remembered she'd survived two years in prison. She could do this. She would do this.

"I want to help you," she said, her voice surprisingly calm. "But first, I need you to be more specific. I don't know what money you mean. Did Jeremy owe you money?"

After a moment of silence, the man laughed. "I'm not buying it. You killed him. That means you took the money."

"Okay, first off, I didn't kill him. Secondly, I honestly have no idea what money you mean. So if you expect me to come up with it, you've got to tell me where it came from."

"As if you don't know." He was snarling, and his anger felt palpable. "You were his wife. He must have told you his plan."

"He asked me for a divorce right before he was murdered," she replied. "If he shared his plans with anyone, it was likely his mistress."

"Amber?" Again the laugh, though this time there was zero humor in it. "I've already checked with her. She says you have it."

"Really?" She allowed a spark of her own anger in her voice. "Because she also said I killed Jeremy. I went to prison because of her testimony. Now, after I was locked up for two long years, she admitted she lied. Therefore, if I were you, I wouldn't believe a single word she said."

He snorted. "Look, I don't want any part of a cat-fight between the two of you. I just want my money. If Amber had known where it was, she would have told me."

"How can you be so sure?" she shot back.

A moment of silence and then he gave a low chuckle that sent chills up her spin. "Because torture always works on people like her. And you." He paused a moment, to allow his words to sink in. "Don't make me have to do to you what I did to her. I promise you, she didn't enjoy it. Hell, she barely survived it."

This guy not only operated from a different reality, but was dangerous. Luckily, in prison she'd had quite a bit of practice in not revealing her fear. "I don't have any money, believe me," she said. "If I did, do you really think I'd be here, bumming off my best friend's older brother? The best I can do is look for it, the same way I'm looking for the person who murdered my husband." She paused, a thought occurring to her. "That wasn't you, was it?"

"Of course not," the caller immediately answered,

scoffing. "Not that he didn't deserve it. But know this. If I'd been the one to end Jeremy's miserable life, I would have gotten him to reveal what he did with the money first."

"How do you know his killer didn't?"

Her quick question seemed to stun him into silence. When he didn't answer, she repeated herself. "How do you know his killer didn't?"

"I don't," he finally admitted. "But it's much more likely Jeremy told you—his wife—where he hid the money."

"Not really," she countered, halfway enjoying the exchange. "Remember, he asked me for a divorce."

"That was a cover story," he told her. "He wanted to remove you from danger. He always told me he planned to return to you once it was safe to do so."

Now her head swam. "You and Jeremy were friends?"

"More like business partners."

Of course. Digesting this, she moved on. "Why would Jeremy think I'd take him back? Especially since he'd had a mistress."

"Enough," the man ordered, the menace back in his voice. "I don't care about any of this. I just want my money. I'll give you one or two weeks."

"Not long enough," she replied. But he'd ended the call.

Feeling shell-shocked, she handed the phone back to Trace. "That was weird." And she repeated everything the caller had said.

When she'd finished, Trace shook his head. "You need to tell Rayna. This guy sounds dangerous, especially since he claimed to have tortured that woman. Since he's now threatening you, the sheriff's department needs to know."

"You're right," she admitted. "But Rayna's going to think drama follows me wherever I go. She did say she had some of Jeremy's personal belongings and I could pick them up next time I'm in town. I hope she has his laptop. Maybe that will give me a clue about what money this guy is referencing."

"If they did have his computer, wouldn't you think they'd have gone through it?"

"Maybe. But who knows what they might have been looking for. And I doubt they'd be able to figure out the passwords to his business accounts. Since he didn't have a partner, there's no one else who could have provided access. Though maybe they sent the laptop to some computer expert at the FBI or something."

This made Trace snort. "I doubt that. This isn't a crime show on television. Small-town, West Texas sheriff's departments operate with limited funds."

"Maybe so, but Rayna is good. I seem to remember she caught two different serial killers."

He allowed the truth of her statement with a quick dip of his head. "Talk to her," he urged. "For your own protection."

"I will," she promised. Suddenly, she wished she could ask him for a hug. The need was so strong, so overwhelming, that she simply shook her head, grabbed her folder and left the room.

Watching Emma walk away, Trace couldn't shake the feeling that he should have done something more.

If they hadn't agreed to keep things strictly platonic, he would have wrapped his arms around her and offered comfort. Even though he wasn't certain she needed it, the truth of the matter was that he freaking ached to hold her.

The more time he spent with Emma and got to know her, the more he liked her. In the past he'd admired her for her skill with horses and of course he'd always found her attractive, but this feeling of kinship was new to him. The trials she'd endured had made her stronger and more resilient. Plus, he found her fun to be around when he wasn't trying to avoid reflecting on how sexy she was.

While he admired her bravery and her determination to clear her name, he didn't like the caller and his demands for his money. He especially didn't like the fact that the guy had been on Trace's property and shot a bowhunter's arrow. Even though he'd asked Emma to contact Rayna and make a report, Trace intended to do the same. He also decided to carry his pistol with him from now on. He'd gotten his concealed handgun license several years ago, so he might as well put it to good use.

Trace considered himself an uncomplicated kind of guy. He liked things quiet and easygoing. Given a choice, he went out of his way to avoid drama.

Now, with Emma's arrival, it seemed drama had found him. Time to start being proactive rather than reactive.

Years ago, Uncle Frank had gone through a period of collecting cameras. He'd kept them stored in his bedroom, some under his bed and others in his closet. Since

Trace had left his uncle's room untouched, he knew they were still there. If he remembered right, Uncle Frank had picked up some used video surveillance cameras at an auction. If they worked, Trace planned to set them up outside the house. Damn if some guy with a bow and arrow would be sneaking around on the property to take any more potshots. All Trace needed was one good picture to give to the sheriff.

Opening the door to Uncle Frank's room, Trace turned on the light and stepped inside. He took a deep breath, inhaling the peculiar mix of scents that still lingered in the air. A combination of pipe smoke and arthritis ointment, mint and leather, the smell brought back the image of his uncle so strongly his chest hurt. Uncle Frank had been more than a father to him and his sister. He'd not only stepped in to raise two young children when no one else would, but he'd loved and encouraged them to reach for their dreams. Damn if he didn't miss the man. Especially now, when he no longer recognized anyone and could only talk about the long distant past. Trace missed not just his physical presence, but the man he used to be.

Which meant, of course, Trace needed to visit him. He made an effort to drive out there at least every other week, so he'd go in the next couple of days. He thought maybe he'd take Emma with him. He worried about leaving her alone with that kook out there.

Dropping to his knees, Trace began his search under the bed. He pulled out box after box of old cameras and video recorders, digging through each and every one carefully, not finding what he needed, and slid them all back under the bed. Taking a deep breath, he turned toward the closet.

Remembering how Uncle Frank had crammed the small space full, Trace opened the door with caution, ready to dodge or catch stuff if it started falling out. Luckily, nothing did.

Inside, along with a few items of Uncle Frank's clothes that hadn't traveled to his new home with him, boxes were stacked on top of boxes on top of boxes, filling every available square inch of space.

Staring, Trace recognized he ought to be glad everything was in a box rather than tossed haphazardly in a pile. Nevertheless, this was going to take some time to go through.

Might as well get started. He rubbed his hands together, took a deep breath and removed one of the top boxes.

Ninety minutes later, still at it, he sat on the edge of the bed and shook his head. It seemed he'd gone down a rabbit hole of old photographs and newspaper clippings, and bits and pieces of the past. He'd been humbled to learn his uncle had kept every elementary school award he and Heather had won, as well as handmade drawings and old report cards.

Of course, while none of that came even remotely close to what he was searching for, he'd allowed himself to get dragged down memory lane.

That needed to stop now. If he was ever going to find the surveillance cameras, he needed to get serious.

And then, just as he slid a box of old photographs away, a snapshot of Heather and Emma caught his eye. They'd both worn their cheerleading uniforms and stood arm in arm, beaming at the camera. They looked so happy and young and carefree, practically radiating happiness.

He remembered that day all too well. He'd come home from college a day early and had wanted to surprise his sister. When he'd seen Emma, something had caught inside his chest. She'd practically glowed with joy. And the beauty of her smile took his breath away.

Damn fool, he told himself, dropping the picture back into the box. There'd been plenty of girls at Texas Tech, but he'd never quite gotten Emma Mc-Bride out of his mind. But by the time he'd come back to Getaway for good, she'd already been married to Jeremy. Later, Trace had been stunned to learn she'd been arrested for his murder.

Heather hadn't believed it. Truth be told, neither had Trace. But life had gone on and all that was past history.

"Oh wow," Emma said from the doorway, startling him. "What on earth are you doing?"

Once he'd explained, she asked if she could help him. "I need something to distract me. Reading through that folder is a bit difficult."

"I can imagine."

Not wanting to get all emotional, he reached into a box and retrieved the photograph. "Look at this. You and Heather from your high school years."

Taking it, she laughed. "I remember this day. Heather and I were so full of ourselves. We'd just completed working out a complicated cheer routine and were on top of the world." Handing him back the picture, she sighed. "Those were the good old days."

Her statement made him think. Though Emma had only been out of high school five years, she'd spent two of those in prison.

"Yes, they were," he agreed. "Here, take this one." Reaching into the still-towering stack, he grabbed another full box and set it down on the floor near her. "If you see anything that even remotely looks like surveillance cameras, let me know. I'm not sure if they'll be packaged or just tossed into one of these boxes."

Grinning, she nodded. "Will do." Dropping to the floor, she sat cross-legged and began digging through her box.

Watching her, he found it difficult to drag his gaze away. Right here, right now, he felt every bit that lovestruck boy, crushing on his younger sister's best friend.

"I bet it's hard not to get distracted," she mused without lifting her head. "There's so much good stuff in here."

"There is," he agreed. "But I really need to locate those cameras and get them installed before the guy with the crossbow decides to shoot any more of his arrows."

Just like that, her smile disappeared, which made him feel terrible. "You're right," she murmured. "I'll try to keep my focus on that."

"Me too," he pledged, grabbing another full box and carrying it over to the bed.

Finally, about forty-five minutes later, Emma held up a box with a photo of what looked like a wireless security camera on the front. "Is this it? There are six of them in this box."

"I think so." Relieved, he got off the bed and dropped down to the carpet next to her. "I'm glad you found them. I wasn't looking forward to going through all those other boxes."

Her smile lit up her face. "I'm glad too. Listen…" She hesitated. "If you ever want help cleaning out this room, count me in. I'm thinking you could have a yard sale or something and make a few dollars."

"Maybe." He shrugged. "I'm not sure how many yard sale shoppers would come this far out into the country. Plus, I feel weird about messing with Uncle Frank's stuff. He's not here, but he's not really gone either."

Though his response made her smile waver a bit, she lifted her chin and agreed. "I get it. But whenever you're ready, you can count on me to help."

Aware if he kept looking at her, he'd likely drown in her blue eyes, he turned his attention to the box of cameras. "I think these will be just what I need. Now I just have to get them installed and figure out how to bring them online."

"Are you one of those men who don't bother to read the instruction book?"

Shocked, he glanced at her. "Though I've been known to skip them a time or two, on something like this, I think I'm going to have to read it. I don't know anything about security cameras."

She met his gaze, her own serious. "Me neither, but if you require my help, I'll be glad to give it. I'm not great with computer issues, but I can hold a ladder if need be."

"I'll take you up on that." Checking his watch, he

pushed to his feet. "Let me check these out really quickly."

"Okay." She glanced around the now-cluttered room. "Did you want me to put these boxes back?"

"If you want. Or I can do it later." Halfway out the door, he turned and eyed her. "If you're serious about helping me, I'll call you when I'm ready, okay?"

"Sure." She'd already gotten to work hefting boxes back into their stacks inside the closet. "This should only take me a minute or two to clean up."

Leaving her to it, Trace carried the box into the kitchen. He opened it on the table, removing all the various components before taking a look at the instruction book. Since he wasn't going to do wired installation, he'd be operating off batteries. This meant he'd have to change them out, but doing so would be less of a hassle than trying to wire everything into an outlet.

After a quick read of the manual, he went to get Emma. She'd just about finished putting the boxes away. In fact, she shoved the last one into the closet when he entered the room.

"There," she said, dusting her hands off on her jeans. "All done. Now the room looks exactly as it did before. A shrine to Uncle Frank."

He glanced at her, then back at the room. "It is, I know." With a shrug, he eyed the packed closet. "It doesn't seem right to touch it. Uncle Frank might not physically live here, but he's still...alive."

"I get it," she replied, her smile apologetic. "Did you figure out the security cameras?"

"Yes. Installing them seems simple enough. If you're still okay with helping me, I'd like to get started immediately. I want one on the barn, one on the pole near the round pen, another with a clear view of the riding arena and the others on the outside of the house."

"Lead the way."

He grinned. "Let's do this. By the way, I found a charger and I've got that phone on it. I'll call the wireless provider and get it activated again. I had it shut down once Uncle Frank went to live in the assisted living facility."

"Thanks. I appreciate it."

As she'd promised, Emma followed him around, handing him tools when necessary and holding the ladder. The installation took a bit longer than he'd expected, but he finally had all six mounted. "Now we just need to get them all online," he said, smiling down at her from the ladder.

Though she smiled back, she seemed distracted. She stepped away, releasing her hold just as he swung himself down. The ladder wobbled, and she lunged for it, but only made things worse. As everything began to tilt, Trace tried to jump from the third rung, but Emma was in the way.

He ended up knocking her down hard, his entire body pressing hers into the ground while the ladder fell the other way.

Chapter 6

With the wind knocked out of her and Trace's full weight pressing her down, Emma struggled to breathe. Trace appeared stunned for a few seconds, but then he pushed himself up off her. "Are you hurt?" he asked, his tone as worried as his expression.

Unable to speak at first, she nodded instead. She used her elbows to try and sit up. "I don't think so," she finally managed. "At least, nothing seems broken."

He reached out, hauling her to her feet. "I'm sorry."

"It was an accident." Peering up at him, she managed a wobbly smile. Parts of her were beginning to ache and she knew she'd likely have several large bruises from her fall.

With a hand on each of her arms, he gazed down at her, the concern in his gaze changing to something else, a smoldering sort of heat she felt all the way to her core. For a few precious seconds, she thought he might kiss her again. In fact, her lips parted in anticipation, because in a flash of heat, she wanted his kiss more than she wanted air.

Instead, he shook his head and released her. She wobbled, just a bit, but mostly because desire still fogged her vision. "Let's go back to the house," he said. "You probably should sit down. I want to get on the computer and see if I can bring these all online."

Struggling to hide her disappointment, she nodded. Maybe because he sensed she was still a bit off-kilter, though she hoped he didn't know why, he took her arm. "Steady," he said. "Come on. I'll help you."

Though she was perfectly capable of walking on her own, she shamelessly allowed him to help her and leaned into his strength. By the time they reached the back door, she'd started to come to her senses and felt more like herself.

As he opened the door, she drew away, managing to send him a thankful smile. "I think I need to soak in the tub," she said, knowing that would help alleviate some of the soreness.

Though his gaze sharpened, he only nodded. "Once I have everything online, I'll show you how to work it too. That way you can also monitor everything."

"I appreciate that," she said softly. And then, before she did anything foolish, she slipped away down the hallway.

Since she'd forgotten to grab bubble bath when they'd gone shopping, she settled for filling the tub with hot water. As she stripped off her clothes, she saw a huge bruise on one hip and another, smaller one on her shin.

Slipping into her bath, she sank up to her neck, sighing with pleasure.

She wasn't sure what to think about this newfound attraction and closeness with Trace. As he'd correctly pointed out after that one amazing kiss, they were business partners, nothing more. She had too much on her plate to even think about any kind of romantic relationship, so she considered herself lucky that he didn't want one either. Though she had to admit, that stung just a little bit more than it should have.

Not only did her soak help with her soreness, but it also clarified her thoughts. Once again, she needed to get back to her goal—clearing her name. Therefore, she needed to stick to her plan. And to do that, she knew she'd have to go back to an old habit she'd long since abandoned. Making lists. Not just lists for groceries and necessities she needed, but a list of questions she wanted to ask the man who'd called her asking for money.

Her list-making habit had driven Jeremy crazy, so at his requests she'd gradually weaned herself off them. Once she'd been locked up, she'd had no need for her lists.

But now… She was a free woman. Lists would help her focus, bring her attention to the tasks at hand.

Determined and quite proud of herself, she dried off, combed her wet hair and got dressed. Then, hair still hanging in damp strands down her back, she headed out to look for a pen and a pad of paper.

"There you are!" Seated at the kitchen table with his laptop open in front of him, Trace sounded pleased. "Not only did I get your phone activated, but I've got the surveillance cameras online. I had to purchase a plan so the video will be stored in the cloud. Come see for yourself."

Curious, she went to take a look. Peering over his shoulder at the grainy black-and-white video, she grimaced. "It's not as high quality as I'd hoped."

"I know. But it isn't like I purchased high tech cameras. This will do just fine. I'm reasonably sure if it captures anyone, we'll be able to get a still shot of his face."

"True." Glancing around the kitchen, she looked back at him. "You wouldn't happen to have a spare pen and pad of paper, would you?"

"Check the drawer next to the refrigerator," he said, still concentrating on his screen. "I usually keep stuff like that in there."

She grabbed a pen and a small pad of lined paper and took a seat across from him at the table. Thinking, she started her list, jotting down everything she could think of that might help her get some answers.

Once she'd done that, she read them over, deciding which one she would do first. "This one," she said out loud.

"This one what?" Trace asked, looking up from his laptop.

"I'm going to visit Amber Trevault," she announced.

"Jeremy's mistress?" Trace immediately frowned. "I think I know why, but how are you planning to find her?"

Pleased with herself, she explained, "Her address was in one of Rayna's reports." She looked slightly embarrassed. "I used your phone and checked her out on social media too, and it doesn't look like she's moved. I hope you don't mind. I didn't look at anything else, I swear."

He waved his hand. "No worries. But don't you think Amber staying put seems kind of strange? Especially since your mysterious caller claims he tortured her."

"I didn't think of that," she admitted. "But you're right. Either he lied, or maybe she deliberately didn't update her social media accounts, because she doesn't want him to be able to find her."

"That makes more sense. After all, why would she continue to live in a place where she'd continue to be in danger?"

His comment made her grimace. Nothing ever seemed to go as easily as she planned. Still, determined to push forward, she continued. "I don't know. Maybe she doesn't have anywhere else to go. Or it's possible that he wasn't being honest. What if they're working together?"

As she spoke, she warmed to her subject. "After all, Amber lied about me under oath. She stood by and watched me go to prison for a crime she knew I didn't commit. In my point of view, she's not exactly an upstanding citizen. For all I know, she might definitely be in on whatever scheme that guy has going."

He acknowledged her point with a nod. "Fair enough. But assuming you're even able to find her, have you considered the possibility that she might not be happy to see you?"

"I have." Emma sighed. "It's a chance I have to take if I'm ever going to get to the bottom of this. Now I not only have to find out who killed Jeremy, but learn exactly what money my unfriendly caller is after."

"Promise me you'll be careful."

Surprised by his concern, she nodded. "Of course. I lost two entire years of my life. I'm not about to endanger myself if I can help it."

Watching her, he considered. "I'd like to go with you," he said. "If that's okay."

She liked that he asked rather than simply demanded to go. But if they were going to keep their relationship on a strictly business basis, she thought that might be crossing a line. When she said so, he frowned.

"Is there a reason that business partners can't also be friends?" he asked, sounding genuinely perplexed.

His question had her smiling, something she seemed to do a lot around him. "Good point," she allowed, feeling more relieved than she thought she would. "And actually, I admit I'd feel better if you did come with me. Backup and all that."

"I think we should be armed."

"You do?" She wasn't sure what to think of his statement. "I don't have my CHL, so I can't legally carry. After what I've been through, I'm not doing anything against the law."

"I don't blame you," he responded. "I'll be armed then. I don't see the point in taking unnecessary chances."

"Fine." With a sigh, she checked her notes. "Let me put her address into your phone and we can go."

"Right now?"

She met his gaze, the familiar sizzle settling low in her belly as she fought the urge to drown in his brown eyes. "Why not?" she asked. "The sooner I do this, the closer I'll be to getting an answer."

He didn't move. "Do you have an actual plan? Like what you plan to do once you confront her?"

Since she didn't, not really, she didn't have a ready answer.

"I thought not." He shook his head. "At least try to jot down whatever questions you might have."

"Good point," she admitted. "I need to note everything I want to know." Like why? Why Amber had been willing to lie under oath, to ensure that another woman, a total stranger, went to prison for a murder she hadn't committed.

"Yes. You do."

He sounded so smug she had to glare at him. Which only made him laugh. "No need for the death stare," he said. "I'm just trying to help."

This time, she laughed. "You're right," she said. "Again. I'll make notes on the way there. By the time I confront Amber—*if* I'm able to actually confront her—I'll be prepared." She glanced at the clock. "How soon can you be ready to go?"

Though he shook his head, he grinned. "You're killing me. All right. Let's go."

After she put the address into his GPS, she tried to conquer her nerves and make her list of questions. To begin with, she had two—the basics. Why had Amber lied? And was it true that the anonymous caller had tortured her? If so, did she know who he was or what this money was that he wanted?

Satisfied, she sat back in her seat and eyed the landscape as Trace drove. She figured she had a fifty-fifty chance of getting Amber to even talk to her, never mind answer any questions. However, she had to at least try.

Amber didn't live in Getaway. Instead, she had a house in a small town west of Abilene called Sweet-water, which was about a forty-five-minute drive from Getaway.

By the time they reached the Sweetwater city limits, Emma felt she'd finally wrestled her nerves under control. After all, it wasn't as if she'd wronged Amber. Since it had been the other way around, Emma felt Amber owed her an explanation.

Still, when they pulled up in front of the address she'd input into the GPS, Emma sat in the truck and eyed the neatly kept older brick ranch home, hating how jittery she felt. Next to her, big and strong and far too handsome, Trace didn't say anything; instead he simply watched her.

"I think I'm ready," she announced, wiping her sweaty palms down the front of her jeans. "How about you?"

The kindness in his gaze told her he understood her nervousness. "I'll be right there behind you," he said, the steady timbre of his voice reassuring.

With a nod, she opened the passenger door and got out of the truck. She waited until Trace had come around and joined her before making her way up the sidewalk. With every step, she rehearsed what she wanted to say, well aware she'd likely get only one chance and didn't want to blow it.

Once they'd reached the front door, she froze. Turning to look at Trace, she knew blind terror was likely written all over her face.

To her surprise, Trace took her hand. "It's going to be all right," he murmured. And then he pressed the doorbell.

A moment later, the door swung open. The red-haired woman who answered bore little resemblance to the woman Emma remembered from her trial.

"Can I help you?" Amber asked, looking from Trace to Emma and back again. Clearly, she didn't recognize Emma at all.

Bracing herself, Emma spoke quickly. "I'm Emma McBride. I was hoping you'd have a few minutes to answer some questions."

At the sound of her name, Amber blanched and took a half step back. "I was informed you'd gotten released. I don't have anything to say to you," she replied, and started to close the door.

"Wait." Desperate, Emma stuck her foot in the door like she'd seen people do on TV. "That man who tortured you, he's been calling me and making threats. I really need to talk to you."

Amber stiffened, the color leaching from her face. "He promised he'd leave me alone," she rasped. Then, as she realized what she'd said, her eyes narrowed. "I'm guessing you're here for the same reason, so let me save you some time. I don't know anything about any missing money. Jeremy never said a word to me about that."

Abandoning her written questions, Emma acted on instinct. "Please. Let us in. I'm afraid that man will do to me what he did to you. He doesn't appear to believe that I don't know either."

Looking from Emma to Trace and back again, Amber finally opened the door and stepped aside. "Quickly," she urged. "I don't want to take a chance that he might see you."

Rapidly moving past her, Emma waited until she'd closed and locked the door. "Is he watching you?"

Amber shrugged, not succeeding in masking the flash of terror that crossed her face. "I don't know. Some days, I think so. Others, I tell myself I'm being paranoid. He's finally stopped calling me, but who knows?"

"Why didn't you move?" The question burst from Emma, making her breath hitch in a gasp as she'd realized what she'd said. She cut a panicked glance toward Trace, but his implacable expression revealed nothing of his thoughts.

Instead of answering, Amber sighed and continued leading the way toward the kitchen. Once there, she motioned at them to take seats at the table.

"I can't leave," she said. "I take care of my disabled younger brother. I not able to work outside the home, so we're barely able to afford the utilities and food for this place, which I own outright since my parents left it to me. There's no way I can relocate."

Emma's heart squeezed in sympathy. She hadn't

planned on liking this woman. Or at the very least, feeling sorry for her.

"I've been wanting to talk to you ever since my trial," Emma said, still standing. "I really want to know why you said those things on the stand, especially since you knew they weren't true."

"About that," Amber said, twisting her hands in front of her, her gaze downcast. "I didn't know they weren't true. I was grieving and all I knew was what Jeremy told me. Jeremy talked a lot of trash about you while we were together, you know. He vented to me about your anger issues and how you threatened to stab him if he was every unfaithful. He said you were insanely jealous and when he was killed, it seemed logical that the betrayed wife would have lashed out."

Logical. "None of that was true. At all. And you were under oath."

"I know, but I truly believed what I was saying. It was the truth as I knew it," Amber explained. "You had every reason. Your husband was cheating on you. A lot of wives would have gone off the deep end."

Emma shook her head. "I didn't even know about you. Jeremy just came to me a couple days before he was killed and asked for a divorce. I had no warning. I was still trying to wrap my mind around that when his body was found."

"And then you were arrested and charged with his murder," Amber finished.

"Yes." Again, Emma glanced toward Trace. He stood close to the doorway, quietly watching. "When my case went to appeal, the conviction was overturned and I was released."

"You were set up," Amber said. "I know that now. And I helped with that, though I didn't know it at the time. And I'm still not sure why. That man—the one who came here and threatened not only me, but my brother—I believe he was behind that."

Now Trace spoke for the first time. "Can you describe him?"

"Sort of. Medium height, slightly stocky build." She grimaced. "To be honest, he looked like just about every local guy in his midforties. Short brown hair, close-cropped beard. Beer gut."

Emma hurriedly made notes. "Did he give you any hints about who he might be or how he knew Jeremy?"

"No. That's the thing. All he kept talking about was the money. He got really mad when I told him I didn't know what money he meant."

"Did he really torture you?" Emma hated to ask the question, but she needed to know how far this man would really go to get answers.

Amber's shudder was telling. "He tied me up," she said slowly, her voice low. "But worse, he went and got my brother Matt. Matt's fourteen." She swallowed hard. "He's got a cognitive deficit. What they used to call developmentally delayed. The doctors say he's mentally around age three."

A single tear slipped down Amber's cheek. "Matt likes everyone. He *liked* this man. That's in his nature. And then, he had to sit there while this man started pinching me." She shook her head. "I tried to keep quiet, because I didn't want to upset my brother. He pinched me *hard*. But as far as torture went, it seemed kind of lame, so I figured it would get worse. You know, ripping off fingernails or cutting off fingers. I watch TV. I know what people like that do."

"Did he?" Emma asked, her tone blunt. "Did he do any of those things?"

"No. I don't think he had the heart. He doesn't seem like a truly evil man, just someone who was ripped off and wants his money back." Amber took a deep breath. "I keep worrying that's going to change. It's got to be frustrating, waiting so long. He seemed pretty certain that you'd know where to find his three million. And now you're out..."

"And I don't know either," Emma finished. "But that theory would certainly explain a lot about his behavior."

"He's big with words. When pinching me didn't work, he described in great detail what he would do to Matt if I didn't tell him what he wanted to know. Matt was there. He *heard*, which made it all doubly horrifying. So yes, while I wasn't actually physically tortured, the mental torture was more than enough."

"I'm so sorry," Emma said, meaning it. "I'm sorry you and your brother had to go through that."

Gaze faraway, Amber appeared to be still lost in her memories of that day. "I don't know how much Matt understood, but I'd say at least some of it. After it was over and that man left, Matt wouldn't speak to me or even look at me for damn near two weeks."

"How'd you get that guy to leave?" Trace asked, arms crossed. "Especially since you couldn't give him the answers he wanted."

"He stayed for hours. Kept talking, making his

threats in the calmest voice, as if he was talking about the weather. I swear I thought about lying, telling him some nonsense just to get him out of my house and away from me and Matt, but I knew he'd come back."

"Besides pinching, did he touch you or your brother?" Emma wanted to know. "Did he physically hurt either of you in any way?"

Expression haunted, Amber nodded. "After a few hours of me telling him I didn't know about his money, he twisted Matt's arm. Hard enough to make him scream. I was tied up and I couldn't get to him. I couldn't protect my brother." Now tears streamed down her face in earnest. She grabbed a paper towel and began blotting at her eyes.

"Did you file a police report?" Trace again, impassive. "When the guy left, did you tell anyone at all about what you'd just been through?"

"I couldn't. He said if I called the police, he'd come back and finish the job. Naturally, I kept quiet. You two are the first people I've spoken to about this." She took a deep breath and then lifted her chin. "I bought a gun and taught myself to shoot. I even got my CHL. So help me, if that man shows up here again, I will defend myself and my brother."

Emma resisted the urge to comfort the other woman, mainly because she couldn't yet forgive how Amber's lies had stolen two years of her life. Instead, she waited silently while Amber got her emotions under control.

"Is there anything else you can tell us?" Emma asked. "Anything at all that might help? That man has given me one or two weeks to find this mysterious money."

"I'm sorry, but I don't have anything." Amber glanced at her watch. "You both need to leave. Matt will be waking up from his nap soon and I'd prefer not to have you here when he does."

Trace followed Emma to the truck, careful to keep himself between her and Amber. Instinctively, he'd taken an active dislike to the woman, especially knowing all the trouble she'd caused Emma. For all they knew, Amber might be unhinged. He wanted to make sure she didn't get the sudden urge to hurt Emma. Back straight, he ignored the impulse to turn around, even though the hairs on the back of his neck prickled a warning.

Once they'd gotten into the truck, he finally glanced at the house. The front door had been closed and there was no sign of Amber. Relief flooded him. He sighed and shook his head. "I'm sorry, but I have no idea what Jeremy saw in her." After all, Jeremy had the good fortune to have a woman like Emma. Someone like Amber could never compare. He kept this part to himself however, since it wasn't the kind of thing one said to their business partner.

"Who knows." Clearly distracted, Emma stared out the passenger side window. "That didn't go at all like I expected."

About to ask her what she meant, the camera app on his phone sounded an alert. Since they were still on a residential street, he pulled the truck over to the side and parked.

"What's wrong?" Emma asked, turning in her seat to stare at him.

"Hopefully nothing," he responded. "Just a second and we'll see." Touching the app icon on his phone's screen, he clicked on the banner that stated One New Alert. It came from the camera he'd mounted near the back door.

With a mixture of fury and disbelief, he watched as a husky man wearing a black cowboy hat pulled low over his forehead broke into Trace's house.

Emma made a sound of outrage as she watched.

"Call Rayna," he ordered as he pulled back out into the road and pressed the gas pedal to the floor. "Ask her to meet us at my place."

While she made the call, he concentrated on getting home. More than anything, he wanted to catch that SOB in the act. Due to the length of time it would take them to get back to the ranch, he knew that would be unlikely, but held on to hope.

Leaving Sweetwater, he blazed the backroads. Though he still drove safely—passing only when allowed—he drove fast. They reached the Gateway city limits in much less time than it would normally take.

He slowed as they went through Getaway proper, not wanting to endanger anyone. Once they'd made it past the other side of the town limits, he picked up speed again.

Other than a few choice curse words muttered under his breath, he didn't speak. Honestly, he was afraid if he did, he might frighten Emma with the depths of his rage. His jaw hurt from clenching his teeth so tightly. Knowing that someone had broken into his house and was going through his things seriously pissed him off.

Finally, they reached the turnoff to the ranch. He took it too fast, causing the tail end of the pickup to shimmy side to side. He easily brought it back under control. They were in the homeward stretch now, and in just a minute or two, he'd either catch the burglar in the act or arrive too late.

As they turned into the driveway, kicking up gravel and skidding once again, Emma made a squeak. Glancing at her, he forced himself to slow. "I'm sure whoever it was is long gone by now," he told her. "But I want you to wait here in the truck just in case they're not."

Eyes wide, Emma nodded. "Look. There's Rayna." She turned to look back, pointing as another vehicle kicked up dust behind them in the driveway. "She must have gotten tied up with something. Please don't go in yet. Wait for her."

"I will," he promised, jumping out and going around to the rear of his truck. Arms crossed, he watched while the sheriff's vehicle skidded to a stop next to his.

Rayna jumped out, pulling her service weapon from her holster. Grimacing, Trace did the same, glad he'd decided to travel armed. "The back door is open," he pointed out, jaw still clenched.

"I'll take that way in," Rayna said, her tone all business. "You take the front. That way if someone is still inside, we cut off their method of escape." She glanced at Emma. "Please wait inside Trace's truck."

"I will." Climbing back inside, Emma closed the door. Glad she'd agreed to stay safe without a fuss, Trace jerked his head in a quick nod.

"Ready?" Rayna asked, drawing his attention back to her.

Heart pounding, he nodded, digging his keys from his pocket as he moved quickly toward the front. That door was still closed and secure. He unlocked the dead bolt quietly and slipped inside.

"Sheriff's department," Rayna shouted, moving from the kitchen to meet Trace in the front of the house. "Clear," she added. "Let's check the bedrooms next."

While Trace moved with the sheriff, he registered the fact that his house looked as if it had been hit by a tornado. Furniture had been turned over, and cushions tossed from the couch. Lamps and picture frames had been swept from the tables, with everything tossed haphazardly on the floor.

The bedrooms, while empty of intruders, looked much the same as the rest of the house.

"I wonder what they were looking for," Rayna said after they'd ascertained the entire house was clear.

"Oh, I have a pretty good idea," Trace replied, his tone grim. "In fact, Emma's got something she needs to tell you. Now is just as good a time as any. Let me go get her."

Once outside, he motioned to Emma that it was okay to exit the truck. She jumped down and jogged over to him. "Is everything okay?" she asked.

"Not really. Whoever broke in tossed the house. Clearly, they were looking for something. And I think we both know what that something might be. It's time to talk to Rayna."

Following him, she nodded. Inside, he led her to the destroyed living room.

Stopping short, she gasped. "Whoa."

"I'll say," Rayna agreed. "The rest of the house looks just as bad. I understand you have something you need to tell me?"

Open-mouthed, Emma continued to take in the damage. She gathered herself enough to nod. "I sure do."

Rayna made notes as Emma explained. While Emma talked, Rayna didn't interrupt, though Trace could tell by the set of the sheriff's jaw that she didn't like what she was hearing.

Finally, Emma wound down, ending with their visit to Amber. She glanced at Trace. "Am I forgetting anything?"

"I don't think so," he said.

"I have questions," Rayna announced. "A lot of them."

While Emma answered the sheriff's questions, Trace began straightening up. Luckily, the intruder didn't appear to have been bent on destruction, just a search. And since Trace had no money hidden inside his house, the burglar hadn't found what he'd been searching for.

Chapter 7

Emma managed to hang on to her composure until the sheriff finished questioning her and left. Taking shaky breaths, she couldn't allow herself to break down yet. As soon as Rayna's cruiser pulled away, she jumped right in to help Trace clean up the wreck of his house.

If she kept busy, she didn't have to think. Still, no matter how hard she worked, she couldn't escape the sharp stab of guilt.

This—all of this—was her fault. She knew it and knew that Trace did as well, though he was too much of a gentleman to say anything. If she'd never asked Trace for help, if he hadn't allowed her to stay, no one would have broken into his home, or shot a lethal hunting arrow at him. Her very presence had not only disrupted his life, but possibly placed him in danger.

If she had any honor, she'd leave. Remove this kind and good man from the equation. The only problem was that her status hadn't changed much since she'd arrived. She still had no job, no money and no place to go.

Nor was she any closer to finding out who'd killed Jeremy.

In short, she felt like an epic failure.

"Cut yourself a break," Trace said when she expressed a tiny portion of her feelings to him. "You've only been here a little over a week. That's barely enough time for anyone to catch their breath and get their bearings."

His kindness once again brought tears to her eyes. "Thank you. I'll try harder," she promised. "I still haven't gotten around to making phone calls to some of my former clients, but mainly because I no longer have their information. I used to keep extremely detailed records. I have no idea what happened to all of that when my stepmother sold the house."

Trace looked up from gathering books from the floor and placing them back on the bookshelf. "Have you tried contacting her?"

"I have no idea how. I don't even know where she went." She swallowed. "We didn't keep in touch after my father died."

"Like I said, I activated your phone. I know you have it with you. Just look for her on social media. That's usually the fastest way to find someone."

Her phone. It had been so long since she'd had

one that she'd managed to forget about it. Glad she hadn't left it here at the house, she pulled it from her back pocket and touched the home button to bring the screen to life. "I'm pretty sure all my social media accounts have gone inactive," she said. "I'll need to work on reactivating them or starting up new accounts, whichever is easier."

His smile sent warmth through her. "You do that. I think you'll see that once you get yourself reestablished, it'll be a lot easier for you to get your horse training business up and running again."

Slowly, she realized he was right. "I used to belong to a lot of local horse groups online. Becoming active in those will definitely be a bonus."

He nodded. "Plus, remember you can do a lot of research about anything on the internet. You can access old news stories and newspaper clippings. That will give you another perspective on Jeremy's murder that will be different than Rayna's report."

All at her fingertips, right there on her phone. Shaking her head, she felt so out of touch. Two years incarcerated had changed her. A lot. She remembered when she'd been accustomed to using her phone for virtually anything. Clearly, she'd gotten out of the habit. Funny how that seemed so long ago, like in another lifetime.

After reactivating her profile, Emma checked her friend list. Despite being offline for over two years, her list appeared to be mostly intact. Evidently, most people either hadn't realized she'd gone inactive or they hadn't cared.

Thinking about what to post, Emma settled for a

brief note stating she was back and ready to take on new clients' horses. Then she went through her friend list, looking for her stepmother, Beth. While she did this, Trace sat across the table from her, scrolling through his own feed.

"Here she is!" Emma exclaimed, staring at Beth's profile, feeling triumphant and apprehensive. "It looks like she's moved to Key West." That made sense, in a weird way. From what Emma remembered, her stepmother loved to party. Emma's father had always shaken his head and laughingly claimed he couldn't hardly keep up with her. Still, he'd loved his second wife, and Beth had seemed to love him back. Emma could only hope Beth had been there for him when he died, especially since Emma had been locked up and could not.

One of her greatest regrets and deepest hurts.

Taking a deep breath, she studied Beth's profile. Her stepmother had lost weight, colored her hair blond and looked tanned and fit. She'd posted numerous photos of herself with large groups of friends, and a tall, silver-haired man who must have been her new beau.

Emma couldn't help but feel Beth wouldn't be happy to hear from her. After all, she was part of the life Beth had left in her rearview mirror. Yet in the days when she and Jeremy had lived with them, Beth and Emma had managed to avoid each other enough to get along. Though Beth had stopped writing Emma after Emma's father had died, until then she'd seemed supportive and had claimed she'd never doubted Emma's innocence.

In the end, Emma sent a PM, writing that she'd gotten out after her case had gone to appeal and was back in Getaway. After mentioning how good Beth looked and how Florida clearly suited her, she ended with asking if Beth knew where she might find her old business records. Though she really wanted to know if Beth had saved anything of Emma's from the house she'd grown up in, she didn't want to press her luck. Knowing her stepmother, Emma guessed Beth had wanted to cut all ties with her past so she could move into her new life unencumbered.

Once finished, Emma began checking out several horse-related groups she'd been a member of. Apprehensive, she posted in several, simply letting it be known that she was once again taking on new clients.

Then, and only then, did she click on Jeremy's profile. The sight of his handsome, smiling face threw her for a loop. She stared a moment, and then registered that hundreds of his friends had posted messages of grief and loss at the time of his passing. She forced herself to read each and every one of them.

Only a few mentioned her and those were not kind. She read them anyway. And then she began checking Jeremy's friend list, wondering if the man who kept calling might be there. While she had no idea what he looked like, she felt it couldn't hurt. She couldn't help but see that females made up disproportionately more of his friends than male. How had she never noticed this before? She wondered if all along Jeremy had been more of a player than she'd realized.

Glancing up at Trace, she found him watching her. He didn't look away, which made butterflies swirl inside her. "I've got to figure out Jeremy's password," she said. "There might be some clue inside his profile or in his private messages."

"What were his favorite things?" he asked. "I'd start there."

She thought for a moment, realizing if she made a list of her former husband's top likes, she'd figure in somewhere near the bottom of the list. "Money, beer and football," she said out loud. "Golf. And the stock market."

If Trace noticed she didn't mention herself, he didn't comment. "Let's make a list of terms associated with those things. Also, if there are any special significant dates, jot those down too."

"Okay." She eyed him curiously. "You seem to know a lot about this topic."

"I watched a documentary about it a while back. Really interesting stuff. Most people, despite being told not to, tend to use the same password for everything."

This made her try to remember if there'd ever been a time when Jeremy had shared a password with her. Unfortunately, she didn't think he had.

Shaking her head, she got to work making a list. Trace scooted his chair over next to her, so close his shoulder bumped hers. She tried to ignore the shiver of awareness that ripped through her, instead focusing on the page and her list.

"Beer," she said. And then listed the three brands Jeremy had preferred. She also wrote down his favorite football team—the Dallas Cowboys—and every term she could think of related to them, including names of the star players.

Trace watched her, adding a few words of his own here and there. Next, they covered golf, which she knew next to nothing about. Trace ended up using his phone to do an internet search for popular golf terms.

From there, they moved on to money. They had a bit of fun with this one, listing all kinds of terms, including slang. Trace's suggestions had Emma laughing.

Next, just in case, Emma wrote down every significant date she could think of, from when she and Jeremy had first met up to their wedding day. Deep inside, she knew it would be highly unlikely for any of these to mean enough to Jeremy to choose as a password. He'd never been a sentimental kind of guy.

They left the stock market for last. Emma glanced from her paper to Trace. "Do you know anything about investing?" she asked.

"No. I take it you don't either."

Slowly, she shook her head. "I mean, Jeremy talked about it a lot, but since I had no idea what he meant and he always got irritated when I asked questions, I stopped paying attention. Buy low and sell high are about the only things I remember."

This made him grin. Staring, she wondered how a simple smile could make a man so sexy. "How about we try some of the others first," he said. "If they don't work, we can circle back to the stock market. I have a feeling a guy like Jeremy would pick something that wasn't work related anyway."

A guy like Jeremy. About to ask him what he meant, she decided against it.

After she'd tried plugging in different passwords, none with any success, she finally had to admit defeat. "It's a good thing they don't lock you out after so many wrong tries," she said, shaking her head.

"It is," he agreed. "Do you mind if I give it a shot?"

"Of course not." She slid her phone over to him, curious.

Intent on the screen, Trace typed one thing after another. "Aha!" he finally exclaimed, his expression triumphant. "I got in."

"What was it?" she asked, accepting the phone back from him. To her astonishment, he shook his head. "I'd rather not say it out loud. If you don't mind, I'd rather you change the password to something you can easily remember."

Now she really wanted to know. "He's gone, Trace. Just tell me. It's not going to make one bit of difference in anything."

Gaze locked on hers, he considered. Then he leaned over and, mouth grazing her ear, murmured two words, one of which was slang for a certain part of the female anatomy.

She froze, her face heating as an electric buzz zinged through her entire body. "Oh," she said faintly. "I, uh, see what you mean."

Though he'd moved back quickly, his gaze had darkened. "I'm sorry," he said. She wasn't sure if he meant for the password or for the effect he'd had on her.

Before she did anything else, she went to Settings

and quickly changed the password. She couldn't imagine what Jeremy had been thinking, typing those two words in every time.

Then again, maybe she could imagine. There might have been a reason her former husband had so many female friends.

"I'm going to check his private messages," she announced. Taking a deep breath, she clicked on the icon.

The private message list was long. And there were several—all from women—that Jeremy had never viewed. A few of them had no doubt come in after Jeremy had been killed.

Those would all be interesting to read, but right now she needed to see if Jeremy had received messages from any male clients. But as she scrolled through them, the only males who sent messages were Jeremy's golf buddies or drinking pals.

Then she remembered he had a separate work page for his investment business. She could only hope he used the same, distasteful password there; otherwise she and Trace would be back at the drawing board trying to guess.

Luckily, Jeremy had used the same password. The first thing she did was go in and change it. Then, she discovered numerous messages from various clients—mostly male. Reading through them, she noted the common threads. Escalating anger, demands for a return phone call and then threats to go to the authorities. More than one person mentioned missing money.

"This is not helpful at all," Emma said, showing

Trace. "However, I'm guessing Rayna might want to see these."

"If she hasn't already." Trace shrugged. "In a murder investigation, I would think law enforcement would be able to compel the social media companies to allow access to the files."

"I'll text and ask her." Emma sent off a quick text message.

Rayna responded immediately:

We reviewed all the private messages in Jeremy's social media accounts, both personal and business. We also interviewed numerous people regarding their statements, and found no correlation to Jeremy's murder.

Emma read it out loud to Trace. "Apparently, this is another dead end."

"Possibly," he admitted. "Though you never know. Maybe Rayna and her team missed something."

"Maybe." Though she didn't believe it.

Another text came through from Rayna:

Don't forget, I've got his laptop and a few other personal belongs that we removed from your parents' home. Let me know when you want to pick them up.

Emma thanked her and said she would. While she'd known Rayna had some of Jeremy's things, she hadn't been sure about the laptop. This was good news. Maybe the computer would have some vital information that could help.

* * *

Watching Emma go through her former husband's private messages made Trace ache for her. The bewilderment and hurt showed plain on her face as she began to realize there had been a side to her husband that she'd never known. He suspected as she delved deeper into his life, more unsavory information would emerge. From what he'd seen so far, Emma would be strong enough to deal with all of it.

He couldn't imagine going to prison for two long years, all the while not only grieving the loss of her husband, but knowing she hadn't committed the crime. Twenty-five months of her life, lost and for what?

After feeding the horses and hauling hay out to the cattle, he returned to the house. Early mornings had become his favorite time of the day. Everything seemed clean and new, fresh with possibilities. That hadn't changed, but now he had the added bonus of seeing Emma's beautiful face too.

Walking into the house, he kicked off his boots and went to look for her.

"Where are you off to?" Emma asked. Curled up under a blanket on the couch, with her coffee cup cradled in both hands, she gazed up at him.

His heart skipped a beat. With her tousled hair and her huge blue eyes still dreamy with sleep, all he could think about was how badly he wanted to kiss her. And more.

"Have you had a cup yet?" she asked, smiling at him, clearly oblivious to his amorous thoughts.

He nodded. He'd snagged his own coffee earlier,

while she'd still been asleep. He'd already been up for a couple hours, needing to get the livestock taken care of before he made the trip into Lubbock. "I'm headed out to attend a cattle auction."

"Oh? Are you selling or buying?"

"Both," he responded. "There's a bull I have my eye on. I'll need to sell some of my stock to raise the money to get him. If I can get him for a reasonable price, I feel he'll have a strong impact on my breeding program."

"Then I hope you get him."

He felt the warmth of that smile all the way to his toes. "Thanks. I'll be gone most of the day. Will you be okay here alone?"

"Of course. I plan to spend some time working with Daisy and also going over Rayna's file."

"Just be careful." Cramming his black Stetson on his head, he hesitated, wanting to say more but aware he shouldn't. In the end, common sense won out and he simply lifted his hand in a wave before heading out the door.

The long drive to Lubbock gave him time to think. Clearly, he'd been alone for a while. Emma McBride occupied his thoughts entirely too much, both sleeping and waking. He burned for her with an intensity that astonished and alarmed him. This was made worse by the fact that she clearly didn't feel the same way.

Of course she didn't. At this point in her life, Emma wasn't looking for a relationship. She'd just gained her freedom after being wrongfully incarcerated. She was a woman on a mission. She burned with the desire to clear her name and have her husband's true killer brought to justice.

He couldn't blame her. If their situation were reversed, he would have felt exactly the same. Even so, knowing this didn't stop him from wanting her. He guessed that was just something he'd have to learn to move past.

When he finally pulled up to the Lubbock Stockyards, he was relieved to find he was an hour early. He got his heifers checked in and moved to their pens before parking his rig and making his way inside. The lot number of the bull he had his eye on wouldn't come up for at least an hour, which was good as his heifers would sell first.

As more and more potential buyers came into the building, Trace got a little nervous. He'd gone ahead and picked out a second-choice bull just in case he lost the first one, but he really hoped he'd get lucky.

The heifers he'd brought came up early and were snapped up quickly. He got a fair price, which pleased him. While waiting, he had to fight the urge to text Emma to make sure everything was all right. He had his phone in his hand, watching the auction, while trying to talk himself out of it.

Just then, the camera app on his phone sounded an alert. Trace opened it, keeping his eye on the action in the arena below him. In disbelief, he watched as a masked man swung what appeared to be a baseball bat at the camera, before it went black. The man, who wore what appeared to be a bandanna over the bottom half of his face, then went around and in the course of a minute, disabled every camera Trace had installed on the house. Trace felt pretty sure the others outside would be next.

How had this guy known Trace would be gone? And also, how had he managed to learn about the cameras? None of that mattered though. Because while this intruder was on the ranch, Emma was home alone. And Trace highly doubted she was aware that she might be in danger.

Fingers shaking, he dialed her number. "Pick up, pick up," he muttered, earning a disgruntled look from the rancher next to him.

Emma answered on the fifth ring, out of breath. "Hey, Trace. What's up?"

Quickly, he told her what he'd seen on the cameras. "He's there. Right now. Are you inside the house?"

"No." Her voice quavered. "I've been working with Daisy. We took a ride down the road to cool off after."

Which meant she wasn't home. Relief flooded him. His knees weak, he allowed himself to drop into his seat. "Don't go home," he said. "Call Rayna first and have her check it out before you even go near the house."

"I will," she promised, her voice steadying. "Did you get your cow?"

Cow. He didn't correct her. "Not yet." Quickly, he checked the lot numbers. The bull he'd come to purchase would be led out next.

"You stay and get that cow," she said fiercely. "I don't want you leaving without it. It's too important. And you're a couple hours away anyway. Fifteen or twenty more minutes won't make a difference."

She was right. "Call Rayna," he urged. Below, they

were leading his bull out into the middle of the arena. "I've got to go. I'll call you back in just a few."

"Bye."

After ending the call, he forced himself to focus on the magnificent animal that he hoped to bring home. A young bull, unproven at stud but with excellent bloodlines. Compared to some of the other bulls, this one was nothing special on paper, so Trace hoped to purchase him for a reasonable price.

Apparently, the rancher next to him had the same idea. Soon, they were the only two left bidding. And the price was rapidly approaching Trace's limit. If the other man didn't back down, Trace would have no choice but to let him have the bull.

Raising his paddle, Trace signaled his willingness to bid again. He waited to see what his competition would do. If the man next to him outbid him, then he'd be the one taking the bull home.

But this time, the other rancher didn't top Trace's bid. Instead, he glanced at Trace, shook his head and turned away.

"Sold," the auctioneer announced. "Sold to the gentleman in the black hat." He pointed at Trace.

Relieved, Trace headed out to pay his marker and collect his bull. Tapping his feet, he waited in line, trying to push down the drumbeat in his head that kept nudging him to get on the road and head home. When his turn came and his account was settled, he even had a little cash left over from the sale of his heifers. This pleased him despite inside being a twisted mass of nerves.

After getting his receipt, he was told where to take

his truck and trailer to load up. He hurried outside, hating the fact that he was so far away and could only wait.

On the way outside, he called Emma again. When she answered, he breathed easier. "Did you get ahold of Rayna?" he asked, unable to keep the concern from coming through in his voice.

"Yes," she replied, her tone solemn. "She ordered me to stay away until she and her deputies could check things out. She also sent one to watch over me just in case. He's here now."

"Good." The worry that had been tying his stomach in knots eased up a little now that she had protection. "I'm glad you're safe."

"Me too. What about you? Did you get your cow?"

"Bull," he corrected, finally. "And yes, I'm on my way to load him up so I can head home."

"That's awesome!" Despite everything currently happening, she sounded genuinely excited. "I can't wait to see him."

"Thanks." His phone beeped, indicating another call. "It's Rayna," he said. "I'm going to have to let you go."

He clicked over to the other call. "Rayna. What did you find?"

"Well, your intruder is long gone." The sheriff sounded matter-of-fact. "He smashed up all your surveillance cameras, and then apparently took off. The house is still locked up tight and we saw no sign of forced entry."

"All my cameras?" he asked. "Did he get the ones on the barn too?"

"I didn't know there were any there. Hold on." Rayna barked an order to someone. "I'm having one of my guys check."

"Good. If they're still there, I can check the feed in the app. I pay extra so it's stored in the cloud."

"Excellent. We might be able to get footage of his vehicle if they're still working."

"And you're sure he's gone?"

"Yes. No one is here. My guys searched everywhere. I sent one of my deputies to stay with Emma and they say no one has gone that way."

Which meant the intruder had left by the main road.

Trace pulled around to the side yard and joined the line of trucks waiting to load.

"The barn cameras are still intact," Rayna announced. "Can you check your feed and let me know if you got anything?"

"Sure. I'll forward it to your phone if I do."

Since there were four other rigs ahead of him, he checked out the camera app. The barn camera feed showed only Emma leading Daisy out from the barn and nothing else, even though he forwarded it all the way until it said Live. Next, he switched to the one near the arena and watched as Emma worked with the paint mare, before fast-forwarding it until she rode the horse out of view of the camera.

And then he waited. This camera had a good view of the driveway. If any of them had been able to catch the intruder coming or going, he felt it would be here.

There. A black pickup truck, a Dodge, he thought, drove past. Forwarding in spurts, Trace saw nothing else until the truck left. Parts of the arena fence obscured any hope he might have had of getting a clear shot of the license plate.

Quickly, he copied the video and texted it to Rayna.

Not much to go on. But better than nothing.

Rayna sent back a quick thank-you and said she'd get to work on it. Meanwhile, she promised to have an armed deputy stay with Emma until Trace made it back home.

He thanked her, resisting the impulse to pound the steering wheel as the line in front of him slowly moved. Briefly, he considered jumping out of his truck and approaching the attendant to see if he could expedite things, but knew that would be akin to cutting in line, so he stayed put.

Finally, the rig in front of him loaded up and left and his turn came.

The transaction went smoothly, and someone led out Trace's new bull and loaded him up in the trailer. After pocketing the bill of sale and the animal's pedigree, Trace climbed back into his truck and pulled away. Finally, he was heading home.

It wasn't until he was on the interstate in the middle of nowhere that it hit him. If she'd been home when the intruder had come by, Emma could have been hurt or worse—killed or tortured. After all, the man clearly believed she held the key to returning his missing money. The thought made him shudder. From this point on, he wondered if he could ever leave Emma home alone. They'd need to step up their efforts to not only find Jeremy's killer, but to unearth what had happened with his investment business. If money was missing, and evidently some was, they'd need to figure out where it had gone and why.

Trace suspected all this would turn out to be tied together with Jeremy's death.

Though he tried to concentrate on the road, or the fact that he'd succeeded in getting the bull he'd wanted, his thoughts kept returning to Emma. Only a few weeks had passed, but his attraction to her had only grown. Not just physically either, though that was a huge component. He actually *liked* her. He felt comfortable around her and realized he'd smiled more since she'd arrived than he had in months. He couldn't imagine what his life would be like without her.

What the actual hell? Heart pounding, mouth dry, he shook his head, as if doing so could help him clear away the realization. He didn't *need* Emma McBride, did he? If not, then why had it hit him like a punch in the gut when he'd understood she could have been in very real danger?

As he drove, eating up the miles, all he could think about was what he wanted to do when he saw her again.

Chapter 8

After the nice young deputy conferred with Rayna, he informed Emma he would be escorting her home. He followed along in his patrol car while she rode Daisy back to the ranch.

Home. She tried not to think about how much the word meant to her, even more so now that she didn't have one of her own. When she and Jeremy had married and moved in with her family, she'd believed him when he'd told her that someday they'd have a home of their own. Starry-eyed, she'd dreamed of what their house would look like, of the children they would have and of growing old together.

What a fool she'd been. Even after her sham of a trial, even after she'd been led off in shackles to prison, she'd mourned him. Jeremy, her husband, had died. He might have wanted to leave her, he'd definitely cheated on her, but he hadn't deserved that. No one did.

She'd had faith at first, in those early months. Justice would prevail, her attorney had told her. He'd appeal. Only he hadn't told her how long such a thing would take.

No matter, she thought, turning the mare onto the driveway, the deputy's car about fifty feet behind her. The past was the past. All she had to look forward to was the future.

Once she finished reconciling the past.

She'd spoken to Amber and had learned exactly nothing. Next up, she needed to see what she might find on Jeremy's laptop.

And her stepmother still had not responded to her private message.

Shaking her head at herself, she dismounted and began brushing down the mare, all under the watchful eye of the deputy. She was glad he didn't seem much for conversation. She wasn't in the mood for small talk, knowing how close she'd come to finding herself in serious trouble. She wished that she could sit down and have an adult conversation with this man so she could make him understand that she too was looking for answers. But after talking with Amber, she'd come to understand such a thing wouldn't be possible.

She'd have to fend him off long enough to figure out the truth.

Once she had the horse taken care of, Emma put her in the stall and debated what to do. She wanted to go in and figure out what she'd make for dinner later. Clearing her throat, she turned to face the deputy. "Is it okay if we go inside? I can get you a glass of iced tea or something."

The man smiled for the first time since arriving. "Thank you, ma'am, but I'll wait outside. No refreshment is necessary. The sheriff instructed me to stay here until Trace gets back. Then after that, several of us will be taking shifts patrolling the place until that guy is caught."

"Outstanding," she said. She not only liked that he took his job seriously, but that living in a small town had its perks. Rayna would do her best to keep Emma safe. "Well, let me know if you get thirsty or anything, okay?"

"Will do," he agreed.

Once inside, Emma poured herself a glass of lemonade and drained half of it in one gulp. Then she sat down at the kitchen table and pulled out her phone.

Checking social media, she blinked at the private message from her stepmother, Beth. Clicking on it, she realized Beth had sent a short response—Call me—along with a phone number. Before she could second-guess herself, Emma dialed it. Heart pounding, she waited while it rang and rang. Figuring the call would likely go to voice mail, she readied herself to leave a message.

Instead, Beth picked up. "Hello?"

"Hi. It's Emma." Talk about a brilliant way to open a dialogue. Emma and Beth had never been truly close and Beth had merely tolerated her husband's daughter. She'd seemed to like Jeremy though. Everyone had liked him.

"Emma." Real warmth colored the other woman's voice. "How are you? I'm glad to hear you got out."

"Thanks." Emma took a deep breath, figuring she might as well get right to the point. "I'm looking for answers. A man who I think is one of Jeremy's former clients is hounding me, asking about his missing money."

"I'm sorry to hear that. What can I do to help?"

Distance truly must make the heart grow fonder. Beth had never once offered to help Emma with anything. "I'm wondering if there's a chance you might have saved any of Jeremy's belongings," Emma began. "I know Rayna has his laptop and a few other things, but was there anything else?"

"Yes," Beth answered immediately. "As a matter of fact, when I sold the house, I boxed up everything that belonged to you and to Jeremy. I wasn't sure what to do with it, so I asked Serenity Rune if she'd hang on to it for a bit. It's likely she still has it. If she knows you're back in town, I'm surprised she hasn't contacted you."

"She did tell Trace to have me stop in and see her," Emma replied. "I admit I put it off, mostly because I wasn't feeling up to hearing one of her mysterious pronouncements."

"I get it." Beth's agreement was yet another surprise. Back when they'd all shared a house, Emma felt the older woman went out of her way to disagree with everything Emma said or did.

"But you should go see her," Beth continued. "She's really an insightful person. She helped me a lot when I was grieving the loss of your father."

This statement made Emma guilty and sad. She'd grieved her father's death too—from prison, unable to attend his funeral. No one had helped her get through it. But she hadn't given more than a passing thought to how Beth might be coping. She should have. Emma and her stepmother might not have always gotten along, but Beth had truly loved Emma's father.

"I'm glad she was there for you," Emma finally managed. "And thank you for saving those things for me."

"You're quite welcome. Feel free to save my number and give me a call if you need anything else."

"I will," Emma promised.

Trace came through the door as Emma ended the call, saving her from staring at her phone as if it had just sprouted wings. "That was Beth," she began, breaking off midsentence as she caught sight of the determined look on his face.

He crossed the room without speaking. When he reached her, he hauled her up against him and covered her mouth with his.

Stunned, she opened her mouth to him and kissed him back, letting the heat and passion carry her away. He felt big and strong, his body rock-solid, his kiss fierce. *This*, she thought, dazed and more turned-on than she could ever remember being. She wanted him and judging from the force of his arousal pressing against her, he felt the same way. Business partners be damned.

Heart pounding, she allowed herself to touch him. To slide her hands under his T-shirt and caress his skin. She'd dreamed of this, longed for it, even though she'd been afraid to allow herself to act on her need.

He sucked in his breath when she splayed her hand across his flat stomach, wondering if she dared to allow herself to stray to the waistband of his jeans. Until now, he'd kept his hands on her backside, pressing her up against him. But as she gave herself free rein to explore, he did the same, his fingers sweeping up the curve of her waist, lingering on her rib cage.

Suddenly feverish with need, her mouth found his again. He matched her urgency with an intensity of his own. Now, instead of tentative touches, they couldn't seem to shed their clothes fast enough.

Naked finally, she stepped back, allowing herself to drink in the splendid masculinity of his body. His gaze dark, he looked at her too. She almost swore his gaze caressed her.

"I've lost too much weight," she said, her nerves getting the best of her as he continued to stare. "I know I'm not as curvy as I was before, but—"

"Shh." He pulled her to him, cupping her breast and tweaking the nipple. "You're beautiful. Stunning. And absolutely perfect."

Now she could have melted into a puddle of desire. Seriously, she'd never understood stories with women who swooned, but maybe now she got it.

Kissing, touching, reveling in each other, somehow they managed to make it to his bedroom. She would have loved it if he'd picked her up and thrown her on the bed. Instead, he lifted his mouth from hers and, with his arousal jutting against her, asked if she was sure.

She almost wept, almost laughed. For so long she'd felt as if she'd had no choice in any part of her life. And now he, clearly as turned on as she was, cared enough about her to make certain she didn't want to stop.

"Trace." Lifting one hand, she placed it alongside his cheek. "Yes, I'm sure. I've never wanted anything more in my life."

At her words, he made a sound, so wild she thrilled to hear it, and claimed her mouth again. She let go of caution, giving in to the need to touch him everywhere. Then he pulled away, opened his nightstand drawer and removed a condom, which he quickly donned.

She almost teased him about being well prepared, but instead simply held out her arms for him to come back too.

Again, their mouths met with passion.

Together, they dropped onto the bed, still kissing and touching, while the ache inside her grew. "I'm ready," she whispered, which made him grin down at her.

"So am I," he growled, the proof hard and thick against her stomach. "But this is our first time and I want to take it slow."

Slow? She didn't want slow—she wanted fast and furious and wild. She gripped his arms tightly, bucking underneath him like an untamed horse. Though his gaze darkened and his breath came faster, somehow he resisted. And then he laughed. Laughed!

The sound aggravated and aroused her.

"Patience," he said, even as his body surged against her thigh.

Patience? She'd shred his patience. One small shift of her body and she'd maneuvered so his swollen shaft touched her slick body.

"Patience," she ground out, even as she teased herself around his engorged tip. "I have zero to spare."

Teeth clenched, he held himself rigid, shaking while clearly fighting to resist. "Slow," he managed, entering her, though not all the way. "I've got to go slow."

"Fast," she countered. "I need you inside of me. Right. Now." She lifted herself, taking more of him inside of her. If he wouldn't move, then by damn she'd do it herself.

She saw his expression change and knew the exact moment he lost his last shred of control.

With a muffled groan, he let loose, ramming himself into her again and again and again. Emma matched him, stroke for stroke, her body quivering as the tension built inside of her. His kiss stole her breath. When she opened her eyes, she realized he was watching her, the rawness of her need reflected back in his dark and fierce gaze.

This pushed her over the edge. Shuddering, she cried out, her body clenching around him as she found her release.

Trace followed a second later, crying out her name as he came.

They held each other as their heartbeats slowed and their breathing got back to normal. Emma felt as if she should say something, but no words would come. Trace didn't seem inclined to speak either.

Finally, he kissed her temple. "That was…"

"Amazing," she finished. She hoped he didn't make some statement about where did they go from here or some such thing.

Instead, he brought the conversation back to where it had been before he'd kissed her.

"Did you say you talked to Beth?" he asked, cradling her in his arms. "How'd that go?"

"Surprisingly well," she replied, more relieved than she should have been. "She left some of my things with Serenity. Jeremy's too."

"That's awesome," he said, yawning. "Rayna mentioned she was going to have her deputies include the ranch in their nightly patrols until this guy is caught."

"Her deputy mentioned that," Emma murmured, hiding her own yawn with her hand. "I'll feel a lot safer that way."

When he tightened his arms around her, Emma smiled and allowed herself to sink into a doze.

She must have fallen deeply asleep, because when she opened her eyes again, she was alone in the bed. Judging from the angle of the shadows on the wall, the sun had nearly set. "Trace?" she called out, feeling oddly vulnerable. When he didn't immediately answer, she threw back the sheet and padded to the bathroom. She took a hot shower, relishing in the way her body ached from lovemaking, refusing to allow herself to wonder if or how this would change things between them. Maybe it didn't have to. Because she wasn't ready, not yet. Maybe not ever.

* * *

Leaving Emma sleeping after the most intense lovemaking he'd ever experienced was more difficult than it should have been. Carefully, he slipped from the bed and made it to the bathroom, where he disposed of his condom before stepping into the shower.

Once he'd dressed, he quietly made his way past the bed where she still slept. Unable to resist, he stood for a heartbeat or two and gazed down at her. In sleep, relaxed, she let go of the worry that sometimes made tiny lines in her smooth forehead. Her full lips were slightly parted, still swollen from his kisses.

Never in his life had he seen a woman more beautiful.

Heart in his throat, he shook his head. How the hell had he managed to allow himself to get emotionally entangled like this? Romance was the last thing either of them needed. But they couldn't go back. Even if he could, he refused to regret the passion they'd shared. No matter what happened after this, he had a gut feeling that Emma would say the same.

Still moving as silently as possible, he made his way out to the living room, where he grabbed a set of car keys from a drawer and his cowboy hat. He grabbed a sheet of paper and left Emma a quick note telling her he'd gone into town so she wouldn't worry. He had a few quick errands to run and though he hated to leave Emma alone, Rayna's promise of frequent patrols made him feel safer. In fact, the instant he got outside, he sent the sheriff a text, letting her know he'd be in town for an hour or two and asking if she'd make sure to keep an eye on his place.

Once he'd gotten an affirmative answer, he walked over to the old Jeep, got inside and prayed the thing would start. Luckily, it did. Now if he could just make it into town, he'd have a great surprise for Emma when he returned.

He called his insurance agent before he left, adding the Jeep to his policy, letting them know he'd pick up his liability card on the way into town. That done, he did exactly that, making a quick stop at his agent's office. From there, he took it for the inspection.

Everything went smoothly. The Jeep passed inspection and he got it registered. Then he filled the tank with gas and headed home. To his astonishment, the old Jeep ran smoothly, which was a relief.

Parking the Jeep next to his truck, he hopped out and went into the house. Emma sat in the kitchen sipping a tall glass of lemonade, her long hair still damp from the shower. She smiled at him when he walked in, making his heart skip a beat. "I wish I'd known you were going into town."

Suddenly tongue-tied, he merely nodded. It still amazed him that Emma didn't seem to have the slightest idea of her own beauty.

When he didn't respond, Emma continued. "I need to stop by Serenity's shop and pick up the items Beth left with her. I know you just got back, but would you mind giving me a ride? If not, we can always go tomorrow."

She'd given him the perfect opening to spring his surprise.

He grinned. "Great news, but no, I won't be driving you. Do you still have a valid Texas driver's license?"

Slowly, she nodded, clearly wondering if he intended to let her use his truck. "Yes. It doesn't expire for another year. Why?"

Trace took a deep breath. "You remember that old Jeep you commented on? I've got her running and just updated the registration. Somehow, she passed inspection. Here." He tossed her a set of keys. "I added the Jeep to my liability policy, but I'll need to get your date of birth and driver's license number so I can add you as the driver."

Expression warring between disbelief and joy, she caught the keys. "You're really going to let me drive it?"

Her question made him laugh. "Yes. After what happened last time, I realized I don't like the idea of you being stuck here at the ranch when I'm gone. You needed your own transportation, so now you have it."

"My own vehicle." She shook her head. "I never expected you to do something so kind and generous."

To his shock, he noticed her eyes had filled with tears. A woman crying was one of the few things he wasn't comfortable dealing with. In fact, he'd do just about anything to make them stop.

"Don't cry," he said hastily. "I did this more for the convenience. That way neither of us are dependent on a single vehicle."

Though she nodded, she continued to dab at the corners of her eyes. He waited, three seconds away from gathering her in his arms, when she spoke.

"Thank you," she said, her voice shaky but strong.

"I don't know how I'll ever repay you, but I promise somehow, someday, I'll figure out a way."

Relieved, he waved away her comment. "No need. The Jeep is yours to use for as long as you want."

When she went very still, an intense look crossing her face, he braced himself. "Why now?" she asked quietly. "When I asked you before, you said no. What happened to change your mind?"

At first, he didn't understand. When he finally got what she meant, he knew he had to be damn careful with his answer. He understood what she thought— that his sudden generosity might be tied up with the fact that they'd made love. That wasn't the case. He could only give her the truth and hope she believed it.

"It's not what you think, Emma," he told her. "On the drive back from Lubbock, after that guy had been on my ranch, disabling my security cameras, I realized you had no way to get away from the ranch if I was gone. That's not acceptable."

Still motionless, she continued to watch him, almost warily. "I decided to get the Jeep drivable before we ended up in bed together," he said. Blunt honesty appeared to be required. "One thing has absolutely nothing to do with the other."

He saw the moment she accepted his explanation. The guarded look left her eyes and she relaxed her stance. "I didn't really think it did, but wanted to make sure," she explained. "I might currently be a bit down on my luck, but…"

"You still have your pride," he finished for her. He ached to reach out and hold her, but sensed now would not be the time. "Emma, we're both adults.

We've been tiptoeing around our attraction to each other for a while now. Yes, we gave in. That doesn't have to change things."

"I agree," she replied. The relief that flashed across her beautiful face wounded him, though he hid it. "We both have needs," she continued. "As long as we can keep ourselves from getting emotionally entangled, I don't see the problem. Do you?"

Emotionally entangled. Damn if he wasn't already more than halfway to hell. Still, if she wanted to be friends with benefits, he'd take what he could get.

Somehow, he managed to nod and smile, hoping it wasn't more like a grimace. "No problem on my end."

"Great. I'll guess I'll dry my hair and drive into Getaway."

Glad he had chores to keep himself busy, he nodded. "I've got a few things to take care of around here. Just be careful when you're in town. As you saw, a lot of people have strong opinions about Jeremy's death."

"That's the understatement of the year." Her wry smile brought a weird lump to his throat. "But yes, I'll definitely be careful. And I'll also have my cell phone with me."

"Good." Unable to look away, he continued to hold her gaze.

"I'm planning to stop by the sheriff's department and pick up Jeremy's laptop and whatever else Rayna has of his. After that, I'll go by Serenity's. When I was younger, I used to love going inside her shop."

"I still do," Trace said. "She's good people. As a matter of fact, I'm going to text you a couple of images I pulled from the video when that guy destroyed my cameras. Would you mind showing them to Serenity and see what she says?"

While Serenity claimed to be psychic, Trace knew many of the local ranchers and farmers poohpoohed the idea. Serenity gave readings and clearly had enough clients between that work and her little store to live off.

"I have to say I'm intrigued," Emma said. "Of course, I'll ask her for you. It's interesting that you put even the smallest amount of stock in Serenity's second sight."

"Don't you?" he asked.

"I haven't ever really thought about it," she admitted. "I grew up hearing my father scoff at everyone who went to her for her psychic readings."

"I get it. A lot of my friends say the same." Trace shrugged. "A lot of people think Serenity is a phony. Others swear by her. Either way, she's a good person and I know Rayna puts a lot of stock in what she has to say. That's why I want her to look at the photos. It couldn't hurt."

"I agree," she said. "Go ahead and send them to me." She got up and moved away, turning and glancing at him over her shoulder. "Trace, I want you to know that I really appreciate you letting me use the Jeep. Someday, like I said earlier, I hope to repay you."

"Just pay it forward," he said, forcing himself to look away from her and down at his phone. "I'm sending now. Just let me know what Serenity has to say about them."

"Will do." She left the room. A moment later, he heard the sound of her blow dryer.

Friends with benefits. Most guys would count their blessings. While he most certainly considered himself blessed that Emma apparently was open to continuing to have mind-blowing sex with him, deep down he wanted more.

He knew he shouldn't, for a myriad of reasons. Too soon, for one. And Emma had just gotten her freedom after spending far too long behind bars. She had some serious stuff to work out. Finding her husband's killer and clearing her name was a lot. On top of that, a random guy had decided to stalk her and demand money she clearly didn't have or know anything about.

He'd be a fool to expect or even desire anything more than what she was willing to give.

Chapter 9

When Emma finally emerged from her bedroom, after having applied a little makeup and putting on her favorite pair of jeans and boots, Trace had left. She had to admit she felt the tiniest bit of relief. She wasn't entirely sure about this new relationship phase they'd evidently entered. Sex with no strings attached. It sounded like a recipe for disaster.

But the sex—oh the sex. She'd never experienced anything so intense, so fulfilling. Quite frankly, it scared the hell out of her. When she wasn't craving it.

Shaking her head, she left the house, trying hard not to catch sight of Trace out near the barn or the fields. The second she stepped outside, she noticed Trace had pulled the bright blue Jeep up onto the driveway. Judging by the way the paint shone, it looked like he'd washed it for her.

Thinking back to her initial thought and what she'd almost accused him of, she blushed. Of course Trace hadn't gotten the Jeep street legal simply because they'd made love—er, had sex. Though she'd only been staying with him a few weeks, she could tell he wasn't that kind of guy.

Eyeing the Jeep, she pushed away a spat of nerves and climbed into the driver's seat and put the key into the ignition. It had been several years since she'd driven, but she felt reasonably confident that she could still do it.

However, she took it slow as she drove down the ranch's long drive, picking up speed after she'd turned onto the two-lane Farm to Market Road. By the time she made it to Getaway, she felt reasonably competent. She was even thinking of giving the Jeep a name.

First up, she visited the sheriff's department. Rayna wasn't in, but she'd left a box up front with Mary for Emma to pick up.

Once Emma had stowed that in the back seat of the Jeep, she drove to downtown Getaway and Serenity's shop. She found a parking spot in front and took a moment to see if she could remember her parallel parking skills. To her surprise, she nailed it on the second try.

Hopping out of the Jeep, she locked it. Amazing how such a simple thing as driving and parking could make her feel as if she could do anything. Good, she thought wryly. She'd need that confidence to help her not only figure out who'd really murdered Jeremy, but to reestablish her horse training business and make a new life.

One thing at a time, she reminded herself. Then she squared her shoulders, lifted her chin and opened the door to Serenity's shop.

Inside, the cloying scent of patchouli wafted in the air. Looking at the stacks of books, the displays of rocks and crystals, interspersed with gaudy floral arrangements, she saw that nothing had changed since the last time she'd visited.

"Emma? Emma McBride?" a cheery voice trilled. "I've been waiting for you to come see me."

Emma turned, smiling as Serenity rushed over, a blur of bright colors and loud patterns, her numerous bracelets jangling as she enveloped Emma in a sandalwood-scented hug.

"It took you way too long, young lady," Serenity scolded as she stepped back, though her eyes twinkled. "Let me take a look at you."

Emma smiled. "I've changed a little," she said. "Being locked up for two years will do that to you."

Serenity shook her head. "I told Rayna you were innocent. Heck, I told everyone I could think of. Sometimes they listen to me, you know. But this time, they took the word of that woman and used it to lock up the wrong person."

"Thank you." The older woman's quiet faith kindled a spark of warmth in Emma's chest. "I'm working on trying to find out the real murderer."

This made Serenity frown. She brushed her frizzy mop of hair away from her face. "That could be dangerous."

"I know." Emma took a deep breath, deciding to tell Serenity everything. "I've already got some man hounding me for money that he claims Jeremy stole from him. He's been calling and stalking us. Just the other day, he disabled the security cameras we'd just installed."

"We?" Serenity's sharp gaze missed nothing. "I've heard that you are staying with Trace Redkin."

"I am. I'm not sure if you remember, but his sister, Heather, and I were best friends. I went there looking for her and he kindly allowed me to stay." She pulled out her phone. "As a matter of fact, he asked me to have you look at some photos and see if you recognize the guy."

"I see." Serenity's smile was kind, though she made no move to take the phone. "Come sit down and have a cup of hot tea with me. I'll take a gander at those pictures then. If you'd like, I can also give you a reading when we're done."

Bemused, Emma agreed. She'd had Serenity read her tea leaves before. Shoving her phone into her back pocket, she followed Serenity toward a small room in the back of the shop, separated by a brightly colored beaded curtain. Equipped with a round table and two chairs, it looked like the perfect place to conduct a séance or use tarot cards.

A small microwave and a single-serve coffee-maker sat on a counter near a sink.

"My break room area," Serenity said, winking. "What kind of tea would you like? I have both green, black and several herbal varieties."

Emma had tried herbal tea once and decided it

wasn't for her. "Black tea, please. English breakfast or Darjeeling if you have it."

"I do." Beaming, Serenity turned on the coffee-maker. While that was warming up, she located the tea. "I still prefer teakettles and loose tea," she said. "But I have to admit, this is so much easier. Even if I can't read tea leaves when I make it this way."

Taking a seat at the table, Emma smiled as Serenity placed a steaming mug of tea in front of her. "I'm disappointed," she said. "I was kind of looking forward to having you read my tea leaves."

Brows arched, Serenity regarded her. "I can still do a reading, hon. Even without tea leaves. Sometimes I simply *see* things."

"I've heard," Emma replied.

A moment later, the older woman brought her own mug and settled herself across the table from Emma. "How is Trace? I haven't seen that boy in a few weeks."

Amused to hear Trace referred to as a boy, Emma shrugged. "He seems okay. He misses his uncle Frank a lot. I think he's planning to visit him soon."

"That is a sad situation," Serenity said, taking a sip of her tea. "I always liked Frank. He was a good guy."

"Yes, he was." Deciding she'd better get to the point before Serenity started talking about her aura or something, Emma sighed. "I talked to my step-mother, Beth, and she said she left some of my belongings here with you for safekeeping."

"Ah yes, I have several boxes in my storeroom," Serenity said, still smiling as she sipped her tea. "It was so nice of Beth to think of you in the middle of all she was going through. Do you know she told me numerous times that she always had faith that you would be exonerated and get out soon?"

"No, I didn't." Stunned, Emma tried to hide it. While Beth had claimed to never doubt Emma's innocence, Emma had thought the older woman hadn't meant it. Beth truly appeared to have either undergone a major personality change or Emma had never really known her. "She didn't really keep in touch after I went to prison. The only time she contacted me was when my father passed away."

Serenity nodded. "I'm sorry for your loss. I hated they wouldn't allow you to attend the funeral."

After all this time, Emma had thought she'd come to terms with her father's death. She'd grieved over missing his funeral and felt at a loss since he'd been cremated and Beth had kept his ashes with her. Emma thought being able to visit his grave might have helped ease her sorrow.

"I hated it too," Emma replied softly. She'd reached the bottom of her teacup. "I've enjoyed visiting with you, but I really need to get going. Would you mind if I got those boxes?"

"Of course not." Yet Serenity didn't move. "But didn't you have some pictures on your phone that you wanted me to look at?"

Emma couldn't believe she'd almost forgotten. "Yes, I do," she replied. Getting out her phone, she opened Trace's text and located the photos. "Here they are," she said, handing it over. "Trace wants to know if you recognize this man."

Serenity frowned as she scrolled through the pictures. "He looks familiar," she finally said. "Though he's not from around here. I've definitely seen him around, but I can't remember where. Or when. It's been a while." She glanced at Emma, her expression thoughtful. "I'm thinking I may have seen him with Jeremy. Which would be weird, since if he was one of your late husband's friends, I'd think you'd recognize him."

"I don't. But I suspect he might have been one of Jeremy's business partners instead of a friend."

"Maybe so," Serenity agreed. "And he's the one who's been bothering you?"

"Yes. He's demanding money that he claims Jeremy stole from him. I'm hoping once I take a look at Jeremy's things, I can maybe figure out what the heck he's talking about."

Handing back the phone, Serenity tilted her head. "Do you think he might have had something to do with Jeremy's murder?"

"I don't know. It's possible. But then again, he could just be one person out of several whom Jeremy might have done wrong, even inadvertently. That's one of the things I'm hoping to get to the bottom of. As far as I can tell, when Jeremy died, no one took over his business. There might be more than one client with money tied up in investments that Jeremy made."

"I see," Serenity said thoughtfully, taking a long sip of her tea. "You've got quite a bit of baggage to deal with, especially considering you've just gotten the chance to reclaim your life."

"That's exactly what I'm trying to do." Emma

stood, feeling a fresh sense of purpose. "Getting to the bottom of everything is the only way I can get my life back." She glanced at her phone to check the time. "Now if you don't mind, I'd like to collect those boxes and be on my way."

"Of course." Serenity heaved herself up amid a jingle of jewelry and strode to a metal bookshelf in the very back of the room. She bent over and picked up a large cardboard box, carrying it over and placing it near Emma's feet. "There are four of these," she said. "And a couple of them are a bit heavy. I can help you carry them out to your car if you'd like."

"If it's no trouble, I'd appreciate it." Emma hefted the first box, slightly surprised at its weight despite Serenity's warning. She waited while the older woman retrieved a second box and together they carried them out to the Jeep.

"I remember this vehicle," Serenity exclaimed. "Trace used to drive this back when he was in college."

"He's loaned it to me for now," Emma said, inordinately proud. "It's in really good shape."

She didn't miss the sharp gaze Serenity sent her way. "Trace is a good guy," Serenity told her. "I'd hate to see him get hurt."

Since there wasn't a way to pretend to miss the warning, all Emma could do was nod. "I'll do my best not to hurt him," she promised, inwardly aware that it would be a lot more likely if she were the one who ended up hurt.

They carried out the final two boxes and then Se-

YOU pick your books –
WE pay for everything.

You get up to FOUR New Books and TWO Mystery Gifts...absolutely FREE

Dear Reader,

I am writing to announce the launch of a huge **FREE BOOKS GIVEAWAY**... and to let you know that YOU are entitled to choose up to FOUR fantastic books that WE pay for.

Try **Harlequin® Desire** books featuring the worlds of the American elite with juicy plot twists, delicious sensuality and intriguing scandal.

Try **Harlequin Presents® Larger-Print** books featuring the glamourous lives of royals and billionaires in a world of exotic locations, where passion knows no bounds.

Or TRY BOTH!

In return, we ask just one favor: Would you please participate in our brief Reader Survey? We'd love to hear from you.

This FREE BOOKS GIVEAWAY means that your introductory shipment is completely free, <u>even the shipping</u>! If you decide to continue, you can look forward to curated monthly shipments of brand-new books from your selected series, always at a discount off the cover price! <u>Plus you can cancel any time</u>. Who could pass up a deal like that?

Sincerely

Pam Powers

Pam Powers
For Harlequin Reader Service

Complete the survey below and return it today to receive up to 4 FREE BOOKS and FREE GIFTS guaranteed!

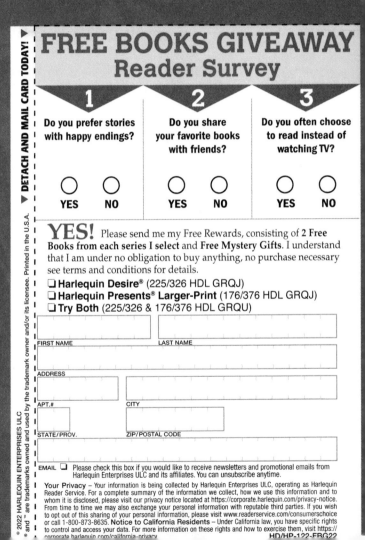

▼ DETACH AND MAIL CARD TODAY! ▼

FREE BOOKS GIVEAWAY
Reader Survey

1
Do you prefer stories with happy endings?

○ YES ○ NO

2
Do you share your favorite books with friends?

○ YES ○ NO

3
Do you often choose to read instead of watching TV?

○ YES ○ NO

YES! Please send me my Free Rewards, consisting of **2 Free Books from each series I select** and **Free Mystery Gifts**. I understand that I am under no obligation to buy anything, no purchase necessary see terms and conditions for details.

❏ Harlequin Desire® (225/326 HDL GRQJ)
❏ Harlequin Presents® Larger-Print (176/376 HDL GRQJ)
❏ Try Both (225/326 & 176/376 HDL GRQU)

FIRST NAME

LAST NAME

ADDRESS

APT.#

CITY

STATE/PROV.

ZIP/POSTAL CODE

EMAIL ❏ Please check this box if you would like to receive newsletters and promotional emails from Harlequin Enterprises ULC and its affiliates. You can unsubscribe anytime.

© 2022 HARLEQUIN ENTERPRISES ULC
® and ™ are trademarks owned by the trademark owner and/or its licensee. Printed in the U.S.A.

HD/HP-122-FBG22

renity hugged her. "Don't be a stranger, Emma Jean. Come see me again soon."

Emma promised she would, smiling slightly at the way Serenity used her first and middle name. Only her father had every called her Emma Jean. Hearing it again made her miss him.

On the drive home, she felt invigorated and thoughtful. She had a lot to look over and maybe here she'd finally get a few answers.

Arriving back at the ranch, she parked the Jeep next to Trace's truck and hopped out. Grabbing one of the lighter boxes, she carried it inside. Once she'd set it down on the living room floor, she spotted Trace sitting in the recliner reading something. "I could use your help," she said. "I have a few more of these in the Jeep."

"Sure." He jumped to his feet. Together they made short work of bringing everything in. "Wow," he said, eyeing the boxes. "Looks like you've got a lot to go through."

"It does." She pointed to the smallest one. "That came from the sheriff's office. The rest were what Beth left with Serenity." Rubbing her hands together, she smiled. "I can't wait to get started. Luckily, right now I have a bit of spare time on my hands."

Just then her phone chimed to indicate a text message. She glanced at the screen and could hardly believe her eyes. "Wow. You're not going to believe this," she said. "One of my former clients wants to talk to me about working with a horse."

Work. Actual, paying work. Even with the bad timing, she wanted to jump up and down and dance around the room. "Maybe my career as a horse trainer is still salvageable after all."

"I never doubted that." Trace smiled. "You're good. People tend to remember that."

She wanted to hug him. Instead, she reread the message on her phone. "I'm going to call them back. Hopefully I can make this happen."

"You can." He dropped back into his recliner and picked up his magazine again. "Go get 'em, Emma."

After Emma had gone into her room to carry on a private conversation with her potential client, Trace eyed the boxes. Though he doubted Emma had realized it yet, this was all that was left of her previous life. Four large boxes and one small. And while some of that had belonged to Jeremy and his business, he'd be willing to bet that Beth had packed away some of Emma's personal belongings too. Clearly, not too many of them, but a few. He couldn't help but wonder how dealing with her past would affect her.

The next day, he and Emma barely interacted. She'd parked herself at the kitchen table, surrounded by ledgers and Jeremy's laptop. She'd worried out loud that she might have trouble getting into the laptop, but apparently Jeremy was one of those people who'd used the same password for everything.

When he returned from repairing some fencing three hours later, he found her still in the same spot, engrossed in her research.

"Having any luck?" he asked.

She looked up, blinking, her expression dazed. "What?" she asked, then as his question registered, she shook her head. "I'm not sure. Investments were made and I think some of them might still be earning money, though it's difficult to tell. Jeremy didn't appear to be very organized. It's like going down rabbit hole after rabbit hole."

"Maybe you should take a break?" he suggested. "How about I make us a couple of sandwiches for lunch?"

Rubbing her temples, she nodded. "That actually sounds great. I think I forgot to eat breakfast."

While he put the sandwiches together, she poured them tall glasses of iced tea. He battled the urge to tell her that he'd missed her, well aware that to even think such a thing would cross boundaries she didn't want crossed.

Lunch made, he opened a bag of corn chips and took a seat. She sat down, closed the laptop and pushed it to one side. "Thank you," she said.

She made short work of demolishing her sandwich. He had to make himself eat, force himself not to sit there and just watch her.

"I needed that," she told him, picking up both their plates and carrying them over to the dishwasher. "All this research has been very time-consuming. I'm hoping in addition to finding out about any missing money, I might get some hints as to who killed Jeremy."

"That's good."

"So far, I haven't found much. And I need to really concentrate on this now, since I finally heard back from Coraline Cotton," she continued. "She's bringing her horse next week. He's named Zotar. I'll need to make sure we have a clean stall ready for him."

"Zotar?" He sat back in his chair. "That's an odd name for a horse."

His comment made her smile. "He's an Arabian. His full name is something much longer and more complicated."

"He's a gelding, I hope. You and I both know some of those Arabs can be high-strung."

"Yes, he's gelded. I checked. You'll never believe what Coraline wants me to work with him on." Then, without waiting for him to ask, she continued. "She wants to ride him in the costume competitions. I don't know if you've ever been to an Arabian horse show, but they spend thousands of dollars on elaborate costumes for both the rider and the horse. Apparently, Zotar is totally freaked out by this."

"I don't blame him," Trace said dryly. "It's been years, but I remember seeing something like that at a horse show somewhere. From what I remember, those costumes have a lot of flowing, jingly pieces. At the time, I remember wondering how the horses were trained to get used to them."

"I guess we're about to find out," Emma replied with a wry smile. "I'm going to approach it from a desensitizing angle."

He nodded. "How much time did she give you?"

"That's just it. She wants him ready for a big show in two weeks, but I told her I have to see how he reacts first."

"Makes sense." He stood, quietly amazed at how much he wanted to linger, but grabbed his hat and crammed it on his head. "I've got to get back to mending fence. Good luck with your research."

"Thanks," she replied. "I'll need it."

No goodbye kiss, he reminded himself, keeping his back straight as he walked out the door.

The rest of the afternoon, with much to occupy his hands but not his mind, he couldn't stop thinking about her. He felt a lot like a teenager with a crush and he didn't like it. But since there didn't appear to be much he could do to change the way he felt, he figured he'd just have to deal with it.

As he was working on the last bit of fence in a piece of his land that bordered a rough gravel road with a small cluster of trees, movement inside the wooded area caught his eye. Instantly alert, he reached for his rifle, figuring it might be a bobcat or maybe a pack of hungry coyotes. Either way, whatever it might be would no doubt be a threat to his livestock.

Trace stood stock-still, waiting for whatever to move again. He pretended to be focused on the fence, though he kept the trees in his line of vision. Instead of a wild animal, he saw a flash of blue and then a man running toward the other side of a slight hill.

The intruder. Emma's stalker. Wishing he'd come here on horseback instead of driving his truck, Trace took off running. The other man had a pretty good head start, but Trace knew if he ran around the other side of the hill, he might be able to cut him off.

Then Trace heard a motorbike starting up. "Damn it," he cursed, increasing his speed even though he knew catching the guy was now a lost cause. He rounded the corner just in time to see the motorbike tearing off down the old gravel road. Though the terrain was tough, that way eventually led to a Farm to Market road from which the guy could easily get to a main highway.

Furious, Trace wanted to punch something. Once again, the stranger had been intruding on Trace's land. What had he been doing? Spying on Trace? Or, more likely, hunting for some mythological missing money?

Mood soured, Trace strode back and finished repairing the last stretch of fence. Then he got into his truck. Instead of heading back to the house, he drove down the beat-up gravel road, going slowly, studying the fields on both sides to see if he could spot anything out of the ordinary.

Finally, he reached an area where spring floods had washed out the road, leaving a deep gully. The motorcycle would definitely have been able to navigate this area, but his truck could not.

Admitting defeat, he decided to call it a day.

Back at the house, he parked. He needed a shower and a beer, in that order. He'd simply avoid the kitchen, mainly because he didn't want to Emma to see him in such a foul mood. He needed to tell her about what he'd seen, mainly so she wouldn't let her guard down, but he wanted to be in a better frame of mind to do it.

As he passed the kitchen, she looked up, her blue eyes slightly unfocused. He lifted his hand in a casual wave, his heart skipping a beat, and continued to his bathroom.

Twenty minutes later, showered and feeling semi-human again, he made his way toward the kitchen. To his surprise, he saw Emma had cleared her research stuff off the table and stood at the stove, stirring something.

"Hey," he said softly, grabbing a beer out of the fridge, opening it and taking a long drink. "Did you knock off for the day?"

Turning, she eyed him. "You look better."

Startled at her insight, he nodded. "I think that guy was lurking around the ranch again." He told her what he'd seen.

She listened, turning every so often to continue to stir whatever she was making. "I guess that means I should be expecting a call again real soon."

"Probably," he agreed. "But he needs to understand, you can't produce his money if you have no idea where it is or if it even exists."

"I think he's beginning to get that," she said. "He must be pretty desperate, since he keeps hanging around."

"You sound almost as if you feel sorry for him."

Turning to stir, she waited a bit before looking back at him and shrugging. "After seeing the mess that was Jeremy's idea of bookkeeping, I kind of get it. Actually, I'm surprised more of his investors aren't coming after me looking for their money."

"That certainly give you a wide pool of people with possible motives for murder," he pointed out.

"I know." She sighed. "That's why this is so frustrating. However, this guy who tortured Amber and is now hounding me is still on the top of my list of suspects. Even though he hasn't done much more than threaten."

"Which is what I'm worried about," Trace said, feeling he owed her the truth. "Any day now he could get tired of waiting and do something awful."

She stared. "I hope not. I'm working really hard to make sense of Jeremy's books."

"Did Jeremy work for an investment firm?" he asked. "Maybe it's time to bring them in and have them help you."

"That's just it," she replied. "From what I can tell, he was operating completely on his own. Which would match what he always told me—that he was starting up his own company."

Then she turned her attention back to whatever she had simmering on the stove. "I'm making dinner. I'm not sure why, but I've been craving chicken and vegetable soup. Comfort food, I guess. I hope you're okay with that."

This made him laugh. "I'm okay with anything you choose to make. And actually, soup sounds great."

After they ate, he insisted on doing the dishes, telling her to go do something relaxing. Rinsing the plates before loading them in the dishwasher, he allowed himself to indulge in a fantasy of Emma taking a bubble bath, and him joining her, naked.

The images had his body hard almost instantly. Which might make walking casually into the living room a problem. Instead, he took a few deep breaths and forced himself to think of something else, anything else besides Emma.

After a few minutes of thinking about repairing fences—which he seemed to spend an inordinate amount of time doing—he'd settled down enough to rejoin Emma.

He found her standing, shifting nervously from foot to foot, as if waiting for him. "What's wrong?" he asked, concerned.

Instead of answering, she walked up to him, smiling that sexy way she had, and pulled him down for a kiss, almost as if she'd known about his fantasy. This time, he didn't hesitate, maybe because she'd been the one to initiate things, but also because they'd decided they could enjoy each other's body without emotional entanglement. She didn't have to know that he was already more than halfway tied up in knots over her.

They ended up in his bed, shedding clothes as they went. The lovemaking was just as passionate, just as intense, as it had been the time before. He barely had time to put on his condom, but he managed. And then she pushed him back onto the bed and straddled him and he forgot about anything else but her.

Later, she slipped from his bed without a word of explanation. Though he pretended to sleep, he waited to see if she'd return. Instead, she apparently went to her own room for the remainder of the night. He told himself that made sense, especially going along with their no-relationship rule, but he couldn't keep from feeling the loss of her body's warmth with an ache that seemed oversize. He must have finally drifted off, because the next thing he knew his phone alarm had come on, letting him know it was time to rise.

Shoving back the covers, Trace struggled to push

back the feeling of dread low in his gut. Today, he'd planned to go to Midland. He always felt this way when he drove into Midland. Still, he always made himself go. Uncle Frank might not realize that Trace visited, but damn if Trace would abandon him. Not now. Not ever.

When he walked into the kitchen for coffee, seeing Emma there raised his spirits a little.

"You look awfully serious for so early in the morning," she commented. "Did you have a rough night?"

Battling the urge to level with her, to tell her how much it bothered him that she'd disappeared after the amazing lovemaking they'd shared, he took a deep breath and answered her question instead.

"No. I slept fine. It's just that I've got to go visit my uncle this morning," Trace explained. "It's a bit of a drive, so I'll be gone most of the day. Do you think you'll be all right here by yourself?"

Emma studied him, her expression serious. "I'd like to go with you," she said. "If that's okay. I always liked your uncle Frank, and I'd sure love to see him."

"He's not the same as you remember." Feeling obliged to warn her, Trace thought of the way his formerly vibrant uncle sat and stared straight ahead, silent. Most times, he didn't even recognize Trace, which hurt far more than it should have.

"I understand," Emma replied softly. "I'd still like to visit him. Unless you'd rather go alone."

He didn't even have to think about it. Guilty as it might make him feel, he'd come to dread his visits to see Uncle Frank. Mostly because he hated seeing the older man a mere shell of himself, but also because he couldn't seem to will away a private, secret hope that this time, his uncle would recognize him. So far, that had never happened.

"I'd welcome the company," he told Emma. "But I know you're busy. You should be aware it will take up most of the day."

She smiled and nodded. "I figured as much. I can really use a break from going through Jeremy's books. It's all starting to run together."

Wanting to hug her, instead he forced himself to grab a mug and make a cup of black coffee. "I'm thinking we need to leave in less than an hour."

"That's fine." She stretched, making him hurriedly avert his gaze so he wouldn't stare at her chest. "I've already showered. I'll just need to change and put on some makeup."

The easy comfort of the domestic scene didn't escape him. He knew he could grow far too comfortable with this, having Emma around to brighten his days. And nights. The thought made his body tingle, despite the bleakness of the day ahead.

Chapter 10

The phone call came on the way to Midland. They'd barely left the Getaway city limits behind when Emma's cell phone rang. She glanced at the screen, noted that she didn't recognize the number and answered anyway.

"Do you have my money yet?" the now-familiar voice asked. "I would hate to have to hurt one of these pretty horses."

Her blood froze. "Are you at the ranch?" she asked, more so Trace could hear.

"I am and you're not. I watched you drive away, you know." He chuckled, as if he found the statement humorous. "I'm getting tired of waiting."

Though her heart rate had tripled, she took a deep breath. Determined to ignore his threats, at least for now, she kept her voice calm. "I've been going through Jeremy's books. I'm assuming you must have made investments with him, right? As soon as I can get everything straightened out, I should be able to tell you where your money is. Of course, I'll need your name in order to do that."

"You're right. Stupidly, I invested with Jeremy." His bark of laughter contained a bitter, cutting edge. "I liked him, thought I could trust him. Until I learned the truth. That guy was the biggest crook around. He was always looking for a way to screw somebody out of money. Mostly, his haul was just relatively small potatoes. Until he met me."

Hardly able to believe what she heard, Emma shook her head. "You sound like you did your research."

"I did," he replied. "Only after I gave him my money. I believed him when he told me he could triple my investment. Stupid me. Instead, he disappeared, along with every cent I'd given him. Next thing I know, I found out you had killed him."

"I didn't kill him," she protested while her mind tried to process what this man had just said. Jeremy had been a crook? She swallowed back the sour taste in her mouth. Why not? He'd been a cheater, forsaking his marriage vows and his wife.

"Let me get this right," she finally managed to say. "You're looking for a large amount of money that my former husband stole? Money that you somehow think I have access to?" A flash of anger spurred her to continue. "Let me tell you something, buddy. While I feel terrible for you, if I were like Jeremy, and I'd had access to that money, I'd be halfway to the Cayman Islands by now. You'd never hear from me again."

"Now you just wait a second," her caller said, sounding slightly nervous for the first time. "I just want what's coming to me."

"What's coming to you should be jail time," she returned, her voice simmering with anger. "You've been harassing me and torturing Amber."

Silence. For a brief moment, she allowed herself to hope she might have actually persuaded him to give up. Then he laughed, a hoarse and somehow evil sound, and she knew she was wrong.

"Did you know horses scream when they're in pain?" he asked, his tone conversational. "I think this black-and-white one is a favorite of yours, isn't it?"

Instead of fear, she saw red.

"If you touch that mare, I will not rest until I hunt you down and make you pay," she promised, so furious she didn't stop to think about her words. "And if I do happen to locate that money, you will never, ever see a single red cent."

Again, she appeared to have stunned him into silence. Emboldened, she continued. "Now get the hell off Trace's ranch and leave me alone. I promise if I happen to find anything legitimately belonging to you, I will figure out a way to let you know."

Then, without waiting for a response, she ended the call.

Glancing over at Trace, she realized her hands were shaking. No surprise there.

"He's at the ranch?" Trace asked, his expression grim. "And threatening to hurt one of the horses?"

"Yes." Still more angry than scared, she inhaled. "We need to go back. We're only twenty minutes away at the most. I can't take the chance of him hurting one of the horses. He threatened Daisy, but they're all at risk."

"I agree." With a quick glance in his rearview mirror, Trace pulled a U-turn. "I have to say, I was impressed by the way you told him off."

"Really?" She shook her head, swallowing to get past the sudden lump in her throat. "I'm actually starting to feel a little bit queasy."

Intent on the road, Trace had picked up speed, going well over the speed limit but not so fast that Emma felt unsafe. "I'm not sure if it was wise or not, but that guy had it coming. I'd actually thought since he'd left you alone for a while, that he'd figured out he was barking up the wrong tree. Maybe even giving up. But from what I heard of your side of the conversation, I see he's not."

"I guess so. If this guy is telling the truth, Jeremy was worse than incompetent. He was a crook. I had no idea he'd been swindling people out of money." She swallowed again, harder this time. "I mean, we were living with my parents, for Pete's sake. The plan was to save money so we could buy our own home. My dad and I were actually proud of him for working so hard to get his own business off the ground. It's difficult to believe that it was all…"

"A lie," he finished for her. "I'm really sorry, Emma."

She couldn't help but notice he'd picked up speed even more. He saw her glancing at the speedometer. "I hate the idea of anything happening to my horses. Or my cattle," he finished grimly.

"I should be the one apologizing to you," she said, now miserable. "None of this would be happening to you if I hadn't showed up on your doorstep."

"Don't." The fierceness of his tone had her blinking. "None of this is your fault. And since I'm the one who agreed to let you stay, I'm also the only one who gets to decide if I regret it. And I don't, Emma McBride. As far as I'm concerned, we're in this together."

Now he had her tearing up. "You're a good man, Trace. I know I keep saying this, but I promise I'll figure out a way to repay you."

He shook his head. "Just clear your name and get your business flourishing again. That's the only repayment I need."

Stunned, Emma couldn't speak. She could only stare, his statement touching her at a level she'd thought she'd lost forever.

That moment, that small kindness on top of so many others, was when she realized she might be falling in love with him. In love. With Trace. Which would be the absolute worse timing on the face of the planet. She consoled herself with the fact that at least he would never, ever know.

They'd just turned off the main road when Trace's phone rang. He answered, listened for a moment and then cleared his throat. "Thank you for letting me know," he said, his voice perfectly polite but off-kilter somehow. "I'll be in touch soon."

Once he'd ended the call, he turned to briefly face her, his expression bleak. "That was the Memory Care Center. Uncle Frank passed away in his bed this morning. The nurse said he went peacefully." Dry-eyed, he returned his attention to the road. "Even if we'd made it to see him, we wouldn't have gotten there in time."

"I'm so sorry." Sensing the pain under his steady voice, Emma touched his shoulder. He'd tensed up, the bunched-up muscles hard under her hand. "Your uncle was a good man."

"Don't." He wrenched himself away. "I can't think about him right now. I'll deal with it later. Let's get to the ranch and make sure the animals are safe first."

Though his rejection stung, this wasn't about her. Removing her hand, she nodded. "I understand," she said.

"I knew you would," he replied.

As soon as they'd pulled up into the driveway, Trace parked and jumped out, hitting the ground running. Caught by surprise, Emma took off after him. He reached the barn before her, grabbing the large sliding door to open it. Just as he began tugging it, he turned and eyed her.

"Maybe you should wait here," he said. "Just in case."

Just in case. She knew what he meant. "No. I'm coming too. If he hurt Daisy, or any of them, I want to see. It's likely I can help them."

Though he shook his head, he didn't argue, instead

yanking the door wide enough for them to enter. Once inside, he flipped on the light switch. Bracing herself, she followed him, dreading what she might see.

No blood, she registered first. In fact, nothing appeared to have been disturbed at all.

Three horses, all in their stalls, swung their large heads to look at them. Daisy, spotting Emma, nickered and walked over to her stall door.

"No blood," Trace said, echoing Emma's thoughts.

"That's encouraging," Emma agreed. She went to Daisy first, slipping inside the stall and greeting the mare. She ran her hands over the horse, checking for swelling or cuts—really anything that might indicate the animal had been abused. She found nothing. Absolutely nothing. Relief flooded her.

"Daisy's okay," she called out. Trace had let himself into Jack's stall and had begun checking the gelding out the same way.

"Same here," he said.

Emma moved on to the third horse, Libby. The gray mare had always been the most placid of horses, and today was no exception. She stood quietly while Emma inspected her, closing her eyes as if she found the interaction pleasant.

"Nothing here either," Emma said, more relief almost causing her knees to buckle. Delayed reaction, she supposed. Somehow, she managed to let herself out of the stall and meet Trace in the aisle. "What now?"

Expression dark, he grimaced. "I need to check on my cattle."

"Let's go." She didn't wait for him to tell her he

wanted to be alone, though she could see it in his face. "Do you want to take the horses or...?"

"Truck," he finished for her. "It's quicker. Though we'll have to do a little walking. You can always wait in the truck if you're not up to that."

"I might just do that," she allowed, wondering if she should at least give him that much private time to gather his thoughts and emotions. She knew he still hadn't processed the fact that his uncle had died. It would likely hit him hard, especially since he'd always regret not being able to see him one last time.

Leaving the barn, she followed him back to his pickup.

They drove down the driveway, turned right on the gravel road, and then a minute later, pulled off onto a rutted dirt trail. As they bounced slowly along, she clenched her teeth and held on to the door handle.

"There they are, closer than I expected," Trace said, pointing toward a cluster of cattle underneath a twisted tree. He began counting under his breath. When he'd finished, he turned toward her and nodded. "All accounted for here. And none of them seem hurt."

She remembered he kept a second herd in another pasture. "Can we get to the other cattle by truck?"

Slowly, he shook his head. "We can get a little closer. But that field is accessible only by foot or by horseback."

"Then let's go. The sooner I know for sure that no animals were harmed, the better I'll feel."

They drove a little bit down the road. Trace pulled over and parked on the grassy edge near an area where two fences met. "It's only a short walk from here," he said. "But again, if you want you can wait in the truck."

"I'll go with you," she said quickly. Though initially she'd thought he'd need private time, now she'd reconsidered. While she wouldn't say it out loud, she didn't want to leave him alone right now. She knew he hadn't yet begun to process his uncle's death and wanted to be with him when the realization hit him.

"Well, come on then."

He helped her over the fence and then took off, striding ahead of her without talking. She started out hurrying to catch up, but then decided not to. As long as she had him in her line of vision, she figured he'd be okay.

Finally, he reached a rise in the land and stopped. When she reached him, she saw the herd clustered around a small pond. Trace stared at them, his mouth moving silently and she knew he was counting.

"They're all there," he told her, his voice suddenly weary. "It looks like we lucked out this time. I'll need to make Rayna aware. Come on, let's get back to the house."

Heart aching for him, she nodded. Together, they walked back to the truck and then rode in silence to the ranch house.

Once he'd ascertained that Emma's stalker hadn't touched any of the animals on his ranch, Trace could breathe a bit easier, though his mind still skittered away from his own devastating phone call. Locked down emotionally, he drove them back to the ranch, parked and once Emma had climbed out, he told her he needed to go for a drive alone to clear his head. Judging from the tightening of her mouth, she didn't like the idea, but she merely nodded and turned and went inside.

He appreciated that more than she would ever know.

Driving away, he didn't consciously choose where to go. He didn't think, or rationalize; he simply drove. Away from town, away from the ranch, out to where the two-lane road stretched into the horizon and the clouds seemed to join the earth and the sky. Going from memory, he pulled off onto a poorly maintained gravel-and-dirt road that wound around the backside of a bluff and when he reached the turnaround spot, he parked instead.

Though this land belonged to another rancher, Trace doubted that man or his family would mind if he hiked to the top of the bluff. He'd done this many times as a teenager, and then again when he'd moved Uncle Frank into the home in Midland. It seemed fitting to come here now, to contemplate his passing.

Contemplate, hell. Come to terms with, actually. Of all the things Trace might have expected, having Uncle Frank die now hadn't been one of them. He'd tried to prepare himself for the eventuality, aware death was always a certainty, but somehow it had caught him off guard.

Before his illness had taken over, Uncle Frank had always seemed larger than life, invincible. When his memory had forsaken him, he'd appeared to shrink inside himself. The man Trace had always looked up to had disappeared, yet Trace had been unable to give up hope that he might return, even if briefly.

Now that hope had been forever extinguished.

Hiking up the gradual incline, wishing he'd thought to grab his cowboy hat from the house, Trace focused on his steps, on putting one foot in front of the other. Loose rocks had a way of making the path treacherous, and his cowboy boots weren't made for hiking. From past experience, he knew when he reached the flat top of the bluff, he'd be able to see for miles. Even as far as his own ranch.

His ranch. Uncle Frank's ranch, really. Trace had lived there, helped run it and loved the place as if it were his own. Now, he supposed it truly would be. Uncle Frank had never married or had children. Trace and Heather, his brother's offspring, had been his closest relatives once their parents had died. They'd been a family, Trace thought, continuing to hike.

Now, with his uncle gone and Heather married and living in California, Trace had no one.

Except Emma. Just the thought of her felt like a soothing balm on his aching heart. Which made absolutely no sense, because he felt quite certain once she solved the mystery of her husband's death and got her career back on track, she'd likely move away too.

Disliking his thoughts, Trace focused on finally reaching the summit. He stood, turning slowly, shading his eyes with his hand and taking in the arid West Texas landscape that he loved. There, he could make out the metal roof of his ranch house, reflecting the sun. Peace stole over him, a sense of certainty that he was exactly where he needed to be. Uncle Frank had lived almost his entire life in this place, and once told Trace he had no regrets. If he'd bewailed the fact of his solitary existence, he'd never said anything to anyone. He'd claimed that taking care of Trace and Heather had been more than enough family for him.

Heather. Trace dug out his phone, dreading the call he needed to make. But his sister deserved to know, so Trace dialed her number.

"I've been expecting this," Heather said when he told her. "Dreading it too. It's difficult, but more for us than for him."

"What do you mean?" Trace wasn't sure how to take her words.

"You know exactly what I mean," Heather chided. "Trace, Uncle Frank had become a shell of himself. He always seemed so vibrant, so full of life. When his illness took over, he began to fade. I'd hate to live like that. You would too."

"You're right," he agreed, even though he found it hard to admit. "But that doesn't make losing him any easier."

"Of course it doesn't." She sighed. "I'm going to miss him, but then I have been missing him for a long time now."

"Me too," he said, his voice raw. "I was on my way to see him and then his nurse called."

"Trace…" Heather hesitated, which was unlike her. "You should know Uncle Frank and I had a serious conversation a few years back, before he got so bad. He made out a will. I told him I didn't want the ranch and was fine with him leaving it all to you. You love it the same way he did."

Now the ache in his heart became a roar. Struggling to find words, he could only drag air into his lungs and exhale.

"Are you all right?" Heather finally asked. "Never mind. I know you're not. I'm just glad you have Emma with you. She's always been great at offering comfort."

"Thanks," he finally managed. "I'll let you know the details of the service when I have them."

"Uncle Frank didn't want one," she told him. "He spoke to me about that several times. He wants to be cremated and have his ashes spread on the ranch."

Stunned, he wasn't sure how to respond. "When did you two discuss all these things?"

"A long time ago," she replied. "Before he started forgetting things. He said he put instructions in his will."

"Why did neither of you involve me in these discussions?" he asked. "I wasn't aware of any of this."

"Because Uncle Frank knew you wouldn't take it well," Heather answered promptly. "He always wanted to protect you. That's why he made all his arrangements way in advance, so you wouldn't have to do anything."

Grateful, Trace didn't know why he felt so surprised. Until his dementia took hold, Uncle Frank had always been on top of things.

"You'll need the will," Heather continued. "The original is inside the top drawer of his desk. He had Theo Devine's office help him draw it up."

"Thanks." Trace almost broke down then, but he held himself together. When and if he allowed himself to give in to his emotions, he wanted to make sure there were no witnesses.

Heather went silent for a moment. "We'll spread his ashes together," she promised. "It'll be a few weeks before I'll even be able to think about coming home, but I know cremation takes time too. Keep me posted, okay?"

Another wave of sorrow rolled over him. It took him a moment of remembering to breathe before he could respond.

"I will."

After ending the call, Trace jammed his phone back into his pocket and returned his attention to the beautiful landscape. Talking to his sister had helped. Suddenly, he regretted sending Emma away. Somehow, she always seemed to know the right thing to say. Plus, he could have used her sympathetic embrace right about now.

Uncle Frank would have liked the person Emma had become. Trace knew the older man had been fond of Heather's best friend during their teenage years. He would have enjoyed seeing Emma all grown-up.

And, with his eagle-sharp gaze, Frank would have picked up on the tangled mess of emotions she inspired in Trace.

Lowering himself to sit on a large boulder, Trace watched the clouds skitter across the bright blue sky, casting shadows on patches of the ground below.

As he sat there, he knew he couldn't let Uncle Frank's life go uncelebrated. While Frank might not have wanted a funeral, Trace wanted to still hold some kind of memorial service. Maybe when it came time to scatter his ashes. He'd discuss it with Heather and Emily and get their opinions, but he felt confident that his uncle would appreciate something like that.

Feeling better, Trace stood and made his way down the trail. He'd nearly reached the halfway point when he heard the crack of a gun. Immediately, a searing pain in his arm made him stumble and fall. Luckily, he was able to grab hold of a bush to keep from tumbling all the way down.

What the…? Looking down at his throbbing arm in disbelief, he realized he'd been shot, just below his shoulder. The damn thing hurt like hell. The bullet had gone in at an angle, which had kept it from exiting the other side. It was now lodged deep inside his arm. Unless he tied off a tourniquet to staunch the flow, the blood loss would be astronomical and he'd lose consciousness long before getting home. Damn if he wasn't already dizzy, swaying on his feet.

Somehow, he got his shirt off. Using his teeth, he tore it and awkwardly got it tied on and just above the wound. Though he knew this was necessary to help stop the blood, it also had the added effect of making it even more painful.

He had no doubt who had done this, but didn't understand why. Pushing to his feet, he turned and tried to see if he could spot the man who'd shot him. Up this high, there weren't many places to hide below, and sure enough, he saw a man carrying a rifle running toward a four-wheeler parked near his truck. Even if Trace hadn't been injured, there was no way he could make it down the path in time to stop his assailant.

In fact, as his vision grayed around the edges, Trace wasn't sure he could make it to the bottom at all. Gritting his teeth, he dug out his phone and called Emma.

When he went to voice mail, he groaned but composed himself enough to leave a message. He asked her to come get him and gave specific directions as to his location. He told her he'd try and get to his truck and if he did, he'd wait for her there.

Then he shoved his phone back into his pocket, took a deep breath and began slowly making his way down.

By some combination of determination and luck, he managed to reach level ground. Just as he staggered over to his truck, his phone rang. Emma. He answered with a weak hello.

"Trace? I'm on my way to get you. Please tell me you're all right."

"I'm still alive." His weak attempt at humor fell flat. "But I'm going to have to ask you to run me to Doc's office. I'll need him to dig a bullet out of my arm."

An hour later, Trace and Emma sat in Doc Truman's kitchen. Though the elderly doctor had long ago retired, he hadn't been able to find anyone else to take his place, so Getaway currently didn't have a practicing physician. As a result, most people drove to either Midland or Abilene, though the old doctor had been known to see one or two in an emergency.

"I'm supposed to report gunshot wounds," Doc said, his gravelly voice steady. "But I'm guessing you don't want me to do that."

"It's fine," Trace managed, glad the local anesthesia had started working. "Do what you have to do. Just please, get that damn bullet out of my arm."

"Just a second." Getting up, the older man returned with a nearly full bottle of whiskey and a glass. He poured three fingers' worth and handed it to Trace. "Maybe you'd better take a few shots of this first. Even though I gave you a local, once I get inside and start digging, it's going to hurt like hell."

"It already does." Trace downed the whiskey in two gulps, shuddering a little at the bitter taste. Immediately, warmth spread through his chest. "Potent stuff."

"It's made for sipping." Doc shrugged. "But for now, it's all I have and it will do the trick. Do you want another?"

Trace didn't hesitate. "Please."

After he'd had his second glass, he felt appropriately blurry. While he'd never been much for hard liquor, he appreciated its effect right now. Emma watched silently, so pale Trace worried about her. "Maybe she should have some of this," he offered, slurring a bit.

"No, thank you," Emma replied. "I have to drive, remember?"

Trace shrugged, wincing as he accidentally moved his arm.

"Are you ready?" the doctor asked.

Trace nodded, not trusting himself to speak. Emma moved around to his other side and took his free hand, holding it nestled in between both of hers.

"You got this," she said quietly, her eyes impossibly huge in her pale face.

Damn, she was beautiful. The last thing he wanted was to appear weak in front of her. "I do," he said, hoping he sounded braver than he felt. He was no stranger to pain, and he'd been in his share of scrapes and had even broken some bones, but this took things to an entirely different level.

"Here we go." Doc worked carefully, though Trace turned his head away to avoid seeing anything. It wasn't that he had an aversion to blood in general, just *his* own blood.

Despite the local anesthesia, despite the whiskey, fire burned inside his arm. He kept his jaw clenched, his mouth shut, and gripped Emma's hand like a lifeline.

"Got it," Doc exclaimed. The bullet made a clinking sound as he dropped it onto his metal tray. "Now all I need to do is clean this up, put in some stitches and a bandage and you should be as good as new. We'll put you on some antibiotics too, just in case."

Though his arm throbbed like hell, Trace managed a lopsided smile. "Thanks, Doc."

A little later, bandaged and absurdly light-headed, Trace stood with Emma's help. When he fumbled for his wallet, Doc waved away his offer of payment. "We can settle up later," he said. "Maybe when you're feeling better, you can invite me over for a nice steak dinner."

"Consider it done," Trace replied, though even he could tell it sounded more like *conshidder itz done*. At this point, he didn't really care. He'd never been much of a drinker and when he imbibed, he preferred an ice-cold beer.

Emma smiled at him. "I think I need to get you home so you can lie down and rest," she said. "Between having surgery while awake and drinking the equivalent of around six shots…"

"Six shots?" Trace shook his head, which had the unfortunate effect of making the room start spinning.

"Come on." Gently, she led him toward the door. "Thank you, Doctor," she said as Doc held it open. "I really appreciate you doing this. I would have hated to have to make a long drive with him in that shape."

"You're welcome."

Though he wasn't sure how, Trace found himself seat-belted in the passenger side of Emma's Jeep. She'd been able to buckle the seat belt without affecting his injured arm, for which he was grateful.

The next thing he knew, Emma called his name. "We're home," she said. "Let's see if we can get you inside."

As she helped him from the Jeep, he tried to stand, but his legs didn't want to work. Luckily, he was able to grip the side of the vehicle until everything stopped spinning. Damn if he was going to pass out here in the driveway and leave Emma with no way to get him inside.

"Are you okay?" Voice concerned, she leaned in close. "If you can't walk, I can try to let you lean on me."

This struck him as funny. He outweighed her by probably eighty pounds. He'd crush her.

"I've got this," he declared, straightening up and

putting one foot in front of the other—even if he zig-zagged a bit—as he made his way toward his back door.

Somehow, he managed to stay upright. She ran ahead of him, opening the door and turning on lights. He went straight toward his bedroom, lowering himself gingerly onto his bed.

For one awful moment, he thought he might get sick. He broke out into a cold sweat, his head throbbing almost as much as his damn arm.

"Let me get you a glass of water," Emma said. "Doc sent you home with some anti-inflammatory pills that might help you sleep."

"Okay." He kicked off his boots, briefly pondered getting undressed and then decided the hell with it. Scooting back on his bed, he propped up both pillows behind his back, preparing to apologize to Emma for everything.

Chapter 11

By the time Emma returned with the water and the pills, Trace had fallen asleep. Or passed out, whichever the case might be. She left the water on the nightstand, along with the plastic bottle of pills, figuring he might need them when he woke.

Seeing Trace injured, indirectly because of her, broke Emma's heart. She'd thought Jeremy's former partner had gone far enough by threatening to injure innocent animals, but to shoot Trace? She didn't understand his twisted logic. Trace had absolutely nothing to do with Jeremy other than the fact that he was sheltering Jeremy's widow. By now the guy should have been able to tell that neither one of them had any idea where this missing money might be.

Quietly making her way back to the kitchen, she

grabbed a glass of iced tea and sat back down in front of the laptop. She had only a few days left until her first horse training client arrived. Despite spending an inordinate amount of time searching, she hadn't gotten any closer to even finding a single hint of who might have killed Jeremy. While she had amassed quite a list of people who might have had reason, that on its own wasn't enough to give her a definitive answer. She kept hoping something would jump out at her, but so far nothing had. Either way, the stalker was right about one thing. There was an awful lot of money unaccounted for, though apparently all that paled compared to the big scam they'd run right before Jeremy died.

There had to be a clue here somewhere. As sloppy as Jeremy appeared to be with his record keeping, she didn't think he had the capacity to hide something that well. She'd find it. She had to. She refused to give up hope.

Staring at the screen until her eyes crossed, she finally stood and stretched. Her stomach growled, reminding her that she hadn't eaten. Neither had Trace, but after all he'd gone through, she doubted he'd be hungry.

She made herself a quick sandwich, ate and checked on Trace. Still sleeping, he let out quiet snores that made her smile. If not for the large white bandage on his arm, she wouldn't have known anything was wrong. She stood in his doorway, watching him sleep, for far longer than she should have. She shook her head at her own foolishness, returned to the laptop and got back to it.

At some point during the night, she must have dozed off. She woke with her neck aching and her back stiff, head pillowed on her arms on top of the kitchen table. She went to her own bed, not wanting to take a chance of disturbing Trace by getting into his bed next to him.

The next thing she knew, her phone alarm woke her. This was her usual 8:00 a.m. alert, though in general she rose long before that.

Not today though. Clearly, she'd stayed up too late poring over that infernal laptop.

First thing, she needed coffee. Stumbling into the kitchen, still in the oversize T-shirt she slept in, she stopped short at the sight of Trace, already seated at the table, a large mug of steaming coffee in front of him. With his brown hair ruffled and morning stubble darkening his rugged chin, he looked good enough to eat.

"Mornin'," he greeted her with a slight smile. "You look like you've had a rough night."

She tried to summon the energy to bristle. "Thanks. I appreciate your kind observation."

This made him wince. "Sorry. If it helps any, I still think you look sexy as hell."

Heat suffused her, bringing a wave of desire. To hide it, she went for the coffeemaker, busying herself with getting her own jolt of wake-me-up.

By the time she turned back around, she had herself under control. She thought.

Somehow, she managed to carry her mug over to the table and take a seat. Trying her best to ignore how badly she wanted to crawl up onto his lap, she took a sip. "Ahh," she said. "This is good. How's your arm?"

He shrugged and immediately grimaced. "It's okay, as long as I don't move it."

"Have you eaten?" she asked, feeling she ought to make them something for breakfast.

"I have. And I made extra for you. There are a couple of breakfast burritos in the fridge. All you need to do is microwave them."

He pushed to his feet, moving slowly. "I've got to go get cleaned up. The doc said showering is out for a few days, so sponge bath it is." His smile contained a hint of wickedness. "I'd ask you if you'd mind helping me with that, but somehow I don't think my arm would survive."

Then, while she was still trying to come up with a response, he turned and ambled out of the room, leaving her once again aching with desire.

She knew she'd best get a move on starting the day herself. With Trace semi-sidelined, she'd need to begin helping with his chores. He couldn't muck out stalls with one arm, nor could he move around large bales of hay.

With so much work to get done, the day went by quickly.

At first, she thought a hay bale might be more than she could manage, but she and Trace devised a plan where she'd help get the bale into the scoop of Trace's tractor and he'd load it onto the pickup that way. Then they'd drive out to the pasture and off-load it for the cattle to eat. He'd had to move the second herd in with the first to make feeding them simpler.

Losing so much time made her realize that every spare moment she could find to research Jeremy's records had to count. Luckily, Trace volunteered to help her, so she gave him the paper files while she stuck to digital ones. This made him feel useful and quite frankly, she was glad to have the help.

On the fifth day of poring through Jeremy's computer files, Emma found a folder marked Private hidden within another folder marked Tax Credits. She'd skipped over checking this one at first, believing it would have little or nothing to do with her investigation. No doubt that was the reason why Jeremy placed his private folder there.

Heart pounding, she let the pointer hover over the file before clicking. No telling what she might find inside. Maybe she'd finally get some of the answers she'd been seeking.

Once she opened the file, inside were several others with only letters for names. Since they were in alphabetical order, Emma clicked on the first one, *A*. She quickly deduced that the *A* stood for Amber. Inside, Jeremy had apparently listed every occasion he spent with his mistress, and had scanned receipts for purchases ranging from jewelry and flowers to dinners and drinks. For a man who hadn't been very organized in his investment business, this kind of meticulous record keeping astounded her.

The second folder, *B*, was all about Emma's stepmother, Beth. Jeremy had many grievances against the older woman, and he'd listed them in chronological order. Once or twice, he'd included photos he'd taken of Beth with his phone. In most of these, Beth appeared completely unaware her picture had been taken. In one, she'd been standing with her back to Jeremy, stirring something on the stove and chatting with Emma's father, who was also in the photo. As she stared at this, Emma's heart ached. She missed her father something fierce.

There were more pictures of Beth. None of them appeared staged in the slightest. Beth vacuuming, Beth reading and talking on her phone. There was even one of Beth asleep on the couch, with the television on in the background.

Judging from just the file, it appeared Jeremy had been stalking Beth. But why? And had Beth ever realized it? This concerned Emma, since as far as she'd known, her stepmother and Jeremy had gotten along just fine. Emma hadn't detected any undertones, sexual or otherwise. She could only hope that Beth had never learned of any of this.

There were no files for *C* or *D*, so the next file was titled *E*. Emma clicked on it, unsurprised to learn this was *her* file. The first thing she saw was a list of dates, each one with a note alongside it, frequently just a single word, like *headache*. It took her scrolling halfway down before she noticed Jeremy had kept a log of every single time she'd refused sex.

Shocked, she swallowed hard, forcing herself to continue reading. For her file, Jeremy hadn't included any photographs or receipts. Instead, he'd made several other lists.

There was one showing who cooked what meal and when. He'd made asterisks beside certain dishes, along with notes indicating whether or not the meal had been good. He'd marked almost everything he'd cooked as good, while hers appeared to be more hit-and-miss.

A third had to do with household chores. Jeremy had kept exhaustive notes on who did what and when, going all the way back to their honeymoon. He'd included laundry, which usually had fallen to Emma, though he'd taken over washing a few of his own clothes, and grocery shopping, something they'd often done together.

Emma couldn't see the point of all this. If he felt he did more than her, he hadn't noted it.

The level of obsessive detail spoke to compulsive behavior, a meticulous sort of record keeping that had been conspicuously absent in Jeremy's financial notes. Which might seem to indicate, she thought with a frown, that those had been staged. Here, in this private folder, she had a growing gut feeling she might locate a second set of books with much more information than the carefree, nonchalant notes she'd read earlier.

Heart pounding, she sat back in her chair and reminded herself to breathe.

Had Rayna seen any of this? Or had she, misled by the title of Tax Credits, skipped that folder entirely? Emma couldn't blame her if she had, especially since she'd almost done the same.

Steeling herself, Emma went to the next letter, F. She couldn't help but wonder if the letter stood for Fraud.

Instead, in what Jeremy had no doubt considered humorous, he had listed every time he'd had fun, which judging by his notes, seemed to be any instance in which he'd been able to enact a bit of petty revenge. It broke Emma's heart to see he'd played a lot of mean-spirited "jokes" on her dad, inwardly laughing behind the older man's back when his father-in-law didn't even realize what Jeremy had done.

Reading this, though she hadn't even made it halfway through the alphabet, made her understand she'd clearly never known the man she'd married. Not at all.

For the first time, she started to grasp why happy-go-lucky Jeremy might have had enemies. On the surface, he played the magnanimous guy, a friend to all. Outgoing, energetic and kind. While inside, he calculated every perceived slight and made sure to enact his own sort of twisted revenge.

Pushing to her feet, she paced around the kitchen, her queasy stomach making her fear she might vomit. When she became aware she'd begun hyperventilating, she stepped out the back door, hoping some fresh air might help.

Trace, walking back from the barn, caught sight of her and hurried over. "Emma? Is everything all right? You look like you've seen a ghost or something. What's wrong?"

At first, she could only shake her head, unable to articulate what she'd learned. She met Trace's kind gaze and that gave her the strength to continue. "Jeremy…" she began, then found herself blinking back tears, "was a monster."

With a muttered oath, Trace pulled her into his arms. Or arm, since he took care to protect his injured one. He simply held her, asking no questions, holding on tight as if the sheer strength of his embrace could chase away whatever demons her past brought out of hiding.

"I never liked that guy," he muttered, which made her smile.

She let herself be comforted, allowed herself to sink into his warmth and solidity. Finally, when tremors no longer racked her and she could move without feeling nauseated, she stepped back out of his arms. "Thank you," she said. "That turned out to be exactly what I needed."

"I take it you found something on Jeremy's laptop?"

Slowly, she nodded. "His secret files. Ugh." She made a face.

"Do you want to talk about it?" he asked, watching her, his own expression enigmatic.

"I'm not sure." But then she found herself telling him about the files under Tax Credits, and the meticulous and exceedingly strange notes and photographs—all of them. "He seemed to have some weird kind of obsession with my stepmother, Beth. I don't know if she was aware of it or not, though judging by the pictures, I can't see how she wouldn't have been."

Trace shook his head. "I'm not sure how to respond to that. I'm sorry. Hopefully you'll be able to find what you need somewhere in those files."

"I hope so. I haven't made it past the letter *F*," she explained. "To tell you the truth, it makes me sick. But I feel pretty confident that somewhere in this mess will be a clue as to who might have murdered Jeremy."

"Good work," Trace said.

"Thanks," Emma replied. "It was a bit tricky. I almost skipped that file myself. Tax Credits has to be one of the most boring subjects on earth, which no doubt is why Jeremy used that title."

Trace nodded. "Are you going to let Rayna know what you've found? You could ask her then."

"I will, once I've read everything." She took a deep breath, almost herself again. "This is something I have to do on my own for right now. But if and when I have something concrete, I promise I'll fill Rayna in."

He kissed her then, a gentle press of his lips against hers. When he lifted his mouth away, she had to battle herself to keep from pulling him back for more.

"Just be careful, Emma. Promise me that. Whoever killed Jeremy is still out there and might not take too kindly to you stirring things back up."

"I know." Sobered, she found her gaze wandering to his still-bandaged arm. "I can't help but think that deranged man who shot you and threatened our livestock is involved. Maybe he hoped Jeremy would tell him where to find the money before he died—I don't know."

"That's entirely possible. The guy does seem unhinged. Rayna even processed some still photos from our video feed and distributed them around, but so far no one has been able to identify him."

She nodded. "I think he believes one of us might be able to recognize him, which could be why he hasn't confronted us face-to-face. Instead, he threatens our livestock on the phone and takes potshots at you."

"Like a damn coward." Trace's expression went black. "He has to know he hit me, but he hasn't called to follow up. Why do you think that might be?"

She thought about it for a moment. "Maybe he realizes he went too far."

"I doubt that. There is no logic behind his actions."

Emma agreed. "I'm of half a mind to pay that Amber woman another visit. I can't shake the feeling there is something she wasn't telling us."

"Promise me you'll wait until my arm is better," he said. "I want to go with you. There's something off about her and I want to make sure you're safe."

Touched, she nodded. "I agree. I've always had a bad feeling about her, but thought that might just be my bias since her false testimony sent me to prison. But I'll wait." She smiled at him. "Just get that arm healed up. That's what matters the most right now."

Try as he might, Trace couldn't figure out the method behind Emma's stalker's madness. So far, the guy had made a bunch of empty threats, destroyed security cameras and shot Trace in the arm. None of this had gotten him one step closer to finding his so-called missing money.

At this point, Trace had begun to wonder if there really *was* any missing money. He couldn't discount the possibility that this guy might be the actual murderer. If the thought had occurred to Emma, she hadn't shared it. Though Trace didn't want to needlessly alarm her, she needed to prepare for the very real possibility that this guy might soon come after her.

"I agree," she said when Trace finally mentioned it to her. "Though I can't exactly go into hiding, nor do I want to. My new client is bringing their horse here tomorrow and despite finding lots of downright weird stuff in Jeremy's computer, I'm not any closer to finding out who killed him." She met Trace's gaze, her blue eyes clear. "However, if this guy is the actual murderer, all he's done is bring attention to himself by his pointless harassment. And we have to take into account that he tortured Amber, using the same story about wanting his missing money."

"True," Trace conceded. "If any of that even happened."

"That same thought occurred to me," she admitted. "And you have to think if Jeremy really did have a stash of ill-gotten funds, where would he have hidden them? Not here, since he'd never been to this ranch. And not with me, due to the fact that he wanted to end our marriage. So where? My parents' old house?"

"We should have Rayna contact the current owners and see if they'd had any break-ins or any problem with some strange man skulking around," Trace said. "If it were me, that's the first place I'd look."

"Do you mind calling her?" Emma asked. "I need to double-check and make sure that stall is ready for my client's horse. I'll be right back."

He watched her from the window, appreciated her confident stride. During the time since she'd arrived at the ranch, he'd watched her go from shut down and self-conscious to a vibrant, fully assured woman. The way she'd been before. He couldn't help but wonder how any man, even one like Jeremy, could fail to appreciate Emma.

He made a quick call and filled Rayna in. She agreed that he had some good points, and promised to investigate, starting with Emma's old family home. Emma returned just as he had ended the call, so he relayed the gist of the conversation to her.

"She promised to keep us informed on anything she finds," he concluded. "Oh, one more thing. Rayna said she got your cell phone records, and the number that called you was different every single time. Which means he was using various burner phones or pay phones. She's trying to track the numbers down, but so far hasn't had any luck."

Emma nodded. "I admit I'm feeling a little discouraged. I haven't made as much progress as I'd like. For some reason, I thought this would be easier."

Her comment had him shaking his head. "Emma, if this had been simple, you'd never have gone to prison. Rayna's sharp and she's a damn good sheriff. You know she did everything she could to investigate."

"Maybe so," Emma shot back. "But I have to admit to feeling just a little bit of resentment. Okay, a lot actually. You can't imagine what it's like to have everyone in your hometown believe you murdered your husband. Or to go to prison, knowing you did no such thing." She held his gaze, her voice wobbling. "I kept thinking it had to be a bad dream and at any minute, I'd wake up. But it wasn't."

Seeing the devastation in her face, the pain in

her voice, shook him to the core. Throat aching, he reached for her and pulled her close. "We'll figure it out, Emma," he promised. "No matter how long it takes."

She held on to him for a moment or two. When she stepped back, determination shone in her eyes. "I know we will. Thanks for having my back. You're a good friend."

Friend.

Somehow, he managed a casual nod. "I'm heading out," he said.

"Where are you going?" she asked.

He grabbed his cowboy hat on the way out the door. "I've got pictures on my phone from our camera feed before that guy destroyed the setup. I'm going to take them into town and see if anyone recognizes him."

"Good idea." Her casual smile ripped away the rest of his torn pride. "And good luck."

He left before he said or did anything stupid, like stalking over to her and kissing her just to prove they were so much more than just friends. Driving, he stewed about it all the way down the drive, telling himself to let it go. Emma had been through a lot, more than most women could endure, and just because his feelings for her had grown, didn't mean she felt the same way. He needed to be okay with that, and wouldn't push her. Either she came to him of her own free will or not at all. He just hoped he could survive if she chose to move in.

Once he reached Main Street, he parked and began the task of going from place to place with his admittedly grainy photograph. He made sure to go into every shop, even Hannah's Craft Store, just in case. By the time he reached Serenity Rune's Metaphysical Store and Flower Shop, he was batting zero.

As he pushed open her front door, an exotic jingling of bells announced his arrival.

"Well, I'll be," Serenity exclaimed, hurrying over to greet him with a huge, patchouli-scented hug. "What brings you here, Mr. Trace?"

"I pulled this still picture off my video security feed. I'm asking around to see if anyone might recognize this guy."

She took the photo from him, studying it intently. "Emma showed me this already. Like I told her, he does look familiar, though I honestly can't say why. She didn't mention that to you?"

"No." He shook his head. "But there's been a lot going on."

"I take it you haven't had any luck so far?"

"Not yet." When she passed it back, he took it and grimaced. "But I haven't been in Rattlesnake Pub or the Bar yet. I figure those plus the Tumbleweed Café would be the most likely. I mean, everyone has to eat and some people enjoy having a drink."

"True, true." Serenity studied him, her gaze intent. "How is your pretty lady doing?"

Since she claimed to be psychic, Trace found the phrasing of her question a bit unsettling. "Emma? She's keeping busy. She's getting her first client horse tomorrow."

Serenity nodded, sending her large earrings swinging. "Has she had any luck with her investigation?"

"Not yet." No way did he plan on going into any detail on that, even if Serenity was one of the nicest people he knew. "Anyway, I've got a lot more places to stop by. Let me know if you think of anything, will you?"

"I will." She followed him to the door. "May I give you one piece of advice?"

Damn. Turning, he braced himself. "Of course."

"Don't give up without a fight," she said. "That's it. My message."

Feeling as if he'd gotten off easy, he nodded. "Thank you. I won't." And then he made his escape.

As he walked down the block to the Rattlesnake Pub, he considered Serenity's words. Her advice could mean anything, he told himself. It might be completely unrelated to Emma, though somehow he doubted that.

At this hour of the day, the pub was mostly empty. The lunch crowd had long ago left and it wasn't time for the after-work bunch. Trace walked up to the bar and greeted Simone, the bartender on duty. With her purple-and-blue mane of hair and colorful tattoos, she looked fierce, until she smiled. "Hey, Trace. Good to see you. It's been a while. Have you come for a beer?"

"Actually, no." He slid the photograph across the bar. "I'm just going around town seeing if anybody might recognize this guy. So far, I haven't had any luck."

Simone studied the picture. "He's been in here," she finally said. "Though not enough to be considered a regular. The few times I've served him, he sat at the bar. And I can't say for sure, but I think at least once he was with a woman."

Trace perked up at that. "Can you describe her?"

"I can try." Simone shrugged. "Tall, dark hair. Very clingy. That's all I can remember."

"Any chance you got either of their names?" Trace asked.

"No. I'm sorry." She handed him back the photo.

"Don't be." Trace smiled. "You've been more help than anyone else."

"Do you mind me asking why you're looking for him? He hasn't done anything illegal, has he? Because I don't like those types of people coming in my bar and causing trouble."

Trace chose his words carefully. "He hasn't been charged with any crimes as of right now."

Picking up on what he didn't say, Simone laughed. "I get it. Leave me your number. If I see him again, I'll give you a call."

Thanking her, he jotted down the information on a cocktail napkin and handed it over. "I really appreciate it," he said. "And I promise I'll come back soon and have that beer."

Next up, Trace stopped by the Tumbleweed Café. He sat in one of the booths by the window with a good view of the parking lot and the entrance, and ordered a slice of banana cream pie with a cup of coffee. His waitress shook her head when he passed her the picture. After pouring his coffee and bringing his pie, at his request, she took the photo with her so she could ask her coworkers. When she returned a few minutes later, she shook her head. "Sorry, but no one recognizes him. Of course, a completely different crew works breakfast and dinner, so if he came in then..."

"Thanks." He accepted the photo back. She left the check, telling him to let her know if he wanted a refill on the coffee. Once he finished off his pie, he left his money on the table, including a generous tip, and headed out.

The Bar, Getaway's other drinking establishment, didn't open until seven, so he couldn't stop there and show his photo.

There were a few other stores on the other side of the street, so he visited them all as he walked back to his truck. Only one person—Dan at the hardware store—thought he might have seen the guy in the photo around, and even then he wasn't sure.

Finally, Trace reached his truck and climbed in to go home. While he hadn't learned much, he didn't consider the afternoon a totally wasted effort, thanks to Simone. Some woman in town or nearby knew this guy, maybe dated him. She might not even know about his past criminal activities.

He decided to make a few other stops before heading home. There were several other stores nearby that weren't located on Main Street. He figured he'd stop by all of those, ensuring he'd checked everywhere.

Chapter 12

After Trace left, Emma decided to keep busy and took Daisy out to work her. In the middle of putting the paint mare through her paces, Emma caught sight of a car making its way up the long drive, kicking up dust in its wake. Mindful of Trace's warning, her first thought was that she was too exposed out there in the middle of the riding arena on horseback.

While she'd taken Trace's advice and kept her Glock .43 in a holster on her back, she didn't like her chances should it come to a gunfight.

Dismounting, she led Daisy out of the arena and tied her to the hitching post near the barn. Emma moved into the doorway of the barn, watching while the battered red Kia parked.

Something about the little car looked familiar and

as the driver emerged a moment later, Emma understood why. Her husband's former mistress Amber had come to pay her a call.

Keeping within the relative shelter of the barn, Emma wondered if she'd been wrong. Maybe Amber had killed Jeremy, and now she was coming to put an end to Emma as well. Or perhaps Amber had lied about not knowing anything about missing money. Emma could think of no real reason why the other woman would come pay her a call.

"I come in peace," Amber announced, holding up her hands to prove she was unarmed. While she walked toward the barn, she continually scanned the landscape around her, almost as if she worried someone might take a potshot at her.

Crazier things had happened. One thing for sure, Emma didn't trust her. Just in case she might need it, Emma withdrew her pistol, holding it loosely at her side.

When Amber passed the hitching post, Emma held up a hand. "You've gone far enough," she said. "What do you want?"

"I came to apologize," Amber replied, once again scanning the horizon. "And maybe warn you. All I can do to make it up to you is tell the truth. Please, I'm not comfortable standing out here in the open. May I come inside?"

Emma backed up a few paces. The door at the other end of the barn aisle stood partly open, letting in some light but providing adequate blockage. "Come on," Emma said. "You should know that I'm armed."

"I don't blame you." Amber's dry tone matched her

wry smile. "It's not safe right now. I hope I'm okay, but I'm not sure about you. Either way, since my false testimony ruined your life, I feel like I need to help you as much as I can."

"Why now?" Emma asked. "Why didn't you do that when I went to see you? What's changed?"

"Because I wasn't prepared." Amber shrugged. "You took me by surprise. I honestly didn't expect to ever see you again." She inhaled sharply. "And he's back. That man who lost all that money. He's come back and is threatening me again."

Steeling herself, Emma stood her ground. "I don't believe you."

Resignation settled over the other woman's pretty features. "Again, I can't say I blame you. But since then, I haven't been able to stop thinking about what happened to you. And since I'm partly to blame for all of it, I decided you needed to know the rest of the story. Or, at least as much as I know."

Emma froze. If—and this was a big if—Amber told her the truth, that would be the first of many puzzle pieces falling into place. "I'm listening," she replied, her voice raspier than she would have liked. She knew better than to let her guard down. Whatever this woman's reason might be for coming to see her, she doubted it had to do with helping in any way unless it also helped Amber.

"As you know, Jeremy stole three million dollars from one of his clients. I don't think he started out trying to take that much, but this guy apparently totally believed in Jeremy and his investment plans."

When Emma, struggling to process the staggering amount of money, started to speak, Amber held up her hand. "I didn't know about it, if that's what you're going to ask."

Slowly, Emma nodded. "Did this man kill Jeremy?"

Amber shrugged. "He says he didn't, but he's probably lying. But then again, who knows? Despite what he did to me and Matt, that guy doesn't seem like the type to shoot someone and then set him on fire. If he had been, I honestly think he would have hurt me or my brother much worse."

Emma had heard enough. "Why are you really here, Amber?"

"Because if you have that money, I want you to tell me. We can work together and get that man arrested."

Was she serious? Eyeing the other woman's expectant expression, Emma figured out she was. Disgusted, Emma shook her head. "I'm sorry, but I can't help you," Emma finally said. "Again, I don't know where the money is. Now you need to get off this property before I call the sheriff."

Amber held up her hands. "I'm going. But I should warn you. I have a feeling this guy is at the end of his patience. He wants his three million dollars and he won't give up until he has it."

Once she'd watched Amber drive away, Emma called the sheriff's office and told Rayna everything, from Amber's revelations to what Emma had found on Jeremy's computer. When she'd finished, Rayna whistled softly. "What a tangled web they wove," she said. "Why am I not surprised that Jeremy's mistress is hoping for a cut of the missing money?"

"Pretty awful, isn't it?" Emma agreed. "But at

least we now know the amount. It's not much to go on, but better than nothing. I just wish I knew the name of the guy Jeremy swindled and who, according to Amber, possibly killed him. Three million is a lot of money. But still, not worth killing someone over."

"True, but then think about the scenario. This guy must have been furious. Maybe he went to confront Jeremy to get his money back. Say Jeremy refused, possibly even laughed. And the guy killed him in a fit of rage."

Stunned at the vivid picture the other woman painted, Emma swallowed. "Do you really think that's what happened?"

"I have no idea," Rayna responded. "It's simply one of many possibilities. With Amber's track record, it's hard to believe anything she says."

"You have a point," Emma replied. "It's such a twisted mess."

"It is, but we have to go on facts, not supposition. I need to have a little chat with Amber. I'll go round her up and do that."

"And I'll continue combing through Jeremy's laptop to see if I can find out who he stole three million dollars from."

"Perfect. Let me know as soon as you can."

Ending the call, Emma went back into the kitchen with the intention of firing up the computer. But the laptop was no longer where she'd left it on the kitchen table. Had she moved it?

A quick and desperate search revealed no sign of it anywhere. The computer had vanished. Instantly, Emma thought of Amber's visit earlier. Had someone come along with her and while Amber distracted Emma, gone into the house and stolen the laptop? That had to be what had happened. No one else had been here and Amber had been with Emma the entire time.

Emma cursed out loud, using slang she'd heard while in prison, furious at her own stupidity.

"Wow," Trace said from the doorway. "That's some creative swearing."

"You're back," she said, surprised. He looked comfortingly big and handsome. She'd never been so glad to see someone in her entire life.

"I am." His smile vanished when she told him what had happened. "I wish we still had those security cameras."

"Me too. The only consolation is that they won't be able to get into the computer unless they know his password."

Still seething, she relayed everything that had happened, including the fact that she'd passed all the information on to Rayna. "Except for the missing laptop," she said. "And I'll notify her about that in a minute. I feel like such an idiot."

"Don't," Trace said, pulling her in for a quick hug. He smelled faintly of incense, which told her he'd stopped at Serenity's for at least a few minutes. "You had no way of knowing. I'm thinking Amber and whoever she's working with figures there must be a clue as to the money's location on that computer."

"Maybe so, but I haven't found it." Trying not to sound too dejected, Emma moved away and redialed Rayna. "While Amber was here talking to me, someone stole Jeremy's laptop," she told her. "I'm thinking it had to have been that guy, working with Amber. She must have let him out before she came up the driveway and kept me distracted long enough for him to grab the computer and leave."

"That makes sense. And it's highly likely that Amber might know the password," Rayna said. "I'm thinking I'll head over there right now and pay her a visit. I promise to keep you posted."

"Are you going to arrest her?" Emma asked, ever hopeful.

"I would if I could," Rayna replied. "But right now, I don't have anything concrete that I can charge her with. Now this other guy, that's another story. I'll just go and have a little chat with her. Maybe I can round him up in the process. I'll give you or Trace a call after I'm done."

Watching Emma's emotions chase each other across her expressive face, Trace realized he'd do anything and everything to help her close out this chapter of her past so she could move forward into the future. A future he could only hope would include him.

"You look lost in thought," Emma commented, touching his arm. "Penny for them?"

He blinked, knowing he couldn't complicate things right now. "I was just trying to separate out what we do know as opposed to random dead ends."

This comment made her brighten, as he'd suspected it would.

"That's a good idea," she said. "Let me grab a pen

and a pad of paper and we can write everything down. I do love my lists."

How could he not smile at that? "Yes, you do," he concurred.

They sat down across from each other at the table, Emma with her legal pad and Trace with his heart full of love, hoping his emotions didn't show in his gaze.

"Okay, here's what we do know," Emma began. "Amber's testimony, whether she truly believed it or not, made sure I'd go to prison. That's in the Facts column. Now in the second column, which I call Suppositions, I can put possible reasons why. One, the real killer got her to do this so they wouldn't be charged and two, to get me out of the way so someone could reclaim their money."

She made her lists and he contributed when he thought of something. Finally, Trace got up and decided to fix them a meal. He'd never particularly cared what he'd eaten before Emma came. He'd eaten a lot of steaks and baked potatoes. Now, he found he actually enjoyed making food for Emma. Her appreciation as she ate, the little sounds of enjoyment she made, were sensual. Watching as she tasted his cooking had become one of the highlights of his day.

"What are you making?" she asked, eyeing him with interest.

Her question made him grin. "I found an interesting recipe for homemade pizza," he replied. "I've already made the dough and it's been rising." He pointed toward a mixing bowl he'd covered with a paper towel. "Next up, I'm going to turn it into a gourmet pizza."

When she heard that, her blue eyes lit up. "I can hardly wait. Is there anything I can do to help?"

"Nope. Just keep me company while I work, if you don't mind."

"As if you have to ask," she replied. "I like the stream-of-consciousness thing we had going while I was making this list. If you think of anything else, no matter how small or remotely connected, please throw it out there."

"I will, though I doubt there's anything we didn't cover."

His comment made her laugh. "True, but you never know. I wonder if Rayna will be able to get the laptop back from Amber."

"I hope so, but I doubt it." He glanced sideways at her. "There's a possibility she wasn't even involved in the theft."

Clearly, that thought had never occurred to her. She tilted her head, considering. "You're thinking whoever stole it might have been watching and waiting for the perfect opportunity?"

"Though I hate that idea, yes. He could have planned to grab it while you were out there working the horse."

"The timing was too coincidental," she argued. After a moment, she sighed. "But maybe you're right. Unless Amber admits taking it, we have no proof."

Slicing mushrooms to go on top of the pizza, he nodded. "If anyone can get to the truth, Rayna can."

After he got the pizza in the oven, he grabbed them a beer and sat down across from her. Though she still held the pen poised to write in case any ideas struck her, she stared into space, lost in her own thoughts.

Not wanting to interrupt her, he poured her beer into a glass and set it down near her. Looking up, she thanked him and took a small sip. "I really just want this all to be over," she mused. "I don't know why, but I truly thought it would be easier to figure out who really killed Jeremy. Of course, I didn't anticipate some guy threatening me over money Jeremy apparently stole from him."

"True. But if it were going to be easy, I would think they would have figured it out long before now," he said, grabbing a couple of plates. "Maybe even before they arrested and charged you with so little evidence."

"I admit I still grapple with that."

The oven timer pinged a few minutes later, indicating the pizza was done. He got it out, sliced it up and placed it in the center of the table.

She grabbed a couple slices and smiled. "This looks amazing."

"Let me know what you think." So intent on watching her, waiting for her reaction, he forgot to get any himself. Naturally, she noticed.

"Aren't you going to eat?" she asked.

"I am." Still watching her, he got a couple slices and took a bite. "Not bad. I think it needs some Parmesan cheese sprinkled on top." He jumped up to get that.

His cell phone rang.

"It's Rayna," Emma said, leaning over to check his

phone, which he'd left on the table. "She's calling you instead of me. Do you want to answer it or should I?"

Since he figured Rayna had decided to call him for a reason, he set down the Parmesan and grabbed his phone. "I'll get it. You go ahead and eat. Hey, Rayna. What's up?"

"Bad news." The sheriff's voice was grim. "I'm at Amber Trevault's house in Sweetwater. Someone got here before me and killed her."

Trace reacted out loud before he had time to think better of it. "She's dead?"

"Unfortunately, yes."

"How?" Trace asked, though he wasn't sure why he wanted to know. Across the table, Emma stared at him, her eyes huge, her pizza untouched.

"Gunshot wound in the back of the head. She was bound and made to kneel. Then she was shot execution style."

Trace cursed. "Any idea how long ago?"

"Pretty damn recent," Rayna said. "The ME is on the way from Abilene. Tell Emma there's no sign of the laptop. Whoever killed Amber must have taken it."

"I'll let her know," Trace replied. "Anything else?"

"Only this." Rayna hesitated, as if trying to weigh her next statement. "It might not be a bad idea for Emma to go somewhere safe until this guy is caught. There's a very real possibility that he might be coming for her next."

Numb, Trace thanked her and hung up the phone. When he looked at Emma, he wasn't surprised that she appeared to be in shock. He couldn't blame her.

"What happened?" she asked, her voice shaking.

Since she deserved the truth, he told her, sparing nothing.

When he'd finished, she shook her head. "She was killed. Over the laptop?"

"We don't know that," he cautioned. "But it's possible. Either way, if she had it, whoever killed her took it."

She nodded, clearly trying to process the news. His heart ached for her—she'd been through so much and now this. He dreaded what he'd have to say next, not sure how she'd react to Rayna's warning.

But Emma beat him to it. "Do you think he's going to come after me next?" she asked.

Again, he could only give her the truth. "Rayna does. She wanted me to ask you if you had somewhere you could go for a while, at least until this guy is caught."

"Hide?" Emma pushed to her feet, her hands fisted in front of her. "This person not only murdered my husband, but stole two entire years of my life. I want to clear my name, and I certainly can't do that while cowering somewhere far away from here."

"While I admire your spirit, I'm not sure risking your life is worth it," he said, wishing he could tell her it would destroy him if anything happened to her. "Maybe you should pay Heather a visit in California, just for a few weeks. I'm sure she'd love to see you, and I'd be more than happy to take care of the plane ticket."

She stared at him, disappointment warring with resolve in her expression. "I'm staying right here," she told him. "I don't have the missing money and by now this guy has surely realized that. And if I get a chance to prove he killed Jeremy, that's worth almost everything to me. Half the people in Getaway still think I murdered my own husband. Plus, my first client is bringing her horse tomorrow."

"I get it, I really do." Not ready to give up, he spread his hands. "But please at least think about it. Not only might you also be putting your client's life at risk by staying, but also her horse. A short break wouldn't hurt anything and could save your life."

"What about you?" she shot back. "Aren't you in danger too because of me? Even if I left, that guy might think I told you where the money is hidden. Did you think of that? Maybe *you* should go visit Heather in Cali."

She had a point. "Fine." He threw up his hands. "We'll both stay here and watch each other's backs."

Keeping her gaze locked on his, she finally nodded. "At least we have an idea of what this guy looks like. For a murderer, he wasn't all that careful."

"Those video cameras were old and cheap. I doubt he realized I set it up to record to my laptop and that I could grab a still shot from it." He grimaced. "For all the good it's done me."

"I've got to believe that something will turn up," she said. "Either someone will recognize him and call you or Rayna, or he'll make a mistake. Either way, none of us can continue like this indefinitely."

He could only hope she was right.

Chapter 13

The shiny red truck towing the matching horse trailer pulled up to the ranch at exactly thirty minutes before Emma's client Marina Vaughan had said she'd be there. She'd texted to let Emma know she was on the way, so Emma kept an eye out the kitchen window as she did dishes. She couldn't stop thinking about Amber and the fact that she'd been killed. The woman had been a liar, true, but no one deserved to die the way she had.

Now at least Emma would have a horse to focus her attention on.

As soon as the rig pulled up to the barn, she headed out. She couldn't wait to meet Zotar. She'd always found Arabian horses beautiful, even if she'd never actually ridden one.

As the tall, elegantly dressed woman climbed out from the truck, Emma psasted a smile on her face and hurried over. With everything going on, she knew now wasn't the best time to take on new clients, but her reputation had already undergone a nearly terminal beating, and she knew a cancellation might be something she'd never recover from. Therefore, she had to take the chance.

"Welcome," Emma said, shaking the other woman's hand. "You must be Marina. I can't wait to meet Zotar."

"He's a good horse," Marina said, going around to the back of the trailer to open it. "Just a little bit skittish, as you'll see."

A moment later, a magnificent gray horse backed out of the trailer. The instant he had all four feet on the ground, he leaped sideways, nearly knocking Marina down. Luckily, she appeared to have been expecting this, as she moved out of the way while keeping a tight hold on the lead.

"Hey there," Emma said, keeping her voice soft and her posture nonthreatening. She moved over a little closer to the horse, noting the animal's flaring nostrils and flattened ears.

Fearing he might rear or strike out, Emma stopped a few feet away.

"He won't hurt you," Marina insisted, despite her iron grip on the lead. "He's not a vicious horse, just easily spooked."

"By what?" Emma asked, glancing around the quiet ranch. It wasn't windy, and there were no machines operating or even any other people or horses anywhere in sight. "I take it he doesn't trailer well?"

"Among other things." Marina sighed. "I think I may have made a huge mistake buying him. He came from a breeder in Colorado and when I saw his photo, I just had to have him. I had a vet check him out before I completed the deal. He's sound and healthy. And gelded," she added. "Unfortunately, he's proud cut. Which is why he acts like a stallion most of the time."

Emma managed to suppress a wince. She'd dealt with one or two proud cut geldings, which meant when they were castrated, one or more of the testes weren't removed.

Despite her efforts, something must have shown on her face.

"Please tell me you think you can help him," Marina exclaimed. "I'm at my wit's end. Several other horse trainers have already given up on him. And you came highly recommended as being able to deal with problem horses."

"Other trainers?" This was the first Emma had heard of this. "Who did you take him to before this?"

At least Marina had the grace to appear embarrassed. "He's been to three," she admitted. "Dave Halsey, Arnold Brawn and Samantha Tibbett."

Maybe because she'd been out of circulation for two years, Emma only recognized one of the names. And that one wasn't good. Arnold Brawn had been around since Emma had been a child. He was known as being heavy-handed and believed in showing animals who was boss. He'd ruined several good horses and dogs before people had finally caught on and stopped hiring him.

"How long did Arnold Brawn have Zotar?" Emma asked, not bothering to keep the concern from her voice.

"Do you mind if we put him in a stall or somewhere first?" Marina said, avoiding the question. "Maybe turn him out in that arena and let him run."

"Sure." Emma watched as the other woman led the horse over to the arena. Once inside, she unclipped the lead from the halter and stepped back. Immediately, Zotar did an odd little skip and jump before bolting off.

Watching him as he ran, Emma had to admit the Arabian was breathtakingly beautiful. His long silver mane and tail flowed out behind him as he ran up one side and down the other. He moved as if he were floating.

"Now do you see why I want to put him in costume?" Marina asked quietly. "That kind of beauty needs to be celebrated."

Emma turned to face the other woman. "How long was he with Arnold Brawn? I'm thinking he left there worse than he was when he went in."

Marina sighed. "A week and a few days. I made an unannounced visit to check on him and caught Brawn beating him. Needless to say, I went home and got my trailer and loaded my horse up immediately. And yes, Zotar wasn't nearly as head shy before I let that awful man near him. It was my fault. I didn't practice due diligence in checking Brawn out."

Right then and there, Emma came really close to

telling Marina she couldn't help her. But at that moment, Zotar trotted over to the fence and nickered.

"He deserves a chance," Marina said quietly, almost as if she'd read Emma's mind. "Please. At least try. You're my final hope."

"I find it difficult to work with a horse if the owner isn't honest with me," Emma said, keeping her gaze trained on the horse. "All you told me was that Zotar wasn't adapting to wearing a costume. That's a far cry from what you're telling me now."

"I know and I apologize. Honestly, I was afraid you wouldn't work with him if I told you everything up front. However, I heard you had been away from horse training for a while, and I figured this might be the perfect opportunity for you to get your name back out there."

"You have me there." Emma knew she should be angry, but all she could muster at the moment was a feeling of defeat. "I get it. I was your last resort."

"Yes, but that's not the only reason I contacted you. Everyone I talked to said you put the horse first. Zotar needs that. Zotar needs you."

Put like that, how could Emma turn Marina down? Not that she'd been about to. She didn't have the luxury of turning away clients and even if she did, Marina was right. Zotar needed her help. She could only hope the beautiful gelding hadn't been brought to her too late.

"I'll work with him," she said, unable to miss hearing Miranda's huge sigh of relief. "But you might as well know this could take a while."

Marina nodded. "I understand. But you'll keep me updated on his progress?"

"Of course. Feel free to drop in and check on his progress anytime."

"I will do that." Beaming, Marina turned to go. Once she had climbed back into her shiny truck and driven away, Emma remained on the outside of the riding arena, watching the restless horse pace inside.

Moving slowly, Emma climbed the wooden fence and perched on the top rail. Zotar swung his large head around to eye her, but when she remained motionless, he took off with his tail held high, flowing out behind him.

"Damn, he's magnificent," Trace said, coming up behind her and leaning in to watch. "That's the one they want to put in a costume?"

"Yes, but it's more than that."

When she finished explaining what the horse had been through, Trace's expression darkened. "Brawn ought to be banned from working with horses. I've heard nothing but bad things about him."

"Me too." Still watching Zotar, who appeared to be struggling with whether or not to react to Trace's presence, she shook her head. "One thing is for sure. This horse is going to be a lot more difficult to work with after having been left with that man."

Trace winced. "Are you up to it?"

"I hope so, though I seriously considered telling his owner that I'd need to cancel." She sighed. "But in the end, Zotar needs help. I just hope I'm able to give it."

"You've got this, Emma." The confidence in

Trace's deep voice made her smile. "If anyone can help that horse, you can."

Over the next several days, Emma took things with Zotar slowly. She lunged him for at least twenty minutes before she even attempted to ride him, and even then she kept to the close confines of the round pen as opposed to the larger riding arena. Riding him felt like a treat. His smooth gait was perfection and he appeared very responsive to her cues.

But the slightest sound made him nervous. A tractor starting up on the other side of the barn had him prancing sideways, tossing his head and trying to take the bit in his teeth. Emma spoke soothingly to him, turning him in small circles until he calmed down.

While working with Zotar would be a challenge, the prospect exhilarated her. She knew once she got the horse where he needed to be, she'd have to work with Marina as well. While there wouldn't be a quick fix by any means, putting the horse and rider on the right path together and helping them stay there would be enough to consider a job well done. She just had to get Zotar there first.

At the end of the week, things were quiet. Too quiet, which made her slightly nervous. She hadn't heard anything else from Rayna, which meant that Amber's killer was still on the loose. The man who'd been demanding money that she didn't have had also gone quiet, and Emma wasn't sure what that meant, if anything.

He'd killed Amber and gotten Jeremy's laptop. Did that mean he'd been able to locate his missing money?

She didn't dare hope, but if that were the case, that might mean he'd leave her alone.

Still, she knew better than to let her guard down. Even if she'd wanted to, Trace continually reminded her to stay alert until the killer was caught. Because Emma didn't want to end up like Amber, she promised she would.

Marina showed up unannounced on day eight. Emma had just begun putting Zotar through his paces and they both watched the red pickup truck pull up. Though he tensed and his nostrils flared, the gray gelding didn't falter, not even when Marina parked, got out and walked over to the arena.

Emma gave her a quick wave, but otherwise deliberately ignored her. As she and Zotar made another trip around the arena, they rode right past the horse's owner.

"He's looking great!" Marina hollered, hoisting herself up to sit on the top rail just after Emma and Zotar had passed.

Zotar's entire body tensed, but Emma kept him moving. They made a second pass, keeping the same steady pace.

Next, Emma urged the gelding into a controlled lope. Zotar flowed into the movement. "He's one of the smoothest horses I've ever ridden," she told Marina.

"I know," Marina answered softly. "And it looks like you've made great progress with him."

Emma slowed the gelding to a walk and then halted in front of the other woman. "Next, I want to work with you riding him."

"Really? That will be awesome."

Dismounting, Emma led Zotar to the gate. "Come and pet him," she said. "Spend some time with him so he understands you're still his person." She handed the reins to Marina and moved away to sit on the top rail while the horse's owner crooned to him and scratched behind his ears.

"That looks like it's going well," Trace said, coming up next to her.

"Surprisingly, it is," Emma replied. "He just needs to learn to trust humans again. Once he sees no one here will hurt him, we're well on our way to getting him trained."

"What about the costume? Do you think he'll ever be able to wear that?"

"Yes." She smiled at Marina, who had begun to lead Zotar over toward them. "Marina, why don't you take him in the barn and remove his saddle and brush him down? I think he'd like that."

"Sure." Beaming, Marina changed direction.

Emma watched until she'd disappeared inside the barn before jumping down and turning to Trace. "I can't stop worrying about that guy."

He nodded. "Me too. That's why I've been hanging around the main barn area, so I could keep an eye out."

"I appreciate it. I just hope he doesn't do anything to spook Zotar. That gelding has just begun to relax and let down his guard. I need to get him as close to finished as I can and let his owner do the rest of the work at her place."

"I agree." He squeezed her shoulder. "I've got to ride out and check on the cattle."

"What about your arm?"

He shrugged. "I'll make it work. Will you be all right here without me?"

She liked that he asked. "Yes. Once Marina leaves, I'm going to work Daisy and then exercise Libby. I'm assuming you'll be riding Jack?"

"I will." Giving her a pointed look, he turned and scanned the entire area. "You're armed?"

"Of course. Though I hate it's come to that."

"Me too," he agreed. "But better safe than dead."

Since there was nothing else she could add to that, she simply nodded. Trace looked as if he might have something else to say, but just then Marina called her. Grateful for the interruption since she'd been fighting the urge to wrap her arms around Trace, Emma headed into the barn to see what the other woman needed.

"I'm very pleased," Marina said, her smile wide. "You've come so far with Zotar in such a short time. You've actually given me hope."

"I'm glad," Emma said, liking the way the horse nuzzled his owner. "We need to talk about setting up a schedule for you to come out. I'll still be working with him, of course, but I'd like you to participate in that as much as you possibly can."

If anything, Marina's smile grew wider. "I'd love that. Let me finish up brushing him and then I can check my calendar in my phone and we can set up a schedule."

"Sounds good." Emma glanced outside, noticing

Trace still remained standing where she'd left him. *Watching over her*, she realized. And damn if the fact that she had a man like Trace in her corner didn't feel good.

Lost in thought, Trace remained standing in the barnyard after Emma went to see what her client needed. He truly admired Emma's skill with the high-strung Arabian. She had an intuitive sort of patience that appeared to be exactly what the gelding needed. And when she started working with the horse's owner, Trace had no doubt Emma would eventually succeed getting Zotar to wear the elaborate Arabian costume.

As long as Amber's killer didn't decide to make an appearance, that is.

Trace didn't like living with uncertain danger looming over his head. His ranch was not only his home, but his place of refuge. Having this man lurking around after some mythical missing money and endangering the woman he loved was simply unacceptable.

Stunned, Trace forced himself to rethink those last words.

The woman he loved.

Trace couldn't move, couldn't breathe. When had this happened? But the more he thought about it, the more he realized he should have known this all along. The question he now faced was what to do about it?

Nothing. The last thing he wanted to do was scare her off. Emma had a lot on her shoulders, including trying to clear her name and reestablish her horse training business, never mind a killer who wanted money she didn't have. He'd keep his feelings to himself and hope someday they might be returned.

Heaving a deep sigh, he headed into the barn to saddle up Jack so he could go check on his herd. Walking past the two women still chatting as Marina brushed her gelding, he hurried into the tack room to grab his gear.

The rest of that week passed uneventfully, despite the constant threat looming over them. Trace managed to keep things casual and friendly with Emma, despite the ever-present desire that had him taking more than one cold shower.

He spent more time than he probably should have watching Emma working with Zotar and his elaborate costume that Marina had left with her. Emma began with putting it on the horse bit by bit, starting with little things such as the fringed and blingedout bridle. Zotar tossed his head at first but seemed to grow accustomed to it, and when he was, Emma moved on to another piece.

Trace didn't really understand the desire to parade a horse around in a bright and fancy costume, but even he had to admit, watching the magnificent horse glide around the arena in the flowing getup was a beautiful thing to see.

Zotar's owner, Marina, could scarcely contain her glee. Working closely with Emma, she'd started coming out every day. Marina became the primary rider, helping Zotar become used to each accoutrement. The final test came when Marina donned her own costume consisting of a gauzy veil, brightly colored pantaloons and a vest, all bedazzled with sequins and fringe. She even had tiny little bells sewn into the costume and they tinkled as she moved.

Zotar froze when she walked out into the arena. At Emma's command, Marina stopped, standing still while the breeze lifted the edges of the fabric, making it float around her body.

Eyes huge, ears flat against his head, Zotar watched Marina, clearly poised to take flight. When Emma controlled him, he pawed the dirt and tossed his head. Emma spoke soothingly to him and then asked Marina to do the same. "Help Zotar understand it's still you under that costume," she said.

Marina did as Emma requested, calling out to her horse in an upbeat tone. Zotar's ears turned forward as he recognized her voice.

Meanwhile, Trace kept his expression neutral, continually scanning the barnyard area and beyond.

His phone rang. Rayna.

"Anything new?" she asked.

"Not really," he replied. "So far, this guy hasn't even contacted Emma."

Rayna said he was likely lying low after murdering Amber, plus he had the laptop to try and decipher to keep him busy. That didn't mean the threat had gone away. On the contrary, once the killer exhausted all means at his disposal to find the missing money, he would turn to Emma as a last resort. And, Rayna had warned, the kid gloves would likely be coming off.

"Kid gloves?" Trace asked, rubbing the site of his gunshot wound in disbelief. "You call this kid gloves?"

"Compared to what he did to Amber, yes." Rayna's stern voice left no room for argument. "We're still investigating that one and I don't have any idea what made him snap and kill her."

Trace swallowed. "Have you found anything that might tie him to Jeremy's murder?"

"Not yet. But I'm not discouraged. We'll keep digging. Sooner or later, this guy is going to make a mistake."

"Keep me posted." Ending the call, Trace could only hope the sheriff was right. He couldn't stand even the thought of Emma being hurt or worse. He knew he'd do whatever he had to do to make sure that never happened.

Emma and Marina were still involved in working with Zotar. Neither had noticed his call. He watched until they were done. Marina left and Emma walked the horse to the barn to brush him down.

Trace followed.

"Why the long face?" Emma asked, looking up from her task. She listened while he relayed his conversation with Rayna. When he'd finished, she nodded. "I get it. We're all being as careful as we can. The ironic thing is if he hadn't stolen the laptop, I might have had a lead on the money's location by now."

"Maybe. Maybe not." Trace couldn't keep the bitterness from his voice. "But if I had three million sitting around, I'd hand it over to that guy just so he'd leave us alone."

His comment made her smile. "Change of subject," she said, patting the horse on his neck. "Today's the big day with Zotar. His final test. We've been working so hard on getting him used to this costume. He's doing well. Now Marina wants to trailer him to the barn at her place. There's a practice event going on with her Arabian costume club. They'll all be there this afternoon and we want to see how Zotar does around other horses and riders who are also in costume."

Trace winced. "I hadn't thought of that. How do you think he's going to do?"

"We won't know until we try. Marina left to get her horse trailer. She'll be back in an hour to pick Zotar up. I'm taking the Jeep and following her. That way if he does well, she can keep him there and I can come home."

He liked the easy way she called the ranch *home*. "Job completed, then?"

"Fingers crossed." She beamed. "Marina's already told me she'll have my check waiting. I expect her to be here at any moment."

"Come here," he said, refusing to overthink things. When she looked up at him in question, her head tilted, he eased her into his arms and kissed her.

A moment later when they broke apart, they were out of breath. "What was that for?" she asked, still smiling.

Several different responses ran through his mind, none of which he could say out loud. Not yet. Instead, he kept his tone light when he answered. "Just because I'm proud of you, Emma McBride. I knew you could help that horse. Now stay safe and be careful. Always keep your eyes open, no matter where you are."

Her smile faded. "Of course. Thank you for the reminder."

A bright red pickup truck with matching horse trailer pulled into the yard. "There's Marina," Emma said, moving away. She glanced back at him over her shoulder. "You stay safe here too, okay?"

"Always." Amazed that she clearly had no idea how he felt, Trace watched as she greeted Marina and the two women went into the barn to fetch Zotar. Unable to help himself, Trace stayed put while they led the gelding out and loaded him up into the trailer.

Marina climbed into her truck and began driving away. Emma followed in her Jeep. And Trace stood still, aching and wondering how he was going to get out of this unscathed.

Over the next several hours, Trace saddled up Jack and checked all his fences. He also wanted to move the cattle in closer, but would need Emma's help to do that. He figured they'd do that tomorrow. He usually kept the herd in the back pastures once the spring storms had subsided, all through the heat of summer and into the fall. But now, with a deranged killer out there looking for methods of revenge, he didn't want to take a chance. It would be way easier to keep an eye on his cattle if they were grazing closer in.

As he took care of numerous small chores, Trace kept a continual eye open for trouble. There weren't a lot of places to hide up close to the ranch proper, so he felt reasonably certain he'd spot any interloper before any trouble could get started. Still, he couldn't entirely suppress the constant worry as he wondered about Emma. He actually got out his phone several times with the intention of texting her, but forced himself to practice restraint. Emma would be careful and since she'd be in the middle of a decent-sized crowd, it seemed less likely anyone would try and harm her.

Still, he couldn't help but feel anxious about Emma's safety. She didn't check in, not even once. He couldn't really blame her. She was working, trying to complete a job, and that alone carried more than enough stress.

He kept busy for several hours and eventually got everything done. With no jobs left unfinished, he reluctantly unsaddled Jack and brushed him down. Now, with excess time on his hands, he needed to still keep occupied so he wouldn't worry.

Libby, his gray mare, could use some exercise. Despite the late-afternoon heat, he saddled her up and took her around the arena several times, relishing the easy gait of a well-trained horse. Though he knew Emma made sure Libby got her fair share of attention, Libby didn't need training like Daisy, the paint mare, did.

Finally, just as he'd finished his ride with Libby, Emma's old Jeep pulled into the yard. Trace had never been so glad to see someone in his entire life.

Aware he needed to keep things casual, he rode Libby over and waited while Emma climbed out of her Jeep.

"We did it!" she exclaimed, holding up a check. "Zotar is ready to compete and Marina paid me. I was too tired to go by the bank and set up an account, but I'll do it tomorrow."

"Good job," he told her, glad he was on horseback so he didn't do anything stupid like try to kiss her. "I knew you could do it. Congratulations."

She grinned. "Thanks. I think I'll go see what I can rustle up to make us for dinner. I'm starving."

Surprised it had gotten so late, he nodded. "I'll go put Libby up and come help you. Unless you'd rather go into town and eat, as a celebration."

"Normally, I'd love that." She glanced down at herself and shook her head. "But I need to eat and then shower. After that, I'd love a glass of wine and to kick back and relax." Hearing herself, she made a face. "Sorry if that sounds like a boring way to celebrate, but today just wore me out."

"Actually, that sounds kind of nice." He thought for a moment. "I took out a couple of steaks to grill tomorrow. How about I cook them tonight, along with baked potatoes or something. I'll do all the work and you can go take a shower while I get everything ready."

"Oh, that would be perfect." Tossing a carefree smile up at him, she took off for the house to do exactly that.

Later, after they'd both eaten their fill, he poured her a second glass of red wine and rinsed off the dishes. Since the afternoon heat had barely subsided, they carried their drinks into the living room instead of out on the patio. He loved the sense of easy companionship he felt around her, at least when he wasn't battling the urge to kiss her. These days, it seemed he spent most of his waking hours semi-aroused, because of her.

"That was wonderful," she said, taking a seat on the couch and inviting him with a smile to sit down beside her.

He didn't dare, at least not yet. He needed to get his

body under control first. Looking at her didn't help. Sated and clearly relaxed, she leaned back into the sofa and stretched out. She'd put on a pair of shorts that showcased her long legs and a T-shirt that did nothing to hide her curves.

Damn, he wanted her.

"What's that smell?" she asked, sniffing. "Are you burning off the grill or something?"

At first, her words didn't register. "Burning off the grill?" But then he smelled it. Smoke. Out here in the country, people were known to burn off brush, but not when it was this windy and therefore, not safe.

"Let me go check that out," he said. "Be right back."

Uneasy, he stepped outside, hoping he could get a fix on the general direction of the smoke.

Instead, he realized his barn was fully engulfed in flames.

The horses! Calling for Emma, he took off at a run. He needed to free the horses before they were burned or suffered smoke inhalation. He didn't have time to see if Emma had heard him and followed.

As he reached for the heavy barn door, one of the horses screamed. The awful sound curdled his stomach. Yanking the door open, he rushed inside, trying to make his way in the thick, black smoke.

At the first stall, Daisy paced and whinnied. He got her out into the aisle, pointed her in the direction of the yard, and yelled at her to go. She needed no urging, taking off at a run.

The fire, feeding off the hay bales in the feed room, jumped the aisle toward the back two stalls, which luckily were empty in preparation for Emma's new client's horses.

The next stall had Jack, his sorrel gelding. Eyes bulging, the horse kicked at the stall door, attempting to get out on his own.

"I'm here," Emma shouted behind him, gasping as she tried to draw in air. "You get Jack, I'll get Libby. We'll need to round them up once we're all out."

She had a point. With the horses this traumatized and terrified, they'd likely run away as far and as fast as they could. Luckily, the ranch was completely fenced and the cattle guards at the gate at the end of the drive would keep them in.

Trace opened Jack's stall, barely getting out of the way as the gelding barreled past, ears flat against his head. A second later, Libby followed suit, running in a blind panic, with Emma staggering out after her.

Once out in the still-smoky air, both Trace and Emma doubled over, trying to catch their breath and expel the smoke from their lungs.

"Did you call 911?" Emma managed to ask in between coughs.

"No time," he gasped, phone in hand. The fire roared, something popped, sending up sparks and another plume of black smoke, and the middle part of the barn's roof caved in. "Dialing now." He pressed the numbers, even though he knew by the time Getaway's volunteer fire department arrived, the barn would be a total loss.

Trace made his report, his voice raspy as hell, and once the dispatcher promised help was on the way, he called Rayna. Despite the hour, she answered on the second ring, sounding wide awake and alert. She listened as Trace told her about the fire and then told him to sit tight as she was on the way.

Ending the call and shoving his phone back into his pocket, Trace turned to face Emma. Clearly in shock, she stood facing the roaring inferno with tears running down her soot-streaked face. Though her eyes were wide-open, they appeared unfocused.

"Emma." He gathered her to him, turning her away from the fire. "It's going to be all right. None of the horses were hurt. I can always rebuild the barn."

Shaking her head, she wrapped her arms around him and held on tight. She smelled like smoke and soot, and he'd have given anything to make her stop trembling.

"This is my fault," she said, her face pressed against his shirt. "None of this would have happened if not for me." When she raised her head to look at him, determination shone in her red-rimmed eyes. "I don't know how or when, but I'm still determined to make it up to you."

"Stop," he told her, pressing a quick kiss on her mouth and then forcing himself to move away. "Let's go round up those horses. The fire department and the sheriff's office are on their way."

Having something to do helped Emma regain her composure and by the time the fire trucks pulled onto their driveway, lights flashing, they'd gotten most of the horses into the arena. Daisy was the only exception. Every time they'd gotten even remotely close to her, she'd waited until they were a few feet away before taking off at a run, tail held high. "I swear she's laughing at us," Trace groused to Emma.

"If the feed hadn't been inside the barn, I could have caught her that way," Emma said. "Let me try once more before the fire truck is here." She walked toward the mare, but then, instead of getting too close, turned and gave the horse her back.

Trace watched as Daisy eyed Emma. Then, apparently curious, the horse walked over and nudged Emma in the back of the head.

"I've got her," Emma said, taking hold of the halter. "Come on, girl. Let's get you put up."

Hurrying ahead of her with the fire sending sparks and black smoke into the sky, Trace couldn't help but feel as if he'd stepped into an alternative universe or maybe a bad dream. Uncle Frank had built that barn with his own hands as a young rancher, and while Trace could and would definitely rebuild, he hated losing one other connection with his uncle.

They'd just closed the gate on the arena when the fire trucks parked, lights still flashing. Trace put his arm around Emma and the two of them stayed out of the firefighters' way while they hooked their hose into the tanker truck and began dousing the fire with water.

While Trace already knew they had come too late to help much, he appreciated their efforts.

"Rayna's here," Emma said, moving out from under his arm.

"What happened?" the sheriff asked, striding over to them.

"Who knows?" Trace said, shaking his head. "Though I have a feeling we'll learn this fire was deliberately set. Likely by the same guy who killed Amber."

"And Jeremy," Emma chimed in.

Rayna's sharp gaze took in Emma's sooty face. "Has he called you? To take credit for this?"

"Not yet." Judging by Emma's grim tone, she fully expected that call to come at any moment. "I just wish I could find that money so I could get him off my back."

"Have you been actively looking for it?" Rayna wanted to know.

"Well, no." Emma tried for a wry smile, but it looked more like a frown. "I mean, I have been trying to find any clues, but that ended once the laptop got stolen."

"Come here, both of you." Arms crossed, Rayna waited until Trace and Emma had crossed the distance that separated them. "Before he took a potshot at you, this guy didn't concern me as much. Then Amber was killed, and now I can't shake my gut feeling that the two of you, especially Emma, are in very real danger. Though I still don't have an identity yet."

Trace nodded. "I agree with you. But we still don't have the missing money, so I'm not sure what this guy will accomplish by hurting us."

"I'm beginning to suspect it's about more than just the money at this point," Rayna said. "I think he's moved on to getting revenge. That's why he killed Amber. And why I think that you, Emma, are in danger. I know we've discussed this, but it's time to go into hiding. Just for a little while, until we can catch this guy."

Chapter 14

Though Emma hated hearing Rayna's pronouncement, she'd begun to think the sheriff might be right. But burning down the barn made no sense, at least not without a follow-up phone call making demands. If the stalker was trying to prove a point, he'd failed.

"No hiding," she said. "Not yet. We haven't heard from that guy since before Amber was killed," she pointed out. "And until the fire inspector says this is actually arson, we don't know that he really set it. Something else might have caused the fire."

Rayna and Trace eyed her with identical skeptical expressions. "Like what, faulty wiring?" Rayna drawled.

"It's possible," Emma argued. "Isn't it, Trace?"

Trace shrugged. She got the sense he wanted to roll his eyes, but he didn't. "Anything is possible," he replied. "I guess we'll just have to wait to hear from the fire department."

He sighed, watching as the firefighters used the water hose to knock back the flames. "They've just about got the fire under control. I know the investigator can't check things until it's mostly out."

"He's already here." Rayna pointed to a gray-haired man in a rumpled suit. "That's Tommy Lockhart. Most of those guys like to come running as soon as the alarms go out. Looks like he's just waiting until they give him the go-ahead."

Nearby in the arena, the horses were still on edge, though they'd gathered in a cluster at the far end, watching the goings-on with swishing tails.

The smoke made breathing difficult, even though the north wind carried most of it away from where they stood. The firefighters worked with an easy rhythm born of experience, and soon they'd managed to battle the flames back to a few scattered hot spots and smoking embers.

The captain went to confer with the fire inspector. Together, the two of them began walking the perimeter of the pile of charred lumber and ashes that remained of the barn. Emma, Trace and Rayna all fell silent as they watched them.

Tommy Lockhart seemed thorough. Emma had to admire the way he braved the smoke and the heat to at least attempt to give things a cursory inspection.

A few minutes later, the fire inspector walked over and after greeting Rayna, introduced himself. Trace shook his hand and asked if he'd been able to learn anything.

"Not really," the other man answered. "On first glance, there weren't any signs of an accelerant. Did you happen to keep anything combustible inside that barn by any chance?"

"No. Just grain and feed and tack, along with the horses." Trace frowned. "Nothing that could have cause this intense of a fire."

"I didn't think so, but it doesn't hurt to ask." Looking down at his clipboard, the inspector made a few notes. "I'll be back out here again tomorrow to have another look. By then, the hot spots should all be out."

Rayna walked with him to his car, leaving Emma and Trace. "This is terrible," Emma said, keeping her voice low. "While it's a blessing your horses are safe, if I were to get any new clients, there isn't any place to put their horses."

Trace put his arm around her shoulder and tugged her close. "Don't worry. We'll figure something out. Looks like I'm going to have to build some temporary shelter for those three horses anyway. I'm thinking a large, three-sided lean-to in that pasture right close to the house."

Grateful for this man, Emma found herself blinking back tears. "Delayed reaction," she replied, in answer to his questioning look.

Rayna returned just then. "I'm going to take off," she told them. "Let me know if you need anything, okay?" Without waiting for an answer, she walked away. A moment later, she returned. "Emma, please put some thought into what I've said. A short time away from here might do wonders."

Emma nodded, murmuring something she hoped the sheriff would take for assent. Trace shook his head, but didn't speak until the sheriff had driven away. "I've got your back," he said, giving her one final hug before releasing her. "Whatever you decide to do."

That night, after all the excitement of the fire, Emma thought she'd have been exhausted. Instead, she didn't have the faintest desire to rest. If she'd been a runner, she would have taken that opportunity to go for a run. However, she went out into the backyard and took a seat on one of the patio chairs. The October air contained just a hint of a chill, but she'd brought a light jacket to combat that. The full moon illuminated the ranch yard, including the eerie husk of where the barn had been. The three horses stood grouped together at one end of the arena, safe and finally calm.

This place, she realized, had the feel of home.

She couldn't stop thinking about Trace's promise. He'd said he had her back. Emma couldn't remember a time when someone else had made her that kind of promise. She truly must be the luckiest woman alive. She had no idea how she'd managed to deserve a man like him.

She also felt like a fool. She'd gotten out of prison with an intent and sharp focus—clearing her name. Instead, she'd made absolutely no progress in that direction and had come close to ruining Trace's life simply by her presence in it. Astoundingly, he didn't seem to mind, which made her feel guilty and grateful. If only things could be simple and straightforward. If only...

Her cell phone rang. It had to be him. Her stalker, the guy who wanted his missing money. Caller ID only showed Private Number. Taking a shaky breath, she answered.

"I'm tired of jacking around," the now-familiar voice said in her ear. "I didn't set your barn on fire. I need my money."

"I don't have it," she said. "I don't know how many times I can tell you that before you believe it, but I don't have the slightest idea where it is." She took a deep breath. "I was trying to see if I could find out something on the laptop before you took it."

"Your husband was a fool," he snarled. "And I was more so for trusting him. I was able to retrieve everything off that computer. There was no reference to the money."

Stunned, she struggled to find the right words. "Then what did he do with it? Three million dollars is a lot to make simply disappear."

"Exactly. And that Amber tried to play me too. She pretended she knew where the money was hidden. She didn't."

"How do you know?" she asked. And then, before he answered, she realized. "You killed her when she wouldn't tell you."

"Amazing how people try to hold on to their lies until the pain starts." His laugh chilled her to the bone.

"Is that why you killed Jeremy?" The question burst from her. She hadn't been expecting to ask; in fact, she'd been avoiding the subject. But now, quite suddenly, she found she wanted to know.

"Killed Jeremy? I didn't kill Jeremy."

"What?" Blinking, she wasn't sure she'd heard him correctly. "But I thought..."

"You thought wrong. Why would I have killed him? He had my money. I believed that he planned to invest it. When I learned he figured otherwise, all I wanted was my money back. I would have had nothing to gain by murdering him."

Brain reeling, she said the first thing that came to mind. "Didn't you confront him, demand your money back and then, when he refused, kill him?"

This made him laugh, which wasn't a pleasant sound. "Of course not. I did what any normal person would do. I called and spoke with him. We made arrangements to meet at his house the next day. Then Jeremy went on the run. He took all of my money and planned to disappear with it. Someone else got to him first."

"But Amber said…" Again, she let her words trail off as she suspected she might have put far too much faith in a woman who was a known liar.

He laughed again, as if he knew her thoughts. "Amber said whatever served her best. I don't know who killed your husband. I honestly thought it was you, thanks to Amber. It was her idea to make sure you went to prison. I think she believed she'd find the money and keep all of it for herself."

Emma's head started to ache. "None of this makes sense," she whispered. "I don't understand."

"I don't care." The bite came back into his tone. "I just want my money."

"If I had it, I'd give it to you," she promised, her voice equally sharp. "It belongs to you anyway." She inhaled sharply as a thought occurred to her. "I think you're looking in the wrong place. If you find Jeremy's killer, you'll likely find the money."

"That's what I've been trying to tell you," he said.

"All along, after I realized it wasn't you, I thought Amber had stolen it. She's the type to kill in cold blood if it benefits her. But I've come to understand I was wrong. She isn't the one."

And now she was dead. Emma needed to remember that. No matter how reasonable this man sounded, how good she found his arguments, he'd killed a woman and no doubt wouldn't hesitate to do so again.

"Problem is," he continued, "no one seems to have any idea who killed him. The guy had a lot of enemies."

Surprised, she considered. "I guess he did. I always thought he had a lot of friends. Clearly, I was wrong."

"We will work on this together," the man announced. "You knew him better than anyone else, including Amber."

"Together how?" she asked, dread souring her stomach. She figured she already knew how he would respond.

"I'm coming for you, of course," he replied. "And you *will* help me until we both get what we want. Otherwise, I can promise you that you'll end up like Amber and her poor brother."

Then he ended the call without waiting for her reply.

Shaken, Emma fumbled with her phone and nearly dropped it. She tried to stand, but since her knees felt like they were about to refuse to support her, she dropped back into the patio chair. "Damn," she muttered. She didn't know what to do. On the one hand, she could take Rayna's advice and go into hiding. But if she did that, she'd likely never learn the truth about who had really killed Jeremy. And this guy, whoever he was, would likely believe she really did have his money.

If she stayed, and did what this man wanted, she might finally get some answers, despite the risk. The truth, which she'd burned for during her entire two years in prison, would finally be revealed. That alone was worth anything and everything.

Except what good would an answer do if she was the only one who knew it? Her reputation would remain ruined. She understood there might be a very real chance she wouldn't make it out of this situation alive. Yet to know…

To know the whole truth would be more valuable than she could express.

The more she thought, the more she realized what her decision would be. Which meant she'd need to keep this entire conversation a secret from Rayna.

But what about Trace? While she knew he'd try to dissuade her and even protect her, she hated hiding anything this important from him. Yet she believed he'd be so hypervigilant, he'd get in the way.

Jeez. Covering her face with her hands, she forced herself to try and be dispassionate. When she moved her hands away, she breathed in and out, attempting to calm her racing heartbeat and center her thoughts.

Was she really considering allowing herself to be captured by the man who'd killed Amber? Even though he'd insisted he hadn't murdered Jeremy, how did she know for sure? She could be putting herself into the hands of a ruthless psychopath.

The sound of the back door opening cut into her thoughts.

"Hey there," Trace said, dropping into the chair next to her, one lock of his dark hair falling over his forehead. He looked so damn handsome her chest ached. "Are you okay? You look upset."

If he only knew.

"Maybe a little," she allowed, well aware he'd see straight through her if she tried to claim she wasn't. In the short time they'd been together, she couldn't help but notice how attuned he'd become to her emotions. And she to his. Suddenly, she understood if she really was going to go through with this insane plan, she wanted to make love to Trace one last time.

Moving quickly, before she allowed herself to doubt or rationalize, she turned to him. "I need you," she murmured, getting up and moving over to sit on his lap. His gaze darkened as she wrapped her arms around him. When she leaned in close and grazed her mouth across his, he met her kiss with the kind of blazing heat that made her lose all sense of rhyme or reason.

Trace didn't know what he'd done to deserve her, but when Emma straddled him on the patio chair in the backyard and kissed him, he felt he'd won the lottery. And then, as passion immediately roared between them, he thought of nothing but the feel of her body on top of him. His arousal had been swift and almost painful in its intensity. Unzipping his jeans, she'd freed him immediately, taking him into her mouth and making love to him until he'd had to beg her to stop before he lost control.

To his relief, she did, standing up and stripping off her clothes with a come-hither smile. Then, blue eyes intense, she climbed back on top of him and took him deep inside of her.

She rode him as if she couldn't get enough, as though she craved him as much as he craved her. Magnificent as she took control, her sensual, sexy-as-hell confidence had him thrusting up to meet her every stroke.

Her release came swiftly, her body clenching around him as she shuddered, calling out his name. He tried like hell to stay the course, to hang on for longer, but her pleasure sent his own ripping through him in waves. As he emptied himself into her, he realized too late that they hadn't used protection.

"It's okay," Emma said when he mentioned that. She'd begun gathering up her clothing, though not getting dressed. "I'm evidently not fertile at all. Jeremy and I tried forever and I never got pregnant."

Though the pain in her eyes made his own heart ache, he decided not to mention that the problem might have been with Jeremy rather than her. Why give her something else to worry about? They'd deal with any consequences resulting from this together.

Instead, he found himself battling the urge to tell her he loved her. Though he had no doubt his feelings were genuine and lasting, he knew she likely wasn't ready to hear them. Not now, not yet, with her life in constant chaos.

Clearly oblivious to his thoughts, she gave him a sleepy smile. "I'm really tired," she said, covering her mouth to hide a huge yawn. "I know we don't usually do this, but would you mind if we shared your bed? I really don't want to sleep alone tonight."

Eyeing her, he could scarcely contain his joy.

"Sure," he said, as casually as he could manage. "I'd like that."

By the time they both slid under the sheets, the thought of lying next to her had him already semi-aroused. Noticing, she gave him a wicked little smile and then kissed him. "Maybe later," she murmured against his mouth. "We've got all night for that. Right now, let's get a little sleep first."

Somehow, he did. He woke once, several hours later, hard and aching, but she slept so peacefully in his arms that he hated to wake her. So he forced himself to think of other things, which wasn't easy with her soft curves so close. Miraculously, he managed to drift back off.

When he woke in the morning and reached for her, he encountered nothing but empty sheets. Clearly, she'd already awakened and had gotten up. Disappointed, he headed for the shower.

After his shower, he dressed quickly, craving coffee and Emma, and not necessarily in that order. He found her in the kitchen, her long hair damp from her own shower, sipping coffee from a large mug.

"Good morning," she said, smiling. Her blue eyes seemed brighter this morning, though he suspected a lot of that had to do with the way his body responded to her.

"I need coffee," he told her, struggling to find anything to say other than how badly he wanted her. Again. Turning his back to her, he got busy making his own cup. The instant it finished brewing, he took a deep sip, burning his mouth.

He needed to stop this, he told himself fiercely.

He knew he could manage to keep his desire under control. After all, he'd done it since practically the moment she'd arrived at the ranch. Plus, he had a lot of work to do. Since the barn fire, he needed to get busy building shelter in the pasture for his horses.

"Are you all right?" she asked, a teasing lilt to her voice. "You seem kind of…tense this morning."

"I've got a lot on my mind," he replied, turning. "I've got to build some temporary lean-to shelters for the horses. I thought I'd get an early start, since it's supposed to rain later today."

"Good idea." Tilting her head, she studied him. "Do you need any help?"

While the idea tempted him, and he always could use an extra set of hands, he knew she'd be more of a distraction. "I'm good," he said. "I know you were planning on working with Daisy today. Would you mind also giving Libby some exercise? She doesn't get ridden often enough."

"I can do that." Her smile lit up the room. "I was thinking of making some oatmeal first. Would you like some?"

"Sure." He drank his coffee while she made them oatmeal. Then they ate breakfast together, in the particular sort of easy domesticity he'd come to enjoy. Even though when he spent any time around her these days, he walked around in a state of arousal. When they'd finished, he shooed her off to dry her hair while he did the dishes. He needed to do something with his hands to prevent him from touching her.

Not trusting himself, he headed out to the pasture

before she returned. Working out there was exactly the kind of demanding physical labor he needed.

The warm October sun felt good as he busied himself with finishing the lean-to. Movement over by the arena caught his eye and he turned to watch Emma head out of the house carrying a saddle. When the barn had burned, they'd lost all of their tack in the fire. One of his neighboring ranchers had driven over bright and early with a couple of used saddles and bridles and bits in the bed of his truck. He'd left them with Trace, refusing to take any money. With no tack room, they had to store them inside the house until the barn could be rebuilt, but they made do.

Emma carried the saddle easily, and she'd draped a bridle and reins over one shoulder. When she reached the arena, all three horses trotted over immediately to greet her.

Aware he'd been standing and staring, he returned his attention to the task at hand. He'd never felt this way about a woman before and knew deep within himself he never would again. Emma was a once-in-a-lifetime, special woman and even if she didn't feel the same way about him, he had to hope she might with time.

As he worked nailing the sheet metal to the frame, he kept catching sight of Emma riding in the arena. He'd seen many accomplished riders over the years, but Emma sat a horse as if she and the horse were one being rather than two. As he watched her urge Daisy into a controlled lope, the fluid movement was a thing of beauty. Chest aching, he forced himself to turn away and get back to work.

Finally, he finished the back of the lean-to. He'd

put the roof on first, and now he just had to finish up the two sides.

His stomach growled, alerting him it was getting close to lunchtime. Since Emma had been kind enough to fix them breakfast, he'd return the favor and make them a couple of sandwiches or something.

He stopped by the arena on the way to the house, passing the pile of ashes and burned lumber that had once been his barn. The fire had also spread to a section of wooden fence bordering the gravel road, taking out a good portion of that. For now, Trace had strung some temporary orange netting along the open area. He planned to repair all that after he finished the lean-to.

Emma smiled at the mention of sandwiches, stating that she could definitely eat. "I've worked up an appetite," she said, leaning over and scratching Daisy on her neck. Glancing at the sky, she stretched. "Isn't this weather beautiful? I love October."

He agreed, barely stopping himself from saying something cheesy like the weather wasn't nearly as beautiful as her. "I'll holler when they're ready," he said instead.

"Perfect."

Inside, he took a few minutes and reheated several meatballs and sauce, put them inside of baguettes, added cheese and then toasted them in the oven. When those were done, he grabbed some chips and went to the back door to let Emma know lunch was ready.

Stepping outside, he opened his mouth to call her. Instead, he froze, taking a second to actually process what he was seeing.

A large man with his arm around Emma's neck

was dragging her toward a pickup truck parked on the gravel road behind the temporary fencing. Emma clearly struggled, but her efforts were futile against the man's strength. He got her to the truck, knocking down the temporary fence on the way, and then, to Trace's horror, sucker punched her. She went limp and then the man threw her into the back seat.

Trace sprinted toward them, well aware he'd never make it in time. As the man climbed into the driver's seat and peeled off, kicking up gravel in his wake, Trace changed direction and ran for his truck instead. Though he doubted he'd be able to catch up with Emma's abductor, damn if he wasn't going to try.

But by the time he got the engine started, drove hell-bent across the barnyard, through the temporary fence, and made it out onto the gravel road, the other truck was nowhere in sight.

Refusing to give up, he continued to tear down the road, rear end sashaying and tires spinning. He made it all the way out to the paved road and stopped at the stop sign, having to admit defeat.

"Damn it," he cursed, slamming his hands onto the steering wheel. He felt like he'd been punched in the stomach. Still unable to believe what had just happened, he dialed Rayna's private number.

"Did you get a license plate?" she asked, making him curse again.

"No. Everything happened so fast." He dragged his hand through his hair. "I was so intent on trying to catch the guy that getting the license plate never occurred to me. I can tell you it was a black Dodge Ram pickup, late model, quad cab, with a lift kit."

"I'll put out an APB," Rayna said. "But since we live in a county where everyone drives a pickup and black is a popular color…"

Though she didn't finish her statement, Trace got her meaning. Finding such a common vehicle wouldn't be easy.

"We have to find her," he insisted. "If anything happens to Emma, I don't know what I'm going to do."

Rayna went silent for a moment. "You love her, don't you?"

Trace saw no point in trying to hide the truth. "With all my heart. If I could find that guy's missing three million dollars, I'd return it to him in a heart-beat if he'd only let her go."

"We'll do our best to find her," Rayna replied. "I've got two people going over Jeremy's financial records. We kept copies of everything, including what Emma found on his laptop. Hopefully someone will find a clue to tell us where he might have stashed the money."

"I'm more worried about what he's going to do to Emma."

"I understand." Rayna's soothing response had him clenching his teeth. "And we're going to do everything we can to find her. I promise to keep you posted."

Trace thanked her and ended the call before he said something else he might regret. Though every word he'd said was the unadulterated truth, he hadn't meant to reveal the way he felt about Emma to the sheriff. Hell, Emma herself didn't even know yet. He could only hope he got the chance to tell her.

Chapter 15

Head and face aching, Emma struggled to hang on to consciousness, even as she drifted in and out. He'd hit her, she realized. Hard. Knocked her out. Unsure where exactly she was, or why she couldn't seem to move, she tried to make sense of what had just happened to her.

Though she'd made up her mind to go along with his plan, she should have known her stalker wouldn't wait. Why had she expected him to call again, to actually give her a choice? Instead, she had just finished working Daisy. She'd left the arena and starting leading the paint mare back toward one of the still-standing hitching posts when the man came out of nowhere.

He'd jumped up from behind a parked tractor, starting the mare, who'd reared up. As she'd struggled to get the horse under control, the man had grabbed Emma from behind, holding her in a death grip around her neck.

Instinct had taken over and she'd fought him, struggling against the ever-tightening grip on her neck. Trace had just gone inside the house. Though she'd opened her mouth to scream, she could barely breathe so all that had emerged was a grunt. She'd clawed at his arm, went for his face, but all that had accomplished was to cut off her air flow more.

Though blackness had grayed the edges of her vision, she'd kicked and hit, using her entire body to attempt to fight him, trying in vain to get away. He'd been strong, and though she never got a really good look at him, he'd seemed larger than she'd expected. All her effort had gone into keeping his arms from tightening around her neck.

While she'd had her pistol in its holster, she hadn't been able to reach it. In fact, it had taken everything she had not to lose consciousness as he'd dragged her from the paddock area toward a pickup parked in the dirt road alongside the field.

She'd prayed Trace would glance out the window while there was still time to help her, but he hadn't. Just in case, she'd dug in her heels, doing everything she could to slow their progress. She'd begun to wonder if this man wouldn't break her neck. Only the knowledge that he'd said he wanted her alive had given her hope.

And then, just as they'd reached his truck, he tightened his grip once more. Too tight. Panic had set in. She hadn't been able to breathe at all. She'd fought him with every ounce of strength she'd possessed but it hadn't been enough. He'd slammed his fist into her face while still choking her. One final gasp, trying to drag enough air into her lungs to stay alive, and then all had gone black.

Now, she knew she was in the back seat of his pickup truck, trussed up like a lamb being taken to the slaughter. She sucked in air through her raw and aching throat, her cheek and eye throbbing, and considered herself lucky to have survived. Barely, she thought, allowing herself to sink into unconsciousness again.

When she came to, she opened her eyes to utter darkness. No light, not even a spark. For a second, she freaked out, thinking maybe she'd been buried alive.

Forcing herself to get up from the floor, first she checked her holster to see if her captor had been foolish enough to leave her with her pistol. Of course not. The holster was empty and the gun was gone.

Next, she put her arms up to gauge the height of the ceiling. When she realized she could stand, she put her arms out and began feeling her way around.

She was in a small, windowless room made of concrete. A tornado shelter, she realized. The kind people sank into the ground next to their homes. Sure enough, as she inched her way forward, she found steps leading up. However, when she got to the metal exit door, she realized it had been locked from the outside.

Emma had always been mildly claustrophobic. The constraints of her situation had her hyperventilating. She tried to make herself stop because if she didn't get a grip, she was going to pass out.

Sitting cross-legged on the floor, she closed her eyes to block out the darkness, and worked on breathing in, breathing out. Slow, deep breaths. Every time a thought about her tomb-like prison popped into her mind, she blocked it. Her heartbeat still raced, but she concentrated on trying to slow it. One of the skills she'd perfected while incarcerated had been the ability to lose herself in meditation. Since she clearly wasn't going anywhere anytime soon, she needed to conserve her body's resources in case she got an opportunity to escape.

Calm, level-headed logic had served her well in prison and that helped her now too. Panic was weakness and accomplished nothing. When she finally felt calm enough to open her eyes again, she knew she had to do a thorough assessment of the room.

Feeling her way along the walls and hoping for no insects, she realized her first impression of a tornado shelter had been correct. Concrete walls, a few bare shelves and the telltale steps leading up to the locked door confirmed it. She stumbled into some furniture, a table and chair most likely, and something else that might be a small bed. The room had been prepared for occupancy. Hopefully, judging by what her captor had said on the phone call, he wouldn't be leaving her alone in here too long.

He'd grabbed her for a purpose. As he'd said, he wanted her help finding the money. She'd be more than happy to help him with that, if doing so helped find Jeremy's killer.

Assuming of course, that he let her go once everything had been accomplished. Or, she forced herself to consider the possibilities, if everything wasn't achieved. There still remained a very real chance they'd never locate the missing money.

Refusing to allow any more negative thoughts, she closed her eyes again. Since she had nothing else to do while locked in this horrible place, she decided to go back to meditation.

A loud sound jolted her out of her flow. Remaining in place, she listened for it to come again. When it did, she identified it as the sound of a heavy dead bolt sliding away from the exit door. Ahh, showtime. Her captor had come to get her.

Light flooded the room, making her squint. When she realized there'd been a light switch on the wall near the door, she shook her head. She'd been sitting in darkness unnecessarily.

"Good evening," a familiar voice said. Though he'd opened the door and turned on the light, he remained outside. "Do you recognize where you are?"

"A tornado shelter," she answered. "Or in my case, a prison cell. Again."

If he caught on to her bitterness, he didn't acknowledge it. "Not just any tornado shelter, my dear. I bought your parents' house, the one you grew up in. This is the same shelter you would have gone to as a child."

Stunned, she swallowed hard. "You bought… Why?"

"Because I thought Jeremy might have hidden the money here and I wanted to be able to tear the place apart searching. I made your stepmother an offer she couldn't refuse."

Which would explain Beth suddenly selling and

moving far, far away. "I take it you didn't find anything?" Emma asked.

"You already know I didn't. Otherwise, why would I have brought you here?"

Fair enough. She made what she hoped sounded like a murmur of agreement.

"Are you ready to help me now?"

Not sure how to respond, she answered in the affirmative.

"Good. I have Jeremy's laptop," he told her. "I'm going to leave it on the top stair. There is a second account on the computer, under your maiden name, with a different password, which I've written on a yellow sticky note for you. I've searched through it, and all that Jeremy had on it was a diary. After reading this, none of it made any sense to me, but it might to you. He seemed awfully fixated on Beth. Take a look at it. I'll be back in the morning with breakfast and coffee."

Without waiting for her to answer, he closed the door. A moment later, she heard the dead bolt slide back in place.

Beth. Judging by all the photos in the file Jeremy had made for her under his Tax Credits header, he had been fixated on her. But Emma hadn't been able to tell exactly why. He'd seemed to resent the older woman, judging by his extensive list of grievances. Now that she'd be able to read his diary, maybe some of that would make sense.

Heart pounding, she glanced around the small concrete room. Having light changed everything. The furniture she'd stumbled into turned out to be a small table with a chair, as well as some sort of narrow cot pushed against the wall.

Next, she climbed up the steps, picked up the laptop and then, just in case, double-checked the door. As she'd expected, it didn't budge.

She carried the computer back, placed it on the table and powered it on, removing the sticky note and studying it. A second account. The notion had never occurred to her. Since Jeremy had been the only one with access to his laptop, she wondered why he'd felt the need. This must mean she was about to read some really personal and strange stuff in his diary.

In addition to clues about what he might have done with the money, maybe she'd finally get an explanation for why he'd cheated and ended their marriage so abruptly.

Sitting down, she used the info on the sticky note and logged in. Clicking on the folder unambiguously titled My Journal, she opened it and began to read.

An hour passed, then two. While Jeremy hadn't been a skilled storyteller, nevertheless seeing the life they'd lived together through his perception—twisted as it might be—was fascinating. And the more she read, the more she realized that her captor had been right. Jeremy's unhealthy obsession with her stepmother, Beth, was revolting.

She couldn't believe she hadn't noticed any of this. According to her former husband, he and Beth had struck up a friendship at first, and then Jeremy's feelings had changed while Beth's hadn't. None of that had deterred him. Jeremy had been used to getting what he wanted, and he'd clearly viewed Beth as a challenge.

The more she read, the queasier and more uneasy she felt. Though she didn't want to believe it, judging from what he'd written, it appeared clear Jeremy planned to have sex with Beth, willing or not. If he'd raped her stepmother while staying in her father's home and while married to her, she thought she might just hurl.

Awful enough to learn her husband was a cheater and a crook. But a sexual predator?

She was a third of the way through before she saw the first mention of money. Jeremy mentioned it casually, talking about meeting with an investor who had deep pockets, though he never listed a name.

For the next several entries, Jeremy appeared to have gone off into some sort of fantasyland, talking about the exotic cars he wanted to buy, the luxurious vacations he wanted to take and how badly he couldn't wait to get out of the horrible hick town of Getaway.

Again, Emma found herself surprised. Clearly, she hadn't ever really known the man she'd married. At all.

She froze as a sudden thought occurred to her. If Jeremy had eventually forced himself on Beth, that would have given the older woman a motive to kill him.

Wait. Frowning, she pushed to her feet and paced around the tiny space. If Beth had been the one who murdered Jeremy, did that also mean she had taken the money?

Continuing to read Jeremy's diary, Emma grew more and more horrified. Instead of forcing himself on Beth, Jeremy worked on getting the older woman to trust him. Since building relationships was one of his special skills, he easily charmed Beth into becoming his friend. And that was when Jeremy hatched his plan.

Since Emma's captor had read all of this before her, she didn't understand how he couldn't see what must have happened. While Jeremy so far never mentioned the missing three million dollars, reading between the lines, Emma could clearly see how he might have used that money as leverage to win Beth over.

Jeremy had loved nothing more than a good chase, and Beth gave him one. When he first wrote about getting rid of Beth's husband, Emma gasped out loud. What the hell? She'd always found the way her father had died puzzling, as he'd never been a big cell phone user to begin with. Him reaching for it while in the tub had never made any sense. But she'd been behind bars and so grief stricken she hadn't asked any questions. While she and Beth had never been close, Emma had never doubted her stepmother's and father's love for each other.

Appalled, she had to stop reading. Jeremy had been dead when her father had died, so that meant... Had Beth killed her own husband? If so, why? Maybe she'd had three million reasons.

Forcing herself to continue, she managed to wade through several more pages of Jeremy comparing Emma, Amber and Beth to each other. And then the journal abruptly ended, midpage.

Emma rubbed her eyes, feeling sick. What a tangled mess. Though she had no proof, she at least now had an idea of where Jeremy might have stashed the money. Or with whom.

Had her captor reached the same conclusion? He had to have realized after reading this that Jeremy had been involved with three women before his death. Since neither Amber nor Emma clearly had the money, that left Beth.

But what if she was wrong? How could she even consider putting a bull's-eye on her stepmother like that when she didn't have proof?

Stomach churning, she needed to figure out a way to escape and take this information to Rayna. But how? Maybe she could convince her captor that she'd figured out some local hiding place where they might look? Except why now? She had no logic behind it, especially since she'd need to cite something she'd read in Jeremy's private journal as giving her the clue.

Jeremy would have bluffed and charmed until he got what he wanted. However, Emma was nothing like him. She'd always considered herself a straightforward sort of person. Lying about anything had never been her forte, which was one of the reasons her conviction for Jeremy's murder had come as such a shock to her.

Still, she had no choice but to lie, and lie well, if she wanted to save her life. She wasn't under any delusions that this man would set her free once he had what he wanted. No, she'd end up like Amber, forever silenced.

Her best bet would be to play off the truth. Use enough to concoct a convincing story, but not enough to allow her captor to deduce what Emma actually suspected had happened.

Since clearly everything started and ended with Beth, she'd work from there. This alternative had to be plausible enough to be believable. No matter what story she tried to come up with, the fact that Beth had up and sold everything and moved out of state put a wrench in things. Emma's captor wasn't stupid. He'd figure it out in an instant.

Sick to her stomach with misery, Emma could only hope something occurred to her before her captor returned.

Imagining what might be happening to Emma drove Trace insane with worry. He couldn't eat, couldn't sleep and could barely function. The horses and cattle needed him, so that familiar routine helped him get through the next day, but he knew he needed to do something. Anything would be better than sitting around waiting for Rayna or someone else to find her. He suspected the longer they waited, the more likely it would be Emma's body they found.

Her captor hadn't called asking for ransom yet either. Rayna had been convinced that would be what happened next. Trace would gladly have given everything he owned if doing so would guarantee Emma's safe return.

The missing three million dollars would definitely do it. If only he could somehow figure out where Jeremy had stashed it.

With little else to occupy his time, Trace decided to try and think the way he imagined someone like Jeremy did. Emma's former husband had acted as if he was a high roller, and everything he did seemed designed to impress.

If Jeremy had found himself in possession of three million dollars, what would a man like him have done with it?

The obvious responses, like buy expensive cars or a fancy house, wouldn't work. No, Jeremy would need to go on the run in order to spend that kind of money without being noticed, and he'd have to do it in small increments, which he wouldn't like.

Now Trace understood why Emma's stalker had been certain Jeremy's girlfriend Amber would have his stolen money. Jeremy would have had to off-load it to someone to keep it hidden for him. And then what if that someone had simply killed Jeremy so that they could keep all that money to themselves?

Making a list of Jeremy's friends, even though Trace knew that Rayna had already likely done the same thing in her initial murder investigation, was easier than he'd thought it would be. Jeremy had kept to a small group of friends, mostly a younger crowd who liked to hang around the Rattlesnake Pub. Since they'd all grown up in Getaway, Trace knew most of their names. Almost without exception, they worked in the family business in town, the local insurance agency, the Realtor's office, and on a lot of the family farms and ranches. None of them had exhibited the kind of lifestyle change that three million dollars would bring.

Even though some time had passed since Jeremy had been killed, Amber still lived in the same small house in Sweetwater. And Emma, the next logical suspect to have been the recipient of Jeremy's stolen money, had languished in prison. Even when she'd been released, she'd come to Trace's ranch to stay. Surely, the fact that she hadn't taken off for somewhere else hadn't been lost on the man who now had her. The fact that he'd continue to harass her for his money spoke to his desperation.

Trace thought back over the chain of events. Jeremy had asked Emma for a divorce and then he'd been killed. His mistress had falsely testified in court, which had led to Emma's conviction. While Emma had been in prison, her father had died. And her stepmother sold the family home and moved away to Florida, which had seemed odd at the time. Now, Trace considered it downright suspicious.

He grabbed his phone and called Rayna. She listened while he told her his thoughts.

"But she didn't leave until at least six months after Jeremy was killed," Rayna said. "And only then because someone made her an offer on the house that she couldn't refuse. That woman went through a lot, losing her husband the way she did."

"How did he die anyway?" Trace asked. "I honestly don't remember."

"Beth wanted to keep it quiet. He was electrocuted while taking a bath. Apparently, he'd plugged his phone in to charge it and answered it while sitting in the tub. It killed him instantly."

Trace shook his head, even though he knew Rayna couldn't see. "No one found that suspicious? A man his age? You'd think he'd know better."

"What are you saying, Trace?" Rayna's no-nonsense, dry tone told him she'd gone from chatting with him as a friend into law-enforcement-officer mode. "Are you accusing Beth McBride of murdering her husband?"

He sighed. "Put that way, it does sound ridiculous. But hear me out. When Emma was going through Jeremy's laptop, she found a file full of photos and notes about Beth. Jeremy clearly had a thing for her. Whether or not she reciprocated at the time, I don't know. But Jeremy liked to impress people. Three million dollars will go a long way toward impressing any woman. What if the two of them made plans? She might have planned to kill her husband, pretending she planned to run away with Jeremy. But something went wrong, so she killed Jeremy first. And then she made sure Emma went away for Jeremy's murder while she made her escape to Florida, along with the missing three million dollars."

"That's a stretch," Rayna said, sounding weary. "But I know anything is possible. I've seen a lot of strange things in my time as sheriff."

"Can you look into it? Please?"

"I will. First I need to see if Beth McBride has made any unusual purchases, like luxury cars or expensive jewelry. I know she got a few hundred thousand for selling the house here in Getaway, but I'll check into what kind of home she purchased in Key West."

"Will you keep me informed?" Trace asked. "I'll dig around and do some of my own research too."

"Of course. But Trace? If Emma's captor calls, don't go saying anything about any of this to him. Our first concern is getting Emma back. Once we have her safely, then all bets are off."

"Understood," he responded, and ended the call. Now he had to either figure out a way to get in contact with the man who'd grabbed Emma, or sit around and wait until he called. Since Trace had never been one for inaction, he got to work on the former.

Trace grabbed Emma's notes from her room and carried them into the kitchen to read. He figured he might as well go over them. Who knew, maybe he'd see something Emma had missed.

Jeremy's apparent obsession with Beth had been one of the things that struck him as odd. He reread everything Emma had written down about that, trying to understand what Jeremy had found so appealing about the older woman. Beth had been attractive, true, but on the few occasions Trace had interacted with her, he'd found her cold, calculating and self-involved. According to Emma, she certainly hadn't made any effort to help her stepdaughter when Emma had been arrested for Jeremy's murder.

Had Jeremy and Beth been having an affair?

And next, had it been a huge coincidence that someone had come along and offered Beth a lot of money to buy her home? He needed to find the address. Surely Emma had it in her stack of paperwork.

After digging through papers, he finally located an envelope among Jeremy's things with the address on it. Now he could find out who'd bought the property. It might be nothing, but all he had to go on.

Opening his laptop, he pulled up the Nolan County appraisal district's web page and typed in the address.

Someone named Nick Gonzales had purchased the house. For some reason, the name sounded familiar.

Trace checked the list Emma had been compiling of Jeremy's clients. Sure enough, Nick Gonzales was one of them. Though the transactions listed for him were all smaller amounts, Trace also knew Jeremy had been keeping a second set of books somewhere. If he'd even written his big one down at all.

Bracing himself for an argument, Trace dialed Rayna once more. "Meet me at 128 Oakmont Street," he said. "Emma's childhood home. Park down the block and wait for me. There's no time to explain. I'm leaving now."

Then, before Rayna even got a chance to speak, he ended the call.

Rayna called back immediately. Trace ignored his ringing phone and ran for his truck. It might just all be a hunch, but this hunch was better than anything else he could come up with.

Since she'd had a shorter distance to drive, Rayna was waiting for him at the far end of Oakmont, where her sheriff's cruiser wouldn't be visible from the house. She got out and waited while he parked, arms crossed. With her fierce scowl and dressed in her official uniform, she looked like a force to be reckoned with.

"I hope you have an explanation," she said. "Because we can't just barge onto a private citizen's property without probable cause."

"Who said anything about barging? I just want to talk to the man," he said, outlining what he'd discovered. "Now admittedly, this is more of a hunch than facts, but—"

"Stop." Rayna held up her hand. "We can knock on

his door and see if this guy is willing to speak with us, but that's it. As an officer of the law, I can't go around acting on hunches. This isn't a crime drama TV show."

"Unless we see something suspicious." Trace eyed her, daring her to contradict him. "Because if there's the slightest chance he's got Emma…"

Slowly, she nodded. "Let's play it by ear and see what happens."

Side by side, they walked up the sidewalk until they reached the house. An older, brick ranch-style home that had been built in the fifties, the place had an unkempt appearance, as if no one had lived there in quite some time. The shrubs needed trimming, the brown grass hadn't been watered and the house itself could have used a fresh coat of paint.

They stepped up to the front door and Rayna rang the bell. No one answered. A moment later, she pressed it again. Nothing.

"Well, it appears no one's home," she said. "We'll have to come back another time."

"You go ahead and go," Trace told her. "I know you can't do anything illegal, but I want to take a look around just in case."

For a moment, it appeared Rayna might argue with him. Instead, she grimaced. "Come on then. We'll take a walk around the perimeter."

"And inside the backyard," he added.

"Unless the gate is locked." She pointed toward the six-foot-tall wooden fence that had clearly seen better days.

"I'll figure out something if it is," he said. "A good gust of wind would likely blow that fence over."

Though Rayna shook her head, she didn't comment.

They moved quickly and quietly as they went down one side of the home, to where a weathered wooden gate hung crookedly on its hinges. Trace tested the handle. To his surprise, it opened.

"Stay close to the side of the house," Rayna told him, sotto voce. "Just in case."

A large evergreen shrub provided ample cover at the rear corner of the house. They stayed behind it, though Trace leaned around to see what he could. "Look." He pointed.

The raised cement and metal door of a tornado shelter occupied a spot in the center of the backyard.

Trace exchanged a look with Rayna.

"That doesn't mean anything," she murmured. "Lots of people have those."

Pointing to a large bar, Trace shook his head. "Not ones that are locked from the outside."

Straightening, Rayna frowned.

Just then, a man came out the back door. He crossed the yard and undid the heavy bolt. With his back to them, he didn't appear aware he had an audience.

"I bet he has Emma down there." Trace glanced at Rayna. "We need to do something."

Grim-faced, she pulled her service weapon from her holster. "I swear, you'd better not be wrong about this guy."

"Sheriff's department," she called out, stepping forward. "Put your hands up where I can see them."

When Trace came thundering down the shelter steps, Emma cried out. They met halfway, he wrapping his arms around her and lifting her up to meet his kiss.

"I'm so glad you found me," she exclaimed, breathless when they finally broke apart. "When I heard the door, I figured that guy was coming back to talk to me."

"He's cuffed and being placed under arrest. Rayna's reading him his rights."

She cried then, unable to believe her ordeal was finally over. "I think I know who killed Jeremy," she told him. "And also where the missing money went."

"Let's get out of here first and you can tell me." He took her arm and helped her up the steps. Once outside, she breathed in the warm air and eyed her captor, now handcuffed and staring at her sullenly. Oddly enough, she felt an odd combination of elation and defeat. She truly didn't want to believe her stepmother had done the things she suspected her of.

"I'm so glad to see you're okay." Rayna hugged her quickly before turning to Trace. "I've called for backup. One of my deputies will be here in a few minutes and will escort Mr. Gonzales to jail. We'll be booking him for kidnapping, among other things. Then I'll take your statement."

Emma nodded, slightly dizzy. Somehow, Trace noticed and steered her over to an old wooden picnic table bench. "Sit," he ordered. "You're not going to believe what I think I've discovered about your stepmother, Beth."

Epilogue

During a walk down the gravel road on a cool December night, Trace proposed. After her stepmother's arrest and full confession to murdering Jeremy and then her husband, Emma had finally been able to clear her name, though the horror over what Beth had done would never leave her. Still, she felt able to move on with her life.

Emma's horse training business had been scaled back slightly while the new barn was being built. Luckily, insurance covered it fully. Emma had also learned when her father had died, he'd left her half of everything in a will that Beth had chosen to ignore. Due to the pending court cases and various legal issues, it could be a long time before she saw any money. Still, the fact that her father hadn't forgotten her helped her feel a lot better.

Life went on. Halloween came and went. Since the ranch's isolation meant they didn't get trick-or-treaters, she and Trace went into town, where they watched the costumed children go up and down Main Street, collecting candy handed out by the merchants. Serenity had smiled wisely when she'd noticed Emma's and Trace's linked hands, and Emma had grinned back at her and winked.

Thanksgiving would have also been a quiet affair, but Rayna invited them over for dinner. They met her husband, Parker, as well as her daughter and mother. Serenity came too, and they all had a wonderful time with good food and lots of laughter.

As December arrived, Emma and Trace finally discussed their burgeoning feelings for each other, though neither had used the *L* word yet. They both agreed to see where things led.

But she knew she loved him and suspected he felt the same way about her. They held hands a lot and sat snuggled together on the couch when they watched TV. And they took long walks on the roads around the ranch, sharing their dreams for the future.

The light went away early this time of the year, so they'd begun taking their walks before dinner, after all the livestock had been taken care of. When Trace tugged her off the road to a small rocky outcropping, she went willingly. And when he dropped to one knee in front of her, her heart caught in her throat. Joy flooded through her, and tears of happiness sprang to her eyes.

Removing his cowboy hat, Trace looked up at her,

love blazing from his gaze. "Will you be my forever partner?" he asked.

"Yes," she managed, crying in earnest now. "Definitely, yes."

The ring fit perfectly, though not as well as the way his mouth fit over hers as he kissed her. "You're right where you belong," he said. "In my arms."

"Right where I belong," she echoed, dizzy with happiness. "Actually…" Pulling back, she smiled up at him. "We're both exactly where we belong. With each other. Partners for life. Soon to be husband and wife."

The silly rhyme had him grinning. Then he kissed her again and no more words were necessary for a good while.

* * * * *

Don't miss out on other exciting
suspenseful reads from Karen Whiddon:

The Spy Switch
Finding the Rancher's Son
Texas Rancher's Hidden Danger
The Widow's Bodyguard
Snowbound Targets
Texas Ranch Justice
The Texas Soldier's Son

Available now wherever
Harlequin Romantic Suspense books
and ebooks are sold!

**WE HOPE YOU ENJOYED
THIS BOOK FROM**

HARLEQUIN
ROMANTIC
SUSPENSE

Danger. Passion. Drama.

These heart-racing page-turners will keep you guessing to the very end. Experience the thrill of unexpected plot twists and irresistible chemistry.

4 NEW BOOKS AVAILABLE EVERY MONTH!

#2203 SHIELDING COLTON'S WITNESS
The Coltons of Colorado • by Linda O. Johnston

US marshal Alexa Colton is assigned to take care of Dane Beaulieu, a vice detective testifying against his partner's murder by a corrupt police chief. Their nine-hour drive becomes a many days' journey as they elude attackers who want them both dead. Despite escalating danger, the chemistry sizzles between them!

#2204 KILLER IN THE HEARTLAND
The Scarecrow Murders • by Carla Cassidy

When widower Lucas Maddox needs a nanny for his three-year-old daughter, he hires local woman Mary Curtis for the job. As they grow closer, Mary is threatened by a mysterious person and murders begin occurring in the small town. Lucas is determined to protect her, but can he let go of the past that holds him hostage?

#2205 HIS CHRISTMAS GUARDIAN
Runaway Ranch • by Cindy Dees

Ex-SEAL and holiday hater Nicholas Kane is no saint. But he and sexy CIA agent Alexander Creed must find a priceless nativity crèche his boss stole and return it before Christmas. Between double-crossings, rogue agents and their own guarded hearts, these spies will need a holiday miracle to find love—and survive!

#2206 SIX DAYS TO LIVE
by Lisa Dodson

It took sixty days for Dr. Marena Dash to fall in love with ex-soldier Coulter McKendrick, who's been injected with a lethal poison, but if she doesn't find an antidote, she'll lose him in six! After a bitter breakup and time apart, he shows up on her doorstep near death and with a trail of people wanting him silenced. Can Marena find the medicine he needs before the clock runs out?

Alex blinked, startled. This man had already done
80 percent of his job for him? Cool. All that was left
now, then, was for him to finish investigating Gray and
kill him.

Nick was speaking. "…got to New York City, I got
lucky. I texted a guy who was brought in for some training
with me about a year back. He was being groomed to
take a spot on the personal security team. At any rate, he
didn't answer my text, but his phone pinged as being in
Manhattan. I tracked it to a restaurant and spotted Gray
having supper there. I've been on his tail ever since. At
least, until you knocked me off him."

"In other words," Alex said, "we need to hightail it over to wherever Gray is bunking down tonight and pick him up before he leaves in the morning."

"If we were working together, it would go something like that," Nick said cautiously.

"Seems to me we're both working toward the same goal. We both want to know what Gray stole. Why not cooperate?" In his own mind, Alex added silently, *And it would have the added benefit of me keeping an eye on you until I figure out just what your role in all of this is.*

Nick nodded readily enough and said a shade too enthusiastically, "That's not a half-bad idea."

Alex snorted to himself. Nick had obviously had the exact same thought—that by running around together, he could keep an eye on Alex, too.

If Nick had, in fact, been pulling a one-man surveillance op for the past week, he had to be dead tired. With nobody to trade off shifts with him, he'd undoubtedly been operating on only short catnaps and practically no sleep for seven days. Which made the fight he'd put up when they met that much more impressive. Alex made a mental note never to tangle with this man in a dark alley when he was fully rested.

Don't miss
His Christmas Guardian *by Cindy Dees,*
available November 2022 wherever
Harlequin Romantic Suspense books and
ebooks are sold.

Harlequin.com

Get 4 FREE REWARDS!

We'll send you 2 FREE Books plus 2 FREE Mystery Gifts.